Praise for Vivian Arend's
Silver Mine

"There's a real chemistry between the characters, laced with humor and snappy dialogue, and no shortage of steamy sex scenes to keep things lively. The result is an entertaining, spicy romance."

~ *Publishers Weekly*

"Arend offers constant action and thrills, and her characters are so captivating and nuanced that readers will have a hard time guessing who the villains really are. With an appealing crossbreed hero and shifter heroine, this book is a keeper!"

~ *RT Book Reviews*

"*Silver Mine* is an outstanding story. The author creates a world that invites readers for the ride of their lives."

~ *Coffee Time Romance Reviews*

"I really liked all the characters that come into play once they are out in the bush... Not to forget some smoking hot panty melting sex scenes between Shelley and Chase."

~ *Guilty Pleasures Book Reviews*

"As much as I've enjoyed Ms. Arend's other books, this latest release is my new favorite... Enjoy. I did."

~ *Literary Nymphs Reviews*

"If you are a fan of shifter stories, I recommend both this series and the Granite Lake Wolves series. You'll find really interesting characters, great storylines with hot romance."

~ *Smexy Books*

Look for these titles by
Vivian Arend

Now Available:

Silver Mine

Vivian Arend

SAMHAIN
PUBLISHING

Samhain Publishing, Ltd.
11821 Mason Montgomery Road, 4B
Cincinnati, OH 45249
www.samhainpublishing.com

Silver Mine
Copyright © 2013 by Vivian Arend
Print ISBN: 978-1-61921-365-4
Digital ISBN: 978-1-60928-878-5

Editing by Anne Scott
Cover by Angela Waters

First Samhain Publishing, Ltd. electronic publication: September 2012
First Samhain Publishing, Ltd. print publication: August 2013

Dedication

For those who call far away or remote places home. North, south or in-between. Give me a shout—I'd love to come visit.

Part One

So gaunt against the gibbous moon
Piercing the silence velvet-piled,
A lone wolf howls his ancient rune—
The fell arch-spirit of the Wild.

O outcast land! O leper land!
Let the lone wolf-cry all express
The hate insensate of thy hand,
Thy heart's abysmal loneliness

"The Land God Forgot"—Robert Service

Chapter One

Chase stood aside to allow the morning sunlight to fall onto the front porch of his log cabin and highlight his handiwork. He attached another piece of duct tape to the rocking-chair arm, circling three times to tighten the sticky material around the wrist he'd strategically placed along the broad armrest. He repeated his actions on the left side before kneeling to secure the young man's ankles, one to each side of the sturdy extended rockers.

Another strand of tape around Jones's naked torso pinned the wolf shifter against the chair back. For extra measure, Chase tore off two more long pieces and pressed them in an X across the shifter's hairy chest.

Finally satisfied, Chase sat in the Adirondack chair next to the rocker and sighed contently.

"You know, if you'd asked, I would have been happy to let you stay." Chase tipped the mouth of his beer bottle toward the silent figure beside him. "It's not that difficult a job, opening your trap and asking permission. Sometimes that's called conversation."

A long slow drink followed. Chase gazed to his left over the tall pine trees crowding the base of the remote wilderness lake as he sipped the cold amber liquid. "Beautiful, isn't it, Jones? I can't think of another place I'd prefer to be. I'm mighty proud of what I've built here."

"Why, yes, Chase, you're right. This is a fine home you've got." Chase raised his voice, matching the higher tones of the arctic wolf shifter as best he could. "And, Chase, I'd sure appreciate getting to stay here while you're gone. I promise to take care of things."

The rocking chair creaked as Jones moaned, his head lolling from the left to the right, mouth gaping open. Chase watched for a sign the young man was coming around. A low snore escaped instead, and Chase shook his head.

"Boy, you don't know how good you got it. I should have tied you to the boat and sent you floating into the middle of the lake. I'm going soft in my old age."

He adjusted his chair to face fully toward the water, ignoring the incapacitated wolf on his right. It was a glorious late June day, and hell if he would allow Jones to mess with the tranquility of the moment. Chase drank slowly, enjoying his view. Summer had officially arrived in the high Yukon, which meant there were only a few pockets of snow left in the shadowy places under the thicker sections of forest. The sun was hot enough the new green grasses were edging toward drying already, the limited growing season of the north a rush of forward motion hurtling toward death.

It was the most serene and idyllic of settings, if he ignored the hairy beast beside him trussed up like a chicken.

Serene, and lonely. Appropriate for most of the men who lived in these parts. Men like him.

Chase laughed as his thoughts followed a familiar path. He could have set his watch on it. Seemed every year this time he tended toward a bout of philosophical musings. He chewed on his bottom lip for a while and debated going fishing. He really should head out again, but until he had dealt with the disaster on two legs next to him, his hunting would have to wait.

Quiet. Nothing disturbed the air but the light creak of the rockers against the wooden deck boards and the wind playing with the pines. He was used to silence. Didn't mean he loved it, but it fit the setting.

Nearly an hour later he woke from a catnap, an extra loud gurgle echoing from the wolf at his side.

"Hello, the house."

There was another thing that was clockwork reliable this time of year. Chase rose smoothly to his feet and stepped to the railing, leaning his flannel-clad elbows on the sturdy log crossbar as he stared across the meadow at the old-timer approaching on an even older horse. A rattle carried across the distance, the beast's easy gait jostling the miner's gold pans and his solid tin coffee pot together like leaves on a wind-blown tree.

Chase waited until his company drew closer before he spoke. He wasn't sure how well Delton's hearing had held up over the past year, and there was no need to rub in the fact the man was getting older. Heck, they were all getting older.

"New saddle," Chase noted.

Delton nodded. "Wilson quit. Passed it on to me."

Silence returned as Delton pulled his horse up and laid the reins over the mare's neck. She was already tugging lazily at the long grass as he slid off her back, hitting the ground without a lot of give in his knees.

Chase hid his wince.

Delton untied a sachet from the saddlebags and tossed it over his shoulder, pausing to pat his horse's withers before approaching the wide porch staircase.

He was at the top of the stoop before his gaze fell on the shiny-striped man propped up like a freaky Christmas tree. Delton didn't stop, just shook his head a little and made for the door.

"I take it the boy's been a pain in the behind."

"You might say that."

Chase followed his friend into the cool of the cabin. The old cougar's low cussing nicely echoed his own thoughts as he glanced at the damage inside his usually pristine home.

Delton wandered to the kitchen, shoving garbage out of the way with his feet. Bags and boxes crackled underfoot, shards of broken dishes snapping like shotgun blasts.

"You looking for something specific, old man?"

His friend dragged the broom from behind the fridge and hoisted it for a moment. "Didn't think you'd mind if I did a little work."

It was so like Delton—so like all the men that Chase cared for. Shit happened. You moved on.

He nodded and turned to grab a garbage bag, stuffing it with the items broken beyond repair like the plates and shredded cushions. Mentally making a list of all the things he'd need to replace as he cleaned methodically alongside Delton.

Silently. Companionably.

The place looked a whole lot better within a short time, and Chase sighed. "You know, you've gone and ruined my plans to make Jones clean up the mess in his wolf form."

"Must have been in his wolf while he caused some of the damage." Delton pointed to the scratched edges of the couch where the raw wood showed in deep gouges. Claws marks marred the corner, like a cat on a scratching post.

"Jones is usually half in his wolf form. The boy's mostly feral—brain just doesn't switch all the way back to human anymore."

And now Chase felt a little bad about having taped the kid to the chair. Wasn't really unexpected Jones had gone insane in the cabin. Although, he hadn't asked to be allowed access in the first place. At the least a little pain might drive home that message of basic politeness.

Delton paused his sweeping, his grey beard sticking up wildly, the perfect image of an out-of-control Grizzly Adams. "You were gone for a few days?"

"Grabbing information from the Miller boys. I plan on heading north soon to track down everyone else who hasn't been in contact during the past couple months. If I can find folks quick enough, I could be in Whitehorse by the third and home by the eighth."

Five days in civilization. It was enough—and the only reason he'd go was he had to. No one else in those parts could handle the trip, and there had to be some contact with the outside world, if only to deal with banking and food orders.

Delton nodded. "I brought you my list. You're a good man, Chase Johnson."

He shrugged. "I'm the only person available. That doesn't make me good, just makes me the one who can do it."

"We ain't gonna argue about this." Delton leaned the broom to the side and motioned toward the kitchen. "I suppose it's too much to assume you've got anything edible in there after Jones took the place apart."

He hadn't even looked. Chase had returned from his trip into the bush and found the tore-apart house and an unconscious wolf shifter half in, half out his front door. "If he's ruined everything in there, I have supplies hidden in the shed. Can I make you supper?"

Delton's gap-toothed grin lit his grizzled and lined face. "You find me some grub, and I'll do the cooking."

Chase's stomach grumbled at the thought of something other than raw game he'd been eating while shifted. "You cook, and I'll care for your horse."

Two hours later Chase wondered if he'd explode if he ate one more biscuit. Also on the pondering list, would the wolf duct-taped out front ever stop snoring at the extreme decibel level and wake up? And three, what promises could he make to convince Delton to move in on a regular basis as chef because, man, the old-timer could cook.

Delton topped up their coffee cups and groaned in satisfaction. "Your stash of supplies is mighty fine. I could stay here and look after things for you while you're gone. I'm getting tired of my bean and rabbit rations."

Having a house sitter was the solution to a number of problems. Chase nodded. "I'd appreciate that. And Jones—well, I guess he can stay around if you're willing to babysit, but I've got two requests."

"Name them." The cougar scratched his belly and yawned, pushing back the empty plates stacked in front of him.

"He's got to do chores every day in human form. No shifting and bringing in game for the table, or some such excuse."

Delton nodded. "I'll try to explain to the boy, but it's not easy when they've already got that touch of the wild in them. What else?"

The grin stretching his cheeks felt good. "Don't release him. Force him to get out of that chair on his own."

"Shit, you're a mean one at times, Chase Johnson."

Chase shrugged. "He's got claws and teeth."

"He's gonna have a lot less hair by the time he gets free." Delton shuddered. "Gonna be like peeling off a Band-Aid. Or them fancy ladies who rip the fur off their privates."

Chase choked on his coffee. "You know about that?"

One bushy brow rose in the air, and Chase snorted at the old man's expression. It wasn't as if shifters were shy about sex, but he hadn't imagined well-groomed women were high on Delton's experience list.

The cougar shook a finger in the air. "Oh Lordy, I've seen more and done more than you'll do in your entire life. Bright lights of Dawson in her heyday—that was an education and a half for a young man."

The old-timer was still chuckling as Chase stood and grabbed the small bag he used for his annual trip. He loaded it with paper and a few writing instruments before draping the handle around his neck, checking to be sure the strap was set wide enough not to choke him once he shifted.

"You heading out already?" Delton asked.

"No use in waiting if you're going to stick around. Sorry for leaving you with the rest of the cleanup." To be honest, he couldn't bear to have to throw anything else away. It would hurt less to simply have the destruction gone when he got back.

Delton waved a hand at him, then braced himself on his knees to push to vertical, bones creaking as he stood. "Least I can do to enjoy a roof over my head for a bit. Good hunting, Chase, and don't worry about anything here. I've got you covered."

Chase stepped outside. The sun was lower, but the sky remained full bright. There was tons of time to get into the bush. He stripped off his clothes and tucked them into the carrying sack, leaving his shoes behind to the side of the door.

A loud snore reverberated off the log walls, and he strode over to stare at Jones. The wolf shifter's head hung back now, tongue dangling as he rattled the windows with his snoring. He was just a youngster, really.

Didn't mean he couldn't learn.

Chase tore one final strip off the roll of duct tape and carefully applied it across both Jones's bushy eyebrows. The shifter wiggled under his touch before settling back into a deep sleep.

It might be evil, but it was just. "That's for shredding my Gramma's quilt."

Chase strolled into the sunshine to take one last look around. Through the cabin windows, Delton was visible wandering back and forth as he cleaned. Jones rocked slowly in the breeze, light glinting off the silver tape. The trees and the clouds and everything seemed so damn peaceful.

Nothing was exactly as it appeared, now was it? Chase mused.

He shifted, body changing into his wild side. Always took a moment to fine-tune his thinking—waiting for the animal to fully form. He stretched, the big paws before him indenting the ground with the weight of his cougar. So, it was the cat's turn to hunt. He wiggled to adjust the sachet against his chest, then padded his way to the trailhead.

He ran.

"No."

"Yes."

"No." Shelley Bradley pulled the stethoscope from her sister's fingers, tugging to get her to release it. "I'm busy."

Caroline gave her an evil grin. "I'm busy, busy, dreadfully busy—"

Oh God, *no*. Shelley slapped a hand over Caroline's mouth. "If you start singing *VeggieTales*, I will be forced to make you watch repeats of *The Muppet Show*."

Caroline's nose wrinkled, her lower face still covered by Shelley's hand.

"Can I let you go? Will you promise to be a good girl and sit quietly while I finish?" Shelley knew her tone of voice would get a reaction if nothing else did. Sure enough, Caroline rolled her eyes back in her head until only the whites showed.

Shelley released her, and they both fell apart with an attack of giggles, Shelley to finish unpacking the box that rested on the shiny metal examining table, her sister to lean against the doorframe that led to the waiting-room area.

"The parts of the clinic you've got completed look great." Caroline gestured around, including Shelley in the sweep. "You look great. *Gack*, you and your damn wolf genes. Put on a few pounds once in a while."

The only thing her wolf genes seemed to be good for. "It's not my fault. I don't even exercise."

Caroline mock glared. "Yeah, well, don't brag."

Shelley smothered her grin. This was the reason she'd come back. Getting her veterinarian training in the south, and the six-month mentorship in Calgary that followed for shifter specialization had been an exciting mental challenge. She'd missed the emotional ties of family though and, as always, the love and acceptance her sister gave was absolute and mind-bogglingly sweet. It felt so good to be back in the same room as her. Same town. But not the same situation as years ago.

Time to head down a new path. Shelley took a deep breath, and crossed all her fingers and toes that returning to Whitehorse would work.

Her sister wandered away a few steps, picking items off the shelf and checking them over. "You heard from Kent lately?"

Another rock-solid family member, although a little harder to track down than Caroline. Their younger brother was constantly on the go. "Other than the weekly email update from last Saturday, no."

"He's too busy seducing half of Ottawa to spend much time online."

Shelley shook her head. "No wonder Mom and Dad followed him out there. They're attempting to keep an eye on a moving target. That boy got all the party genes that missed me."

"Don't sell yourself short," Caroline scolded. "You're a ton of fun."

Her instant and involuntary snort of disbelief was so intense it hurt. Shelley gave her sister *the look*.

"Really," Caroline insisted. "I mean it. In fact, I want you to come out tonight with me. Please?"

Drat. She'd been dreading this topic coming up, and Caroline had gone there way faster than expected. Why was it so hard for her sister to understand? "Honey, I might have moved back to Whitehorse. That doesn't mean I'm going to dive into pack activities."

"It's not a pack event—it's the whole city. Music, games...come on. You're going to miss Canada Day celebrations just to avoid seeing pack?"

Damn right. She'd do more than miss a party to avoid some of the cold-blooded jerks who'd made her life miserable when she was young. "I'm here because Whitehorse needs a new vet who can confidentially deal with shifters. I love the Territory, and I want to be close to you. The pack as an official entity can go stuff itself as far as I'm concerned. So, yes, avoidance is a fine option."

The concern on Caroline's face deepened. "You know you can't hide from them forever."

"I don't intend to." Shelley closed the door on the supply cupboard and took apart the shipping box for recycling. "I'm going to be acting as a kind of doctor to them, for heaven's sake. How is that avoidance? Plus, I already contacted the Takhini Alpha and—"

"When?" Caroline snapped upright. "I'm his secretary. How the heck did you get to him without me knowing?"

Interesting reaction. Shelley stopped her unpacking to observe her sister more carefully. Caroline's near-panicked response seemed out of place. "There's something you're not telling me."

Caroline blinked. "No. I'm just surprised. Usually I have his entire agenda memorized. And he didn't say anything about you calling."

Because she hadn't called. She'd gotten a human kid to drop off a note. That alone should have gotten his curiosity up enough to agree to wait. "It's fine. He knows there's a new wolf in town, and that I'll get together with him at some convenient time."

Like...*never*, but that was beside the point.

Caroline pushed the party invitation again, but Shelley ignored her, methodically placing supplies on the shelves. Her older sister had never seemed to learn the word *no*. While her determined assaults could be frustrating at times, like now when Shelley was on the wrong end of one, her *never give up* spirit was also inspiring. Fully human, Caroline managed to

21

hold her own amidst the wolf pack of Whitehorse in a way that Shelley admired.

Wished that she could imitate, to be frank. And planned to imitate.

The rest of the family had left the north looking for more accepting packs. Shelley had left for the longest time as well, but Whitehorse was where she wanted to live.

This time it was going to be on her terms. That was the bottom line. Pack or no pack, this was going to be home.

Caroline sighed, stopped her rambling and slipped into the main area. "Fine. I'll change the topic since you're being all Sphinx-like. You hired someone for the front desk?"

Shelley joined her, admiring the tall glass windows that let in the July sunshine. "Not yet. I'm still waiting for a few permits to finish clearing. I'm not going to be able to officially open until mid-August, so there's no rush. There's a bit more work to be done in here, like the flooring, and I haven't completed the surgery area in the back. I also want more shelving, and to finish the boarding and exercise yard. That kind of thing."

"I can get someone—"

"No." Seemed as if she was saying that word a lot, but it was necessary. "Caro, I'm doing great. I know you want to help, but I don't need a big sister fixing things for me and making things easier. There's tons of time to get the shop ready, and I want to do the work myself. What I want for us is to spend time together. To enjoy life."

The glint in Caroline's eyes warned Shelley she'd made a mistake. "Awesome. Then you're going to come over for supper before the celebration? We can enjoy each other's company a little before dealing with the crowds. There's no fireworks, not with how light it is in the evening, but the music they have planned should be great."

Shoot. Walked into that one. "Oh, Caroline..."

Her sister batted her lashes. "I'll make your favourites."

The dinner invite was tempting, and there were positive points to meeting the pack in a public setting, but tonight was too soon. Caroline would be surrounded by wolves, and Shelley wasn't ready for that yet. "No supper, but..." she raised a hand to stop Caroline's protests, "...fine, I will come to the Canada Day party. If you're willing to sit off to the side and avoid pack."

Caroline's instant smile lit her eyes. "We can totally do that. They're all hanging at the Rotary Peace Park. We can sit beside the SS Klondike paddlewheeler and listen to the band from there. The reflections off the Yukon River will be pretty. Deal?"

It was a start. A start to finding her place in the north, which in itself was huge, since she'd never fit in before. "Deal."

A soft brush against her ankles was followed by a loud insistent purr as Enigma demanded to be picked up. She hoisted the tiny black creature and settled him in her arms for a cuddle.

Caroline gasped, the sound breaking apart into laughter. "Oh my God, Shelley, you have a cat?"

She nodded as Enigma opened his mouth and meowed. "He's a rescue. Loves to be scratched right—"

"You've *got* to be kidding. A cat. Shell—owning a pet is strange enough, but a cat?"

"You got some weird biases for a human who grew up in a shifter home." Shelley buried her face in Enigma's soft fur and breathed deeply. "He's been nothing but giving to me. Far more than your typical feline. We get along fine."

Caroline rearranged her face into a semiserious mode with some effort. "Love me, love my cat? Fine, Shelley, he is rather gorgeous."

23

She brushed a hand down Enigma's back, and the feline rewarded her with a rumbling purr.

Shelley smiled as she passed the small ball of fur over to her sister.

It was a start.

Chapter Two

Chase leapt from the high cab of the trucker's rig and waved his thanks as the man geared up and headed away along the Alaskan highway. The trip into Whitehorse had never taken such a short time before.

He hoisted his backpack and started down the long, steep road that led into town. The fresh air made his nose twitch after being confined for the past four hours, the trucker's heavy foot on the gas moving them southbound on the Klondike Highway at more than legal speeds.

Still, Chase couldn't complain too hard. He'd grabbed all the needed information and paperwork from the men double-quick this time around. Arriving in Whitehorse on July first meant he could possibly be out of town by the fourth, if all went well. He adjusted his pack to stop the strap's weight from hitting the raw parts of the claw wound on his shoulder.

One of the downsides of being a Good Samaritan. The loners he cared for were prone to be wilder than your average shifter. The puma he'd accidentally cornered had slashed first, asked questions later. After the fact, the man had been very apologetic, but that hadn't removed the four long gouges Chase carried over his scapula. Worse, the damn wound didn't seem to get any better, no matter how many times he shifted.

The scent of coffee drew him forward like a siren's call. He stopped in the doorway of a small café, checking the occupants with his nose and eyes before fully committing to entering.

There was a reason he didn't live in town on a regular basis.

Two wolves looked up at him from where they sat in the corner. They narrowed their eyes but stayed put, staring intently as if judging him. Chase nodded politely, and that seemed enough to put them at ease.

He took the chance and strode forward.

The blinding smile he received from the pretty girl behind the counter was as enjoyable as the lingering deep roast of the coffee beans in the air.

"What can I get you?" She was checking him out. *Hot damn.* Chase pushed down the urges that had no right to be rising in a public place, even if it had been a long time since he'd been with a lady.

Another good reason to come to town. Maybe he should try for more than once a year.

"Coffee." He dug in his pocket as he checked the baked goods on the counter, secretly checking out the goods behind the counter at the same time. Oh yeah, there was one bonus to being in the big city that he fully intended to take advantage of. "Couple brownies, three of them gingersnaps and a piece of the apple pie."

She laughed softly. "You've got a sweet tooth."

Chase leaned his hip against the counter and admired the soft swell of her breasts peeking from the low scoop of her top. "Some things are sweeter than others."

Another giggle escaped, and he grinned as she turned to get his order together. Maybe the extra days in town wouldn't be a hardship after all.

There was a tap on his shoulder, and Chase stiffened, cursing inside that he'd lost focus and ignored that he was in unsafe territory.

Women were distracting creatures.

He twisted slowly to see one of the wolves standing nearby. The man slouched lazily, his body language screaming friend, not enemy.

"Hey. Come and join us once you've got your things." The dark-haired man leaned past him and whistled softly at the server. "Carly, put his order on my tab."

She slipped apple pie onto a plate and nodded. "Sure, Shaun. You and Evan want anything else?"

"Well, if you're offering..." He winked, and she shook her head at him, a smirk on her face.

"Your fiancée is going to tear your ears off if she hears about you flirting."

"Who's flirting? I just want some pie." Shaun's outraged tone made Chase smile. Okay, not all wolves were assholes, and it seemed he'd found a couple of the good ones.

Shaun slipped away, and Chase took a moment to look around more closely as he waited for his order. The walls of the coffee shop were covered with artwork, price tags attached to each one. Local artists, from the looks of it. Some good, some not so good. The rest of the place was an eclectic mix. Straight-backed chairs sat at sturdy tables—people with open laptops clicking madly through colourful screens. Overstuffed chairs tucked into the places between, people reading books or staring at thin metal book-shaped objects. Low music played in the background.

He accepted the tray of goodies from Carly and joined the wolves in the corner. He didn't recognize either of them from his previous trips into Whitehorse—must be new to the pack.

Maybe he could get a hint of the way things were operating from these two before he had to approach the current leadership.

Once he'd lowered the tray to the table, the second wolf rose to his feet and offered a hand. "Evan Stone. You look as if you could use a bit more than a coffee and a few snacks."

Chase shrugged. He might be leaner than your average wolf, but he wasn't about to explain his specific shifter metabolism problems to anyone on a first meeting. "It's as good a place as any to start. I can get steaks aplenty back home. Baked goods? Not so much."

Evan nodded, and they all sat, pulling plates forward and digging in enthusiastically. When shifters were hungry, there was not much that stopped them from enjoying their food.

The pie and one of the brownies went down first as a base. Two cups of coffee later, Chase came up for air to find both wolves grinning at him. Damn, he'd done it again—totally lost track of where he was. This wasn't his style. If he'd been this inattentive in the bush, he never would have lasted.

"Thank you for the food." Chase nodded at Evan who seemed to be the one in charge.

Evan leaned back, tilting his chair until the top rail hit the wall. "No worries. Like I said, you look as if you could use it. You north Yukon?"

"Mid. Keno area is home."

That was all it took. Shaun whistled, long and low. "You don't look like a crazed maniac—no offense meant. I thought most of that area was pack-less. Pretty dangerous territory for your average wolf."

The tension between them didn't exactly rise, but Chase made sure he had a clear space to defend himself, just in case. "Packless doesn't always mean without morals. And pack living doesn't suit everyone. That's all."

Evan and Shaun glanced at each other, as if making some kind of decision. Chase was ready to grab his things and head out—if there were going to be any issues he'd prefer to be dealing with the right people. He wasn't making trouble, wasn't doing anything unusual.

He buried the dry comment in his head that muttered *you are unusual.*

"Why do you smell different?" Evan eased back again, Shaun leaning away this time as well. Somehow they'd made a decision in his favour, which seemed odd, but hell if he was going to argue.

The cause for his unusual scent wasn't a secret—he just didn't share until asked. "Métis ancestry."

"Holy shit." Evan came to life. "What's your second form? Because I can smell your wolf, but he's buried deep. The other side seems stronger."

"You know about Métis?" Chase wasn't sure if this was good or stunk to high heaven. "I've only met three people I didn't have to explain it to."

"And I'm not one of them," Shaun complained. "What the hell does that mean? I thought you were a wolf."

Evan shook his head, the look of delight on his face as bizarre as it was reassuring. "Dual nature. I heard of a wolf/wolverine once, and there were rumors of a wolf/polar bear crossbreed back in my old pack territory by Hudson Bay. The French Voyageurs who married the First Nations mixed the shifter blood, and for some reason the European strain breed true. Well, not *true*—instead of the kids being one kind of shifter or the other like usual, the next generation could shift into *either* of their parents' clans."

Shaun's mouth gaped open.

Evan elbowed him in the side. "You never take history in school? Louis Riel? Red River Rebellion?"

"Fuck you. That was a long time ago."

"The rebellion, or your schooling? Because maybe you need to head back and get a refresher. Doesn't look good in front of visitors, you being a dumb-ass and all."

Chase watched silently as the two of them bantered. Not your typical pack, that's for sure. And definitely not like the solitude-loving men he'd just touched base with far to the north.

The unorthodox bitch session was entertaining to say the least. He considered sneaking away before they concluded, but the cut-downs were too comical to leave.

They both stopped in mid-sentence and turned to face him, two dark-haired men who radiated power, and Chase swallowed his amusement. *Shit.* He'd made another mistake in judgment. Stuck out in the bush for so long where authority was often imposed with a tree branch instead of shifter hierarchy, he'd missed the now all-too-noticeable clues. "You guys are leadership."

Evan nodded curtly. "I took over Takhini last August. You got a specific need, you ask me." He tilted his head to the left to indicate the other man whose eyes were still a little wild. "Shaun's Beta, new to the role. We're just getting a few things established. I take it you haven't been out this way for a while."

The damn Alpha of Takhini sat across from him. *Sheesh*, Chase had lost all his hard-learned civilization skills. "I came out last July. Same reason as this time. I'll only be in town for a few days, and I'm not looking for trouble."

Shaun frowned. "We never said you were. You need a ride anywhere, though? A place to stay while in town?"

This was so not happening. "You're serious?"

Evan snorted. "You've been packless for too long. A Beta just offered you a place to stay. You want it or not?"

This was as fine a moment as any to test the waters. "What if I say not?"

Shaun shrugged. "No hair off my chest."

The remembrance of leaving poor Jones lashed to the chair stole through his mind, and Chase winced. In hindsight, he might have been a touch rough on the boy. "It's not that I don't appreciate the offer, but I'm not interested in staying in a pack house. It wouldn't be a good idea."

Shaun's indifference slid away as his attention sharpened. "If you're worried about troubles because you're from out of town, don't be. The pack's not about to go around our authority."

Just what he wanted. "And maybe having people ordered to tolerate me isn't something I enjoy. So, not to seem ungrateful, but I'll take care of myself for the night."

Evan's firm pat on his shoulder reassured him there was no harm caused by his insistence. "A ride though? We can drop you anywhere. By the way, you didn't mention the specifics of your reason to visit Whitehorse."

That wasn't a secret either. Chase pulled out his papers, including his shopping list, and showed it to Evan. He kept the others' to-do lists tucked aside—it was one thing to share his personal information and another to let a virtual stranger, Alpha or not, know exactly how many men were scattered through the bush in the Keno area.

Evan scanned the stack, his expression unreadable. "I can't imagine. Supplies for an entire year all at one go. How the hell you know how much to buy?"

"Stays about the same. If I guess wrong, I can always radio for someone from Dawson to do a drop, but Whitehorse is far cheaper to deal with. Plus my bank is here."

The papers were passed back without another word, near indolence in Evan's attitude now. "And that's more than I need to know. I'm not interested in your finances. Not unless you ask for help, and that seems to be low on your list of things to do—the asking-for-help business."

Chase remained still, waiting for the next question.

Shaun whooped as he shot to his feet, turning to flick a salute Chase's direction. "Lovely to meet you. Drop by the Moonshine Inn if you decide you need anything. Later."

He rushed out the door without a second glance.

Evan and Chase exchanged puzzled looks before turning streetward. Shaun raced up to a pretty African American, swept her off her feet, and kissed her madly.

Evan laughed. "It's okay. We're not all insane. That's his mate—she's been gone for a week, and he didn't expect her to be back for a few more days."

An itch tickled up the back of Chase's spine. The mention of mates was enough to make most of his type twitchy.

After one final nod, the Takhini Alpha rose and left. Chase sat alone in the corner of the café, the remains of their repast cleared away quickly by the efficient Carly.

"Can I get you anything else?" She smiled at him again, that flirtatious lilt to her voice, but for some reason he wasn't interested anymore.

He shook his head. If he wanted a little female companionship this week, he'd have to look elsewhere. She wasn't a wolf, not by her scent, so it was safe enough in terms of avoiding pack.

But something wasn't sitting right. Maybe the visit had been too much companionship after all his time alone. Even Delton wasn't real intrusive company. Heck, often the man was so quiet the two of them could be in the same room for an entire day and not get in each other's way.

The Takhini leaders vibrated with life and energy. Power of an entirely different type than mere hierarchy. The kind of vitality that was scary on a whole different level to a man who after years of isolation felt at home staring at the side of a mountain for days on end.

Solitude called to him like a wild creature, and he could hardly wait to discharge his duties and return to the bush. He picked up his pack, carefully draped it over his left shoulder and escaped into the street to find his room for the night.

Evan watched the Métis from a distance, not wanting to crowd the man, but not willing yet to drop his curiosity. And with Shaun distracted by Gem's early return, there was no use in trying to do any more planning for the Grand Master Plan, as Shaun had taken to calling it. Evan laughed as he tracked Chase. Hell, he could hear his Beta using capital letters every time he said the words, like some freaky Pooh Bear imitation.

It was damn time, though, for the Grand Master Plan to be implemented. All along Evan's goal had been to rejoin the two rival Whitehorse packs into one, amalgamating the dominant Takhini wolves with the more elusive Miles Canyon pack, and it was taking bloody forever to figure out how to go about it. There weren't many places in the world that two packs sat in such close proximity to each other, and for good reason.

Territory wars were common in the old days, violence and bloodshed hidden in the more violent nature of the historic settling of the wilderness. Now the battlefields were more likely to involve spreadsheets and accountants than shotguns and hangings.

Evan didn't mind a good fight. A physical challenge that would make his wolf side howl. But there was a subtle beauty in taking an opponent totally unaware—and that was far more possible in the financial world than while wearing his wolf skin.

Chase disappeared into a boarding house, and Evan relaxed. It was a wolf-friendly accommodation, but not one frequented by the pack. Which was good, because even though he'd teased for the details of why the lone wolf was visiting, Evan had failed to push for the other information the man hadn't shared—what his second shifter form was.

But the tickling sensation at the back of his throat was enough to let Evan suspect it might be cat-based. Just what he needed dropping in at the pack house, driving all the less sensible members crazy. *Not.*

He didn't even want to think about triggering his damn allergies. Evan pulled out a tissue and blew his nose, wondering if he'd turn into a sniffling, sneezing mess if he happened to be around when Chase changed.

Although—Métis. *Damn.* Evan pondered the logistics of the shifting business but got distracted by the buzz of his cell phone.

"Evan here."

"You won the bid." His accountant's pleased tones spread happiness all the way to Evan's toes. "And there were no second glances at all. Business as usual. You're now official owner of three more shops in town. Congrats."

Celebrations weren't going to be scheduled until he'd gotten a little farther down the road on his plans, but it was a start. "What about the college? Any word on the housing project?"

The other man went on for a while, sharing details. Evan made mental notes as he strode back to the hotel the pack owned. The new landscaping they were finishing around the parking lot had turned the old landmark's tired façade into a special feature, with sitting areas and fountains.

If he was going to put the place on the map, getting more of the seasonal visitors to stop at the Moonshine Inn and Pub was vital. Money was only part of the project—they had to keep traffic coming.

The wide glass doors slid open with a soft sigh as he approached, the tinkling water fountains in the lobby a refreshing contrast to wash away the street noise.

Behind the front desk, Caroline, his highly efficient head receptionist and personal assistant, raised her head and smiled. Evan made his way over, nodding at a few of the pack who were working as bellboys or cleaning staff to keep the place immaculate.

"You've had a couple calls you should return, and there are questions from both the bakery and the pizza place about your order for the party tonight. I've arranged for the rest of the supplies—drinks and such, but you'd better deal with the food. Oh, and just so you know, I'm not going to be at the pack party. I've made other plans. I hope you don't mind."

"I guess not. You want to drop by later, you're always welcome."

He checked the lobby, but there were no human visitors in sight. Well, no humans other than Caroline. He tugged her against his body and enjoyed the way she softened, accepting his kiss with enthusiasm. Hmm, yeah. She wasn't his mate, but their arrangement as bed partners suited him fine. Evan slipped his fingers around her ass and held her close as their kiss deepened.

She smiled when he finally let her up for air. "You're not getting your work done this way."

"Maybe I need you to come and take a few notes in my office. That would be more efficient."

Another itch tickled his nose, and he jerked back before he sneezed in her face. Damn, he must be coming down with a cold.

The heat that rose to her eyes was gratifying, though. "I'd love to join you, but there's no one else on the front desk for an hour. You'll just have to deal with the food for the party all by your lonesome."

Evan sighed, tweaking her butt before he headed into the back. "I hate being efficient all by myself."

She waved him off and returned to her organizing, and once again he speculated why she'd suggested they pair up. Having her as a partner had done wonders for his ability to finally get things happening in the pack—until she'd moved in with him he'd experienced constant disruptions from female wolves wanting to get a piece of him, or more accurately a piece of the pack.

The higher rank the wolf, the higher their partner was considered. Since Evan hadn't had a sniff of a mate in all his nearly forty years, the arrangement with Caroline was working well, even with her a human. Especially since she was a human.

At least he knew she wasn't using him to get ahead in the wolf game.

Evan dropped the papers she'd given him onto his desk and opened his computer, distraction taking over as he considered the next stage of taking all of Whitehorse under his control.

Chapter Three

Shelley lay back on the thick blanket and stared at the blue sky. "I've missed this."

Caroline leaned over her, a shank of her blonde hair falling across her face. "Missed what? Me? Eating too many corn dogs and potato chips?"

"Of course I missed you." Shelley sighed happily, pointing upward. "But I mean the light. It's ten p.m. and it's still light out. I feel as if I've got forever to get things accomplished when I'm up north."

"It's pretty, but it's an illusion. You wait until the sky tells you to go to bed and you'll end up a basket case within a week," Caroline warned.

Shelley sat up and looked around. True to Caroline's word, there weren't any of the Takhini pack in the people congregating around them looking for spots on the grass beside the giant paddlewheeler that was now dry-docked and used as a museum. A few *were* wolves, but most of those were strangers—visitors or Miles Canyon pack, she wasn't sure. They eyed her and Caroline with caution before giving them a wide berth, which was very weird in a way.

She was the last wolf ever to intimidate anyone. "You hear anything about the Canyon pack? What they're up to? Who's leading?"

Caroline's head snapped her direction. "Why? You're not thinking about joining them, are you?"

This wasn't the time for getting into a detailed conversation. "Just curious, that's all." Although, if she did plan on joining a pack, the other side might be better than the pack of her youth.

Caroline jabbed her in the arm. "No way. No bloody way. You know Dad always warned us about them."

Sheesh. "Warned what? That they were mean and to avoid them? Man, Caroline, it's not as if I got such good treatment from the Takhini pack that I'm dying to return to the bosom of my childhood."

Caroline opened her mouth then reluctantly shook her head. "I know. You got a raw deal, but things have changed. Evan's a totally different Alpha than the one who was in charge when we were kids."

Her suspicions tweaked again. "There's something you're not telling me about this Evan guy. You make it sound as if he's some super-wolf."

Caroline busied herself with the picnic basket, guilt written in her every move, and Shelley decided to drop the topic. Concentrate instead on the music, the visit with her sister. Issues like pack politics, of north and south packs, and being treated like a dog could wait. She needed to put her burdens aside for the night.

She squeezed Caroline's shoulder, waiting until her sister looked up. "Let's make a deal. Tonight we don't try to discuss any of the million things we need to discuss, and we stick to the fun things. Like...people watching."

Caroline's smile was spontaneous. "Who Would You Do?"

"Oh no..." Shelley laughed. "You aren't going to make me play that again."

Her sister's grin got bigger. "It's safe. I promise I won't tell anyone. Unless you want to guess *boxers versus briefs.* That's always entertaining, and a totally harmless way to get some kicks."

"Until you dare me to go ask them what they're actually wearing, it's safe. At that point the danger levels become a little iffier."

Shelley looked into the slowly gathering crowd. Checked out the guys. It was a teenager's game, and she wasn't a teen anymore. She'd learned a lot about her sexuality while in the lower latitudes getting her veterinary training. Wolves liked sex, and she hadn't denied herself in that area. In many ways, it had been easier when there weren't all kinds of questions and expectations involved with the sex.

And humans far out-numbered shifters in the south. Not like here where she figured a third of the population of the Yukon had shifter blood—whether they knew it or not.

Caroline pointed toward the street. "I'll go first, even though it's far tougher for me to actually find someone. I mean, I know a lot of them and adding in their personalities makes me go *ick*. See the man by the bike rack locking up the bike? *Nom nom.* He's easy on the eyes."

Dark-haired, obviously muscular. Shelley snorted. "You haven't changed your type at all. I could have picked him for you."

Caroline actually blushed. "Yeah, yeah. Now your turn. If you were going to get naked and sweaty with someone, you would pick...?"

Shelley twisted slowly, checking all the men. Some of the guys with partners, some alone. Some tall, some short, many muscular like Caroline's stereotypical lust. The night was warm enough there was a lot of skin showing. Shorts, muscle shirts. Even a few groups of guys swaggering as they did a Venice

Beach imitation and pumped out pushups and flexed in that "look at me" and yet casual kind of way.

Nobody caught her eye. Maybe they were all too blatant. She'd had enough of wolf posturing over the years. And while she liked a guy in shape, she didn't need the nearly grotesque musculature of some of the pimped-out, pretty boys—

Oh my. Her gaze stuttered to a stop. *He* wasn't typical. His hair was short and blond, nearly white it was so light. Unlike the posers, he was fully clothed, sturdy but lightweight cotton slacks covering his long legs, a button shirt with slightly worn patches on the elbows. Tall. Lean. A light shadow on his chin and cheeks not quite covering paler skin—as if he'd shaved recently for the first time in a while. The whole *kinda, but not, scruffy* thing totally did it for her.

Caroline turned to follow her gaze, frowning slightly. "I don't know him."

"As if you could know everyone in town." Shelley's mouth was actually watering. Okay, him not being a Whitehorse local was better than she had anticipated. Complications of dealing with pack aside, she wasn't looking for a relationship.

But the drool factor on the man was seriously high.

"Okay. You have a winner. And yeah, your type has changed since you've been gone," Caroline teased. "I thought you were going to marry a dark-haired prince and live in a castle."

"Oh, sheesh, when I was eight. You were going to travel around the world. When's that happening?"

Caroline shrugged. "Priorities change. I like it here in Whitehorse. I wanted to stay, and...I know you don't want to talk about pack tonight, and that's fine, but I have to mention again things have improved. The current leadership team is

great. You will not have the troubles you had before. I
guarantee it.""

Shelley felt that strange sensation repeat—the one that
meant Carline was both telling the truth and keeping something
from her. "Thanks. And we'll talk more tomorrow."

She snuck another glance at the man as he strolled toward
the paddlewheeler, his gaze taking in everything around him.
He seemed to be avoiding the crowds, clinging to the perimeter
of the park. Even the way he moved made her heart race. He
had a confident gait, yet somewhat like she'd seen in the wild
animals she'd worked with. Nothing tame about him. Maybe he
was an explorer, or from some South American country.

She wanted to go and ask him, and even that urge made
her nervous. This was supposed to be a game, a teasing way to
find out things about your friends.

But at that moment the idea of *doing* the silver stranger
sounded very pleasant indeed.

Chase looked over the gathering, pissed off that he was
slightly nervous at being around this many people. He'd never
thought of himself as a real recluse, not even with living
isolated in the bush, but it was clear that over the past year
he'd lost a little more of his ability to cope with crowds.

Whatever. He focused on the parts he enjoyed—especially
the laughter. Living amongst outcasts there wasn't a lot of
mirth in his life, and he savoured the current *joie de vivre* in the
air.

And the kids. Running, playing. Wasn't likely he'd ever
have any of his own, but he didn't mind a little dose of watching
others'.

Laughter rang out on his left and caught his attention. Not
far away, two women reclined side by side on a blanket, one

blonde like the girl at the shop today, the other darker in colouring. He soaked in their happy tones, attempting to catch a glimpse of the brunette's face, but the blonde was directly between them.

Chase hesitated for all of a minute before deciding what the hell. He turned and stalked around the edge of the park, deliberately not looking in the women's direction.

Hunting. Just like sneaking up on a deer, you had to make sure they didn't know you were coming. He kept track with his peripheral vision to be sure she didn't sneak away. More glimpses teased him—a flash of a smile, her gaze darting around the park. She was wary, cautious. He liked that she seemed more observant than the other woman, and he wondered if the brunette might be a shifter.

He'd know soon enough. He slipped into the thin row of trees on the park's perimeter before changing direction. It only took a moment to cut back around the gathering by weaving through the parking lot. The cars made as good a cover as any rocks or boulders in the bush, and by the time he'd gotten into position he was smiling.

It was always enjoyable, getting his target within his sights.

And there she was. She had pulled her dark hair back and secured it with something, the heavy ponytail draped over one shoulder. Her skin wasn't as dark as the shifters he'd met that afternoon, but there had to be First Nations blood in her family line. While his own skin tones were far more European, leaving him pale in the winter, her colouring made her skin glow as if with a light tan. The blonde said something and they both laughed again, and Chase soaked in the sound like a treasure. He could listen to her laugh all day long.

He had to assume the other noises she'd make in pleasure would be enjoyable as well.

He stepped forward, suddenly not sure why his feet were moving. There was still time to retreat if he wanted to, but then again, why? The worst that could happen was for her to turn him down. And the best?

There was still a lot of evening ahead of them.

He'd taken not even three steps forward before she turned and their gazes met. She had beautiful dark brown eyes, but it was the clear interest in them that fascinated him more than the colouring. She swallowed hard, hands tugging on her companion's shirt. The blonde stopped speaking and swung to examine him as well, and now he was the prey instead of the predator.

Only the fact he'd never run away before kept him from fleeing in near terror.

From two women. Blast it.

Good thing Delton couldn't see him now or he'd lose all points with the old-timer. He screwed up his courage and stopped at the side of their blanket.

"Evening. Are you having a good time?" Even in his own ears he sounded rusty and stinted.

The brunette nodded, her gaze trickling down the front of his shirt so slowly it felt as if her fingers ran over his naked skin.

The blonde shot to her knees, hand thrust forward. "Hi, I'm Caroline. This is my sister. Wonderful party, isn't it? And you are...?"

So, she was the protective one. He accepted the handshake, surprised by the firmness of her grasp. "Chase Johnson. Just visiting for a few days, and in time to enjoy the event."

He turned with anticipation, squatting to offering his hand to the other woman.

She swallowed again, slower to reach out and place her fingers in his. "Shelley. Welcome to Whitehorse."

The touch of her palm to his was electrifying. All his anticipation totally underestimated the impact as her scent wrapped around him.

Wolf. Definitely wolf, but...not pack. There was a change that occurred when someone hung out with dozens of other shifters for long periods of time, and she didn't have it. There was another scent clinging to her that made him nearly fall over backward.

Cat?

Impossible. The odds against there being another crossbreed exactly like himself were astronomical. He held her hand and her gaze, and allowed the confusion to wash away in the glow of exactly how good it felt to touch her.

"*Ahem.*"

Shelley stared at him, her mouth a small O of shock. He rubbed his thumb over her knuckles, and the answering flash of excitement in her eyes made his body thrill. Oh yes, this would be a good *good* night if he had any choice in the matter.

"Yoo-hoo, earth to Shelley."

His fascinating woman didn't move her gaze away while she answered her sister. "What?"

Caroline's volume dropped to a mere whisper. "I want to know if this is one of those shifter things. Because if it is, which is what it looks like, and you two stripping and going for it is on the agenda, I suggest you remember where you are."

The interesting fact that the human knew about shifters was kind of crowded over by the images she'd conjured up by the words "stripping and going for it". Chase took another deep breath and allowed the sweet scent of Shelley's arousal to soak into his system. "We can control it."

"You're not mates, are you?"

Shelley's eyes snapped wide, and she jerked her fingers from his.

Chase paused. Checked inside. He was very attracted to the woman, that was true, and his wolf seemed to be the more attentive of the two sides of his nature, but even that beast wasn't demanding any more than usual when presented with someone he was attracted to. Wolves liked sex. Period. "It's not a mating thing."

"Oh God, no, not mates." Shelley spat out the words at the same time as he did, as if desperate to make the declaration.

The panic on her part seemed out of place, especially in light of their undeniable physical lust. Chase fought his desire to sweep the woman up like a caveman and remove her to a private place where they could ravish each other until they were both rather exhausted.

He was curious why her words seemed in total opposition to what her body so loudly stated.

A series of loud bangs sounded from their right. Caroline and the crowd of humans around them all jerked their heads to see what caused the disturbance, but the man in front of Shelley didn't so much as twitch. As his visual contact remained unbroken, the pounding in her chest kicked up a notch.

She had no wolf, or at least not one that would come to the surface for more than brief moments, and never enough to allow her to shift. And with no real wolf, she could have no mate—that much the Omegas and pack leadership had been able to dreg up from historical records. Outcast, unwanted.

Neither human enough to be tolerated nor mutant enough to be despised, it had taken years before she'd found a place of peace in her heart for who she was.

Not-wolf. Not-human. Just...Shelley.

But staring into this man's eyes? For one split second when Caroline had asked if they were mates, Shelley had experienced that torturous twist in her belly of longing for something that could never be.

Chase adjusted position, lowering his trim body to the grass on the edge of their blanket. The rush of voices around them rose in laughter, but he remained silent. Still staring.

She curled her arms around her torso, and his gaze fell, traveling over her slowly, methodically. Shelley's elusive wolf side was as active as she ever got, bumping upward and signaling high interest in the sexy stranger. A line of goose bumps rose on her arm, and when he stroked the back of his fingers up her forearm, she bit her lips to stop from groaning.

Instead, she leaned back slightly. "Stop that."

Chase shook his head and blinked, drawing his hand away in a flustered manner. "I beg your pardon. I don't know—sorry. I won't do it again."

Her heart fell, because her entire body was screaming for him to do it again, and do more.

But he was a shifter, and she didn't fool around with shifters. Not anymore. That way led madness.

She nodded tightly. "No worries. We're just leaving. I hope you have a good trip to Whitehorse. Make sure you check out the Moonshine Inn. Best beer in town, I hear."

She reached down to grab the blanket, her other hand pulling the basket closer, frantic to escape. Chase held up his hand to stop her.

"Don't. I didn't mean to make you leave. It's time to call it a night anyway."

He rose to his feet, Shelley scrambling to follow. "I'm sorry, I'm being totally rude, but it's just—"

His smile lit his face, knocked off the rough edges and made him even more handsome. "You don't need to explain. I feel your discomfort, and upsetting you was never my intention. Have a nice evening with your sister."

He dipped his chin, and regret arrived, but not hard enough for her to actually stop him from walking away. Although the sight of his ass in those faded, well-fitting pants made her mouth water.

Something hit her arm, and she turned to discover Caroline glaring at her. Shelley rubbed her bruised biceps. "Ouch. What's that for?"

"You turkey. That's not how you're supposed to act around a good-looking fellow like that."

"He's only in town for a few days. He's a shifter."

"You nearly swallowed your tongue, he pushed all your buttons." Caroline stared over the field, and Shelley followed her line of vision just in time for Chase to disappear into the crowds wandering the street fair. "Lost opportunity, that's all I'm saying, Shell."

"Oh, stop it." She collapsed back to the blanket, some of the fun and happiness of the past hours gone. "I'm getting settled in, and I don't need a man to make me happy. Or complete. Or...whatever."

Caroline grinned. "Okay, fine, but at least acknowledge that even if you don't want one for long term, men are dandy things to enjoy for the short term."

"I don't want to talk sex with you, sis."

"You are such a weird wolf." Caroline squeezed her tight as if to ease the sting from her words. "Talking about sex with wolves is like breathing. Since you insist, I'll zip my mouth after this, but at some point please reconsider your stand on abstinence. Because frankly, your moaning will drive me nuts since I know some action would make you a whole lot more relaxed."

How her sister had managed to adapt to the wolf culture so well amazed her. "You're such a weird human."

Caroline laughed.

Another *oooh* rose from the crowd as a huge batch of balloons were released into the air, filling the bright sky with a rainbow of colour as the wind got hold of them. Some swirled in circles, back eddying in the twisted currents over the Yukon River before escaping into the higher airstreams and lofting into the north.

Shelley watched the bits of latex and ribbon spread out, impossible to gather back, each carrying a tiny piece of bright pollution into the vast wilderness of the territory. Pretty, yet destructive.

The ache inside to belong felt bigger than before, and she sighed. Part of her loneliness was her own choice. Her own decision to live life this way. She'd planned to take the positive with the negative, but the lingering scent of the sexy shifter made her reconsider.

Perhaps she had a few items on her list she should consider revising. Maybe the next time she met someone who turned her on, she could have a little fun—even if they were a shifter.

Life was supposed to be about change. It was high time she remembered that.

Chapter Four

Caroline plopped the steaming coffee down on the bedside table and watched as Evan slowly woke. He rolled over, sniffing toward the rising aroma.

"You are a goddess," he moaned.

With the sheet tangled around his naked body he looked like a Greek god, so they were even for once. "You're so easy to please."

He grinned and rearranged himself until he was level enough to pull back a deep sip. "You know it. I'm a simple man, really."

She sat on the edge of the bed and admired him. This whole sleeping-with-the-Alpha thing was working out way better than she'd expected. He was a generous lover, and besides that, their friendship had remained rock solid. "I've got news for you, once your brain cells engage."

"Spill." He sat up and leaned against the headboard. Evan crossed his arms behind his head, biceps bulging nicely.

Hmmm, distracting. Caroline shook herself back to attention.

"There's been a rash of hotel bookings. I think you're right—the bear shindig that was making all that noise up north is moving location from Dawson City to Whitehorse."

His relaxed persona vanished. "Damn, really? I mean, hey, about time..."

She laughed. "You tricky bastard. You were just guessing."

Evan grimaced. "No, I figured they'd head here, I just hoped it would be later than sooner. You ever have a crowd of bear shifters around?"

Caroline thought through previous conventions that had been held in the hotel while she'd worked there. "When I was young my stepdad took us to West Edmonton Mall, and we ran into a huge bear gathering—something to do with the hockey season—but up north? Never."

"They aren't normal guests, let's just put it that way." Evan took another swallow of his coffee then pointed his cup at her. "Book them carefully. Try to find out alliances when they call, and place them on different floors. That might help matters."

"Don't think we need to worry. Sounds as if each faction is taking a different part of the city. We've got the Harrison clan registering."

Evan whistled.

"That good, eh?" she asked.

"He's one of the bigwigs this time around. Last rumors I heard, he might end up in charge of the whole shooting match."

"I still don't believe bears vote to organize their territories."

Evan grinned at her over his mug. "Yeah, the wolf way is so much more exciting. Blood matches, throats being ripped apart in surprise attacks..."

She deliberately yawned. "Right. The buyouts you're fooling around with right now simply thrill me to pieces."

Was she an adrenaline junkie? Maybe it was wrong for her to be energized by a potentially volatile situation in Whitehorse, but this was part of the reason she'd always gotten along with shifters.

Evan rolled his eyes as he put his cup aside. "Damn, you're happy about this."

Oops. She hid her delight a little harder. "No, of course not."

"You are so."

"Am not."

Evan lunged forward and grabbed her by the wrist, dragging her toward him and flipping her under his body. He settled in nicely, his weight trapping her in place. "You. Are. Trouble. With a capital T."

"Takes one to know one..."

Evan lowered his head and kissed her neck. "Mischief is your middle name. I'm still not exactly sure why you were so keen on us becoming lovers, but I will say the last few weeks have certainly been interesting."

A shiver shook her. "I've kind of enjoyed myself as well."

He tucked his nose against her throat and took a deep, deep breath.

Caroline slapped his bare shoulder. "Stop that. No matter how hard you sniff me, it's not going to change the facts. I'm not your mate."

He shook his head sorrowfully. "Too damn bad, because you, my darling, are a pistol."

She rocked her hips under him. "You, sir, have a pistol. Care to show me your ammunition?"

He rolled them again, placing her on top. "All this talk of guns. It's just not right for a Canadian girl. You're supposed to be a pacifist. A peacemaker."

She wiggled until she straddled his hips. "I like a good fight as much as the next girl."

"You like to fight far more than the next girl."

"Which is why, right now, I'm the perfect partner for you. Temporary partner."

Evan cupped her face gently. "I do like you, Caroline Bradley. Now, come and wake me up properly with your own dirty, peacekeeping self."

She stripped off her top and enjoyed the lust that rose in his eyes. The concerns of hotel organization during the upcoming bear territory talks could wait.

"I thought you'd never ask..."

The buzzer on the other side of the door went off for about three seconds before switching to a high-pitched squeal that stopped abruptly. Chase already had his finger off the button, but not far enough to avoid the snap of an electrical shock.

"Shit." He backed away from the glass door and wiggled his fingers to relieve the pain. "Dammit."

He was still cussing lightly when the glass door opened half an inch then jerked to a stop before he could see into the clinic.

"You got the place booby-trapped?" he grumbled. "I was told you were the place to visit, but if you're electrocuting patients, I'll wait until the next time I'm in town."

The door wiggled, gaining another inch clearance. "I don't know why anyone told you to come here. The clinic's not open. I'm still getting all the bugs out of the system."

Something crashed as the woman spoke, but even the distraction couldn't stop him from recognizing that voice.

Oh no. Shelley.

Chase was three seconds away from hightailing it without seeing anyone. Because seeing her wasn't a good idea.

"Just a second. I think I've got it." Shelley wiggled the door and he was caught. The door swung wide open, and they were back to being trapped in a time warp—staring at each other.

Her hair was a mess. Bits of plaster and wood decorated the unruly tangle. There was a streak of paint across her cheek and nose, her T-shirt also dabbled with spots. A thin T-shirt, so well-worn he imagined it would be soft under his fingers. It was certainly thin enough he could tell she wasn't wearing a bra, and her nipples were—

She snapped upright, and he jerked his gaze back to her face.

"The clinic's not open yet," she repeated.

If this weren't important, he would have so walked away. But inside, that place where his wolf and cat selves were prone to take over at times? They'd made it clear they wanted this. "I have to see a...doctor. Before I go bush again."

Her cheeks brightened. "Oh. Right."

She swallowed hard but moved out of the way. He stepped in over the remains of a pallet filled with tile, set exactly where it shouldn't have been for access to the main room. There were broken tiles piled in one corner of the shop and a cutter beside them. "Having troubles with the flooring?"

Shelley sighed. "Well, actually, yeah. But I think I've figured it out. Come on. If you really need to be here, I'll wash my hands and we can talk. My office is pretty much done."

She led him into a nicely organized room with an efficient-looking desk and file system. And only about three feet of floor space. "This won't work."

She'd already settled behind the desk, obviously using it as a safety barrier between them. "We can talk here first. We'll go elsewhere if needed."

Chase shrugged. "You're the doctor."

"Vet. I have vet training." She frowned. "You sure you need to see me?"

He nodded. "Shifted form isn't healing. I hope you can tell me why."

She pulled out a pad of paper and asked him questions. The usual overall health and history. When he mentioned his Métis blood, her eyes widened but she stayed professional. Now that she was over her initial shock, she'd slipped into the smoothest bedside manner he'd ever seen.

His cock got hard just thinking about beds and her at the same time.

Her scent floored him. This time, it wasn't just the wolf that was interested, but the cougar as well, and that bastard was the pickiest thing when it came to females.

"Chase."

He'd gone and lost all train of thought. "Sorry. What?"

"I asked if you've got the injury in all three forms? Since you're Métis."

He shook his head. "No. Or, I don't think so. I've only shifted to the cat and back to human since the accident."

She nodded and laid aside the notepad. "Follow me. You're right. This space won't be big enough for your cougar. I would like to examine all your forms, please, if you don't mind."

He followed her into the back where there was a large stainless steel table in a sparkling clean examining room. Now his troubles started, more than the fact he had to hide his erection from her. Damn, she smelt good. "I don't mind, but I might not be able to oblige."

Shelley paused in the middle of washing her hands. "Reason?"

"Can't control the shift."

Her face went white, and for a second he thought she might actually pass out on him. She clutched the sides of the sink. "No control? But you can shift when you want?"

He nodded, loosing the top button on his shirt. "I can go furry, but the beasts decide who gets to come out and play, so to speak. My wolf's been pouting lately. Only been the cat showing up."

She took a deep breath. "Okay, that might make it a little more difficult, but let's see what we can do." She patted the top of the table. "First, if you don't mind. Sit here and let me see the marks on your human form."

She turned away under the excuse of grabbing her instruments, but honestly she couldn't bear to watch him strip off his shirt. The buttons had sounded loud in her ears, and the thought of having this delicious man half-naked in her office— oh boy.

She was a dirty pervert, the thoughts running through her brain.

The past three nights she'd been thinking about him and her lost opportunity at the party. Caroline had been kind and stopped teasing after only a couple more digs. Shelley had been the one to administer chastisement for the next while. She could have had a man in her bed, but instead she was making herself come in the middle of the night, waking up to feverish dreams, all of which involved Chase.

Now he was here and she had to touch him.

She was either being punished or rewarded, and she wasn't sure which.

"I'm ready."

Slow and steady, there was a teasing lilt to his voice, as if he knew she was hiding as she gathered tools. Shelley braced herself and lifted her chin as she turned back.

She should have grabbed a towel to catch her drool. My, oh my, he was a fine specimen. Sharply muscular, the combination of wolf and cat turning his leanness into hard lines. "You must have the most incredible metabolism," she commented.

"Hard to take in too many calories, that's for sure."

Ripped. Strong. Shelley took his blood pressure and did all the routine checks as stoically as possible, but there was no way to stop him from scenting how turned on she was. His skin was hot under her fingers as she removed the blood pressure cuff from his biceps, and she fought to not linger as she held the stethoscope to his chest.

Sweet mercy, the hair on his chest was thicker than your average wolf—perhaps his cat nature coming to the fore. She imagined petting him, playing her fingertips through the soft curls. Working her way lower until—

It wasn't professional of her to think that way. It wasn't professional to be feeling any of the things she was feeling, but damn if she could stop herself.

She moved faster, rushing through the steps, trying to keep her focus on what she needed to do, which was *not* leaning over to lick him.

Not even once.

A strong grip wrapped around her wrist, trapping her in place.

"Shelley. Slow down. We should talk about this."

"Talk about what?"

"This."

He tugged her between his legs and lifted her chin as his lips covered hers.

It was oh, so wrong and oh, so right. Shelley let the stethoscope fall from her fingers and gave into the urge to press her fingers against his pelt and run her hands up his chest. He'd wrapped a hand around the back of her neck and controlled her, kissing her softly but insistently. His tongue stroking hers, lips teasing and demanding a response. They weren't diminishing, they weren't going away, the urges inside her.

But they also weren't uncontrollable. It was lust, pure and simple, not a frantic mating urge, and that made her feel a little better. Maybe she'd kick her own ass in a few minutes, but for the next sixty seconds she was going to take this in and enjoy every second.

Hmm, she'd set the examination tables at the right height for her to check dogs, cats and other pets without having to stoop or lift up. That put his groin and hers nicely in line and as he kissed her—no, as she now kissed him, heat transferred between them in the most delightful way. He stroked her hair, his other hand slipping behind her back and pressing her against him. Her T-shirt could have evaporated for all the barrier it provided. Her nipples tightened, her sex ached for a touch. The only part of her body truly happy was her mouth because he tasted so. Damn. Good.

Shelley wiggled forward, just a teeny bit, and it wasn't enough. She was ready to ignite, and he was the flame she'd been waiting for. He nibbled his way along her jaw, and she dug her fingernails into his shoulders.

His sudden gasp froze her in position. There was something sticky under her hand, and she realized she'd manhandled his injury.

"Oh Lordy, why didn't you stop me?" Guilt jerked her into action as she spun from his grasp and basically threw herself behind him to see what damage she'd caused.

There were no words. More correctly, the words she wanted to say disappeared as she pulled her professionalism back into place, ready to accept his well-deserved rebuke. Four jagged lines tore down his back. Starting near his neck, they splayed toward his side, red, swollen and hot, and where she'd broken the scab, weeping.

"I'm so sorry." She moved to grab antiseptic and cleaned the cuts as best she could. Chase didn't say a word, but she was saying enough inside for the two of them.

Idiot. Not only had she crossed the line between a patient/doctor relationship, she'd been totally distracted in the first place. His medical history could have waited—she should have looked at his injury at the start.

Of course, this was the weird part of being a shifter who was a vet. It was assumed her human first-aid training in conjunction with the vet specialization made her a better person to visit than a mere human-only doctor/vet.

Not many vets could handle having their patients shift on them, so there was that.

Chase spoke over his shoulder. "If you're done beating yourself up, let me shift. I've cleaned that cut a dozen times. You're just wasting your supplies."

Shelley slowed. Forced herself to move to where she could look him in the eye. "That was inexcusable of me. I'm sorry."

A lazy, relaxed grin broke free. "It was inexcusable. Don't you ever run away again when we're in the middle of a scorching-hot kiss."

Shelley pulled her jaw off the floor, stepping back as Chase slid off the table and stalked her.

"I shouldn't have kissed you."

"But you didn't. I kissed you." Chase stroked her again, his touch so gentle on her cheek she wanted to lean her head against his fingers and stay that way.

He would have had her crowded against the wall if she hadn't slammed up a hand between them. "Chase. Stop. This...*thing*...between us. Can we ignore it for a few minutes and let me see your other form? Please."

His dark eyes sparkled and he caught her fingers in his hand. Lifted her hand and kissed her knuckles before setting her free. "But we are going to talk about this. Tonight."

She nodded. At this point she'd agree to anything to get a little space between them. She needed time to allow the buzz of sexual urgency racing through her body to slow.

He dropped his hands to his waist and popped open the top button on his jeans.

Oh no. Oh no, *no, no.* Professionalism vanished as he dragged down his zipper. "Let me know when you've shifted..."

She fled.

Chapter Five

There was a big ol' grin on his face, he was sure of it. The cuts on his back stung like the blazes, but there was no way he'd give up a second of the sweet kiss she'd bestowed on him. It was a lovely start to what he hoped would be a fabulous final evening in the big city.

He stripped off his jeans, tossing them over the back of a nearby chair. A short stretch, to settle his muscles, and he shifted, the transition flowing with less ease than normal. For a moment his switch from one sort of being to another almost paused, and the usual pleasant buzz of endorphins was sorely lacking. He snarled his displeasure.

The feel-good sensation of shifting was typically one of the high points of his day.

At least his cougar arrived as he'd expected. Shelley briefly snuck her head around the corner before she stepped into the room.

"Holy moly, you are a big son of a gun."

Chase took his time as he lay out to his maximum length. He'd told her he wouldn't fit in her office.

She rolled her eyes. "Yes, you're a typical cat. Gloating because you were right. Fine. Now that you're comfortable, let me see if I can spot any differences in your wound in this form."

She moved around him, scraping a little, taking a blood sample. She talked under her breath as she worked.

It wasn't as if he could answer back, but it was a trifle disconcerting to hear her muttering references to her veterinary textbooks under her breath.

He gave a mental shrug. A cat was a cat was a cat, he guessed.

Something soft and warm rubbed along his hind leg. He twitched lightly, attempting not to disturb Shelley where she was currently working near his left forepaw. She had the cutest little frown on her face, tongue sticking out as if she were concentrating.

A tiny set of needles jabbed him in what would have been his ankle if he were human, and he snarled.

"Oh, stop being such a baby. Enigma isn't hurting you." She pressed a pad against his wounds. He snorted. She'd changed mannerisms completely—it was easy to tell which of his forms she felt most comfortable around.

Something light but with really sharp claws crawled its way up his hindquarters. Teeny tiny pinpricks changed to the whisper-light tread of a feline. The beastie's scent was familiar, and Chase realized it was the cat he'd smelt on Shelley the other night.

She was all wolf. With a cat hanging around her veterinary offices.

"I need to pop this under the microscope and take some pictures. Don't move for a minute." Shelley patted his side then stood, her hips swaying nicely as she paced toward the door and out of the room.

In his animal form, he couldn't appreciate her quite the same way as in his human. The brain patterns were slightly different. He was still himself, but the beast nature was more interested in basics like food and fucking. He liked to think his human side had a little more depth, but after that kiss, there were a few animalistic-based things his human side would also like to explore a whole lot more.

Ice picks fastened on his ear, and he reached with his right paw to bat the offending creature off. A blob of black fell to one side, weight tugging at him as the tiny beast kept its teeth locked in a death grip. Chase lowered his head carefully until the black ball of fuzz rested on the ground. Finally the pinchers released, and a little pink tongue slipped out to touch his muzzle.

Oh boy.

Chase lay trapped by the tiny creature as it moved full force into caring for him. The teeny paw resting on Chase's sensitive nose made sure he stayed in place as the cat—Enigma—groomed him.

So much for being the biggest, baddest dude in the room. He knew his place in this hierarchy, and it appeared the fur ball outranked all of them. At least for the moment.

A soft laugh alerted him to Shelley's return a moment before she scooped up the cat. "Oh you. Stop bossing everyone around. Sorry about that, Chase. He's not afraid of anything. Okay, I've got a shot to give you that will boost your healing during your next shift. I'll need to examine you again in your human form to check your reaction. Do you have an issue with needles? And don't be brave and fake it if you do, because I'd prefer to know now than when I've got three hundred pounds of cat passed out on top of my foot or something."

Chase scooted upward until he rested comfortably on his front paws and was able to stare into her eyes again. He shook his head. Needles were fine.

It was the getting-back-to-human bit he was most interested in.

She seemed to know where his thoughts had gone, and her face flushed. His anticipation rose higher. No matter what she'd said at the park, she wasn't unaware of him as a man. If he wasn't completely incapable of a little old-fashioned seduction, this could be an interesting evening.

The slide of the needle into his flesh barely registered. She was good. And she smelt amazing, which might have helped to distract him.

She pressed the injection spot with a bit of cotton. "It's a trifle strange to treat a shifter. I'm fairly confident you're not about to bite me or pounce on me like a wild animal might, but there's always that edge of uncertainty. Thanks for being so calm about this."

Chase lowered his head.

"I'll let you—"

He shifted, standing as he completed the transformation. No way was he giving her time to leave the room while he changed. "You're very gentle with your instruments. Thank you. Now what did you need to see on this form?"

She was standing only inches away. Shelley's gaze dropped almost involuntarily to his groin, and she twisted her head away rapidly as his cock rose to full attention.

"I want to make sure the shot bolstered your shifter cells enough that the cuts have begun to heal." She gestured to the examining table. "If you could sit again. Turn your back to me."

She spoke to the wall the entire time.

He'd never seen such a shy shifter before. It was kinda cute.

The steel of the tabletop was cold under his naked butt. Her fingers on his back were light, delicate, and so hot he swore he might catch on fire.

"Does it look any better?" he asked.

"Not like I had hoped. You say it's been seven days?"

He calculated back to double-check. "Eight at the most."

"And you've never had any trouble healing before?"

"Never." He pivoted until his legs touched her side. She was so intent on examining his back she barely seemed to notice his slow approach. "I'm a healthy man. Don't do anything to excess, take care of myself."

That brought another furtive peek at his body. Chase grinned.

Shelley walked away, tapping her fingers against her lips. "I've only seen a case like this mentioned a couple times. I need to do some research. Need to check your white-blood-cell count. I should probably contact my mentor—because this is way beyond what I expected for my first solo case." She spun to face him. "You have to stay in town for a couple of days until I get the results."

Oh hell, no. "Don't think I can do that."

She plopped her fists on her hips, looking damn adorable as she did so. "Look, Chase. You came here looking for medical attention. That makes me responsible for you."

"I have responsibilities as well." He shrugged. "Gotta get back north before the boys think I'm gone for good."

"It's only a couple more days, not a month."

"You could convince me to stay..." He stroked her arm again. Such soft skin. He couldn't get enough of touching her.

Her jaw hung open as she gaped at him. "Convince you to stay? How about I use a shot of knockout gas and let you sleep for a while? Maybe that's what your body needs to finish healing."

She might be protesting, but she wasn't moving out of his reach. "I doubt you want to drug me up. Why you getting so prickly? I like you. You like me. I'm not going to hurt you."

If she'd really been saying no like she had the other night at the park he'd have dropped this. Certainly wouldn't have sat in the buff and dragged in breath after breath of her intoxicating aroma.

But she was saying yes with everything but her words.

Shelley sighed and shook her head. She grabbed a bandage and turned him away to patch him up. "Old habits die hard. I'm a bit of a loner. Not used to someone being nice to be nice."

"Oh, I'm not nice..." Chase caught her against his side and squeezed her. She smacked him on the top of his head and he let go in a hurry. "Ouch."

"Behave. I'm trying to explain something. Just because my body reacts to yours doesn't mean I have to respond."

She tugged again, and he stood and rotated as instructed. "I'm not asking to move in with you."

"I know, it's just..." Shelley growled with frustration. Slapped on a final bit of tape more forcefully than the rest. "Sex is complicated."

"Now I know you're not a typical shifter. Sex is one of the simplest things in our world."

This time she crowded him and his pulse sped up. Oh yeah, a power play from her side of the equation would be fine. There he was, pinned against the wall, or at least as pinned as a six-foot-plus male could be by a five-foot-something female. Shelley stared up at him. "I will get them to rush the tests. I want you to stay for one more night."

He caught hold of her hips and tugged her against his body. "I can see my way to cooperating with that request."

Warm, willing hands cupped his face and brought his head toward hers. Their mouths close, her heated breath fanning over his cheek. His cock was rigid against her body, trapped between them, and the faint pressure was the merest promise of what he really needed. One more inch, a little farther. He slid his hands up her torso to meld them together in anticipation of her kiss.

She turned her head aside at the last moment and whispered in his ear, "You stay, but I'm not having sex with you. I have professional and personal limits, and I will not cross them again."

Suddenly he was holding air, the warmth of her body evaporating as she grabbed his clothes from the floor and tossed them at him. Instinctively he caught them.

Instinct was the only thing still working.

"Well, damn."

Shelley paused in the doorway. "Trust me, I'm not happy either. But at the same time, this is what I have to do."

"You have to frustrate me? I didn't see that on the patient/doctor forms."

She snorted as Chase reluctantly dragged on his jeans. "I'll add that in as one of the options to check off next time. I...can't."

She was still staring as he finished zipping. "I have nowhere to stay. Just saying."

"But you—"

"Had a place. Gave it up, since I figured I was heading home. You got a couch for me to bunk on?"

"You could stay at the pack house..." There was dead silence for all of ten seconds. They both laughed uncomfortably at the same time as the truth of that suggestion hit. "No, I guess you couldn't at that."

"I'm just a poor man with an injury my doctor wants to treat tomorrow. I won't be any trouble."

Shelley bit her lip.

"Not unless you want me to be trouble, that is." Chase pulled his shirt over the bandages. It still ached like the blazes, but other portions of his anatomy felt worse.

"Fine. You can stay with me. But we're not sleeping together."

"You're the one in charge." At least until he convinced her otherwise. "I can give you a hand with the flooring if you have medical stuff to do."

"Seriously? You know how to tile?"

Chase nodded. "And I can fix the doorbell. Unless you enjoy waking up your patients before they enter the office."

Her face brightened, the sexual tension between them fading slightly. "I would appreciate your help very much."

She showed him what she'd been doing, and he set to work, the task mindless as he cut and placed the tiles in pattern. Off in the other room, she moved though the lab with an easy competence. It was companionable and relaxed.

Chase turned back to the pile of work. He'd save the seduction for tonight.

Chapter Six

She'd discovered a new form of torture. First, having given in to kissing the sexy shifter, her body assumed that was the all-clear signal for more than just a wildly inappropriate moment. Her work in the lab had helped distract her for a while, as did drafting up a message to her mentor back in Calgary, but her constant awareness of him was, well, constant.

He'd managed to lay out over ninety-percent of the tiles she'd been struggling with, so now she was astonished at his work ethic as well as wanting to slurp him up like an ice-cream cone.

And then she'd brought him home. Her apartment overlooking the Yukon River seemed a lot smaller with him in it. He wasn't loud. Or big, he was just right freaking *there,* and she really wanted a piece of him.

Her wolf was nowhere to be found. The elusive creature wasn't the one making her drool at the moment. No, after kick-starting her libido the beast had retreated as much as possible, so there was no way to excuse this as one of those freaky *other* things.

She had the hots for the man. Period. And what she was going to do about it was absolutely nothing.

Maybe.

She turned up the enthusiasm to hide her need to jump him. "Pizza?"

"Perfect. You order, I'll buy." Chase dropped onto the couch and stretched out his long limbs. He took up the entire space.

Well, not really, but it seemed everywhere she looked, there he was. "I like everything, so order whatever you want."

Shelley grabbed the TV remote and tossed it at him. "Here, have a blast. Pick what you want to watch."

She called the pizza shop, ordered a couple extra large with double meat and three side salads. Remembering his metabolism, she added wings to the order, figuring anything that was leftover she'd send north with him.

When she turned back he was still sprawled out, but he'd turned away from the TV and was watching her intently.

"Nothing interesting on?"

Chase's heated grin stroked her. "You told me to watch whatever I liked. That's what I'm doing."

Oh boy. The zap of sexual lust was instant and bad. Real bad. "Why are you doing this?"

His gaze dropped over her like a caress. "Doing what?"

Shelley hid behind the kitchen island and crossed her arms. "Doing that. That look. Your comments. I said no sex."

"You said no sex in the office. We're not in the office anymore. Besides, I'm not even touching you."

Growling with frustration would just show how much he was getting to her. "Chase. Stop it."

He shrugged. "If you're positive you don't want to have sex, I'll stop."

"Really?" And why did she feel more disappointed in that comment than she should?

"Really. But if you wanted to fool around a little, I'm game for that."

Sheesh. "You are persistent."

He rose smoothly, and again all the images in her brain were of exotic hunters taking sight of their prey and never letting up the hunt. "I'm not some kind of asshole who will hound you until I get what I want."

Laughing seemed inappropriate, but she did it anyway. "You're not hounding me? Definitions are different where you come from."

"I'm reacting to what your body is telling me. That's why I'm now suggesting alternatives." Chase slid his fingers along her cheek, his thumb stroking her lower lip. "You like me. You're attracted to me."

She couldn't speak. Not without drooling, his touch was so addictive. Shelley nodded.

"But for some reason you don't want to let out the side of us that enjoys sex." He shrugged. "I'm not going to push you to find out why, but damn if I won't suggest we can do other things without sex. If it's only the big bad deed making you hesitate."

"You sure you're not a politician?"

"Hell, no. They eat politicians where I'm from."

Shelley discovered her hands stroking him. Bad hands, to take control like that. "You're very reasonable. Far more reasonable than most men. Or shifters."

"I'm not typical."

He said it so dryly Shelley lost control and snorted in amusement. "No. No, you certainly aren't."

Chase brought them closer. His fingers in her hair, smoothing the strands away from her face. "So does that option interest you at all?"

"The no-sex sex?"

"Fooling around. As far as you want to go. I'll follow your lead, but I want to touch you. Make you feel good."

A shiver of temptation struck. And when he brought their mouths together again, part of the decision was made.

Damn, the man could kiss. He was so sneaky she didn't even register when he picked her up and carried her across the room. He must have, though, because suddenly she was sitting on his lap on her couch, straddling him in fact. That wicked tongue of his brushed along the rim of her ear before he dipped inside, and she shivered.

Goose bumps, check. Body aching for a touch, check. He kissed the hollow of her throat, and she was lost.

No-sex sex was awesome. This? This she could totally do.

She grabbed her T-shirt and stripped it off, pleased to see his eyes widen.

"Sweet mercy, woman."

Being small enough to go braless had its moments. "You too. I promise not to scratch your injury."

"I like nails. Don't worry about it." He tore off his shirt, and a second later she was crushed against that oh-so-warm and furry chest. Fingers irresistibly drawn to stroke and weave through the thick tangle.

Then their lips were back together, giving her time to explore his mouth with her tongue. To trace his teeth, to nibble on his lips.

She clutched his forearms to make sure she stayed away from the cuts on his back. He grabbed her hips and tugged her in tighter, her open legs making her ride along the thick seam of his jeans. The thick ridge of him under that seam.

He lifted her as if she weighed nothing and licked his way to her nipple.

Shelley arched against his mouth. "Yes. Perfect."

If she'd expected the same slow tease she'd gotten in his kiss, she'd have been more surprised. But the flash in his eyes gave a split-second's warning so when he latched on and sucked hard, she only kinda screamed.

He released pressure but applied his tongue diligently, and she moaned out her happiness. When he pulled off with a pop a moment later, Shelley smiled at him.

"You having fun?" he asked.

She pivoted her hips over his hard-on as an answer, pleased to watch his eyes roll back. "Tons. You?"

"Oh, yeah." He jerked her forward and took the other breast under attack, and this time she out-and-out shrieked as he nipped the sensitive tip.

Behind them the door flew open, and a growling and furious male charged into the room, power radiating off him. Pizza boxes flew every direction as the dark-haired stranger growled, "Get your hands off her, you bastard."

Through the blur of confusion, switching from sexual excitement to shock at being invaded, facts slowly percolated to the surface.

There was a wolf in her living room.

Well, one other than the Métis cross-blood she'd been happily riding like a pony. This one looked a trifle more intimidating as he stomped across the room toward them. Chase did his best to help cover her, only that meant he actually had his hands cupping her breasts as she rotated and tried to snatch up her discarded T-shirt.

Out of the corner of her eye, Shelley spotted Caroline entering the room, plastic bags dangling from her hands.

"Shelley? You okay?"

Face flaming-hot, she debated the best way to dig out of this hole.

Chase took part of the decision away from her, cradling her head and pressing her face to the V of his neck. That meant only her naked back faced the newcomers. Thank heavens she hadn't ditched her pants or she'd be mooning them. "She's fine. You mind?"

"Shit." That deep masculine voice again. There was a moment's scrambling that Shelley assumed were feet shuffling on the floor. "You're not in trouble."

Caroline laughed. "Well, that's kind of obvious. What did you come running in here like Rambo for, idiot?"

A loud slap. "Ouch. Stop it, Caro. She screamed. You said she was alone, and when I heard her scream I assumed—"

"Oh, pick up the pizza. Make yourself useful." Caroline's exasperation rang loud and clear.

Chase snickered. He spoke quietly in her ear. "You have guests."

Lordy. And here she was topless. "Brilliant deduction."

"I take it you didn't invite them."

She shook her head, and just to drive herself crazy, she relaxed against his warm torso. All her lovely non-sex sex thoughts slipped away. Because if she didn't miss her guess, Caroline had brought this new guy over to meet her or something.

"Shell, I'm going to take Evan for a quick tour of your...bathroom. Go ahead, we'll be gone for a couple minutes."

A hurried whispered conversation moved across the room and vanished behind the click of a door. Chase lifted her chin and smiled at her, that lazy, sexy smile that melted her defenses. He was looking her over with a touch of regret in his eyes. "I guess this means we're taking a breather."

She couldn't resist stroking his chest one last time. "I guess. Sorry. Looks as if my sister got it into her head to cheer me up or something."

Feather-light touches of his fingertips over her nipples made her catch her breath. He sighed again. "Damn shame. You're gorgeous."

He handed her T-shirt over before retrieving his own, rising to help gather the rest of the food supplies. "They accosted your pizza-delivery guy."

Shelley joined him in the kitchen, reaching to prepare drinks. "Poor pizza dude. Hey, you're staying, right?"

He nodded, his slow movements belying the strength he'd shown her moments before. "You entertain the Alpha of the Takhini pack often?"

Her body went numb and the two-liter bottle of pop in her right hand slipped from her fingers. Chase caught it just before it could hit the floor and explode.

Alpha?

She stared at her bathroom. "Caroline brought over the Takhini Alpha?"

"His name is Evan. Met him the other day. Seemed a decent enough fellow."

The bathroom door creaked open, and two heads peered around the corner, one the familiar blonde of her sister, who Shelley had every intention of killing ASAP, and the other a darkly handsome wolf. Who, yes, was obviously some kind of chief pooh-bah because even across the room his mere presence made her wolf tremble.

"Can we come out?" Caroline asked. "Is it safe?"

Evan stood in the hallway, a bundle of sexy muscle and power. "As if it was dangerous before. She had no top on—to your average male a half-naked woman isn't the scariest thing on the planet—"

Shelley watched in amazement as her sister stepped in front of what had to be the top wolf of the territory and firmly grabbed him by the ears. "My sister. Naked. Don't ever put those two words together in the same sentence if you want to keep your nuts. Got it?"

Chase opened the pop bottle. The resulting fizz drew all their attention his direction. "Anyone want a drink?"

There was a moment of silence before they all seemed to decide pretending none of it had ever happened was the best idea. Caroline grabbed plates, drinks were poured, pizza and wings piled high. Someone turned on music in the background, and suddenly Shelley found herself sitting on the edge of the couch next to a relaxed Chase as he lifted the first piece of pizza in a toast.

"To life, and just how damn amusing it is."

Evan's grin widened as he returned the salute. "So, you have a successful stay in town?"

"Mostly." Chase tilted his head toward Shelley. "She's still looking into a few things for me, but everything else is done for the year. I won't be troubling your territory until next July."

The guys chatted a little more, but Shelley only listened with half an ear. Caroline had brought the Alpha to her house, and from the way he was curled up next to Caroline at the table, stealing food off her plate, they were an item.

Shelley's head spun. Caroline and the pack Alpha? How in the world had that happened?

Caroline seemed to be trying to send her clues with head signals, but this mess was far too complicated to settle with head jerks, rolled eyes and grimaces.

Shelley rose to her feet. "You boys excuse us? We need to talk for a minute."

She grabbed her sister by the hand and dragged her from the room. Neither of them spoke until they were safely ensconced in the bedroom where she'd unpacked all of her things. Bright sheets and curtains made up the decor, her treasures proudly displayed. A comforting place to deal with a very uncomfortable topic.

She whirled on his sister. "What the hell?"

"Sorry, but I never expected you to have Mr. Yummy in your apartment. I wouldn't have interrupted if I'd known. Good for you—"

"That's not what I'm talking about, and you know it. You're sleeping with the Alpha? You've gone insane. The pack women are going to rip you to shreds. What was he thinking? How could you do this?"

"Stop with the twenty questions already. I'm fine. We're fine. It's a business arrangement." Caroline had the grace to flush as Shelley took a long, pointed sniff and raised a brow. "Okay, more than business, but really, that's what started it. And the pack is fine. I kicked a few butts, and now the girls are more than happy to behave around me. It's okay, it is."

Shelley stopped tugging on her hair before she made herself bald, but the urge remained. "And you didn't feel the need to tell me this before because...?"

Caroline stiffened. "It wasn't any of your business."

Shelley gasped. "How can you say that? You know how much I've been dreading contacting the pack, and here you are sleeping with the damn Alpha. You didn't think I would want to know that tidbit before you rushed into my apartment?"

"Sorry about that. And I did mean well. That's why I brought him in alone, ahead of time. Thought you could get to know him a little before having to face down anyone else."

Shelley took a few calming breaths. Outside the window, the light shone so brightly it could have been midday instead of early evening. The sun streamed in and highlighted her treasures, her memories from years spent in the south. Where she'd trained and grown and...tried to find a way to be happy without being a full wolf.

It burned inside to have to admit that her fully human half-sister fit into shifter society better than she did. But the jealousy eating her inside was her own issue, not Caroline's. "I know you didn't mean anything but the best, but damn it if you don't make me want to curl into a ball sometimes and just give the hell up."

Caroline's face registered her shock. "My God, no. That's not what I want. I wanted you to have a place you can call home. Where you feel comfortable. I wanted—"

"I know." Shelley grabbed her sister's hands and hung on tight. "And I love you for it, but it still makes me so damn mad. You work hard. I know you do, but it seems whatever you want to accomplish, happens."

Her fingers were squeezed in return. "And you don't work hard? Overachievers, all of us. Our dad taught us well. Stand on your own, get your training. Find what you want..."

"Fight for it. I know, Caro, but—"

Her voice broke, and Shelley twisted free, turning to stare out the window. The tears welling up in her eyes were supposed to be gone and done with.

"Shell?"

She shrugged. "I have done that. Fought for what I wanted. I went to school, finished top in my class. I've skimped and saved to have enough to start the office here. Heck, even coming back to Whitehorse is a trouble I asked for and I'm going to succeed. I will find my place in this pack, but the most important thing I want, I just can't—"

The words choked off, unable to get past the lump in her throat.

A pair of arms surrounded her as Caroline hugged her from behind. Her chin resting on Shelley's shoulder, they stood together for a moment before her sister sighed. "Your wolf, right?"

Shelley nodded.

"That's the one battle no one can help you with. And that there might not be a way to win."

She would have cursed, but all her curses had been spent years ago. "It's a hell of a thing, Caro. To be a wolf who can't shift. And there's no way to describe that pain to you, and nothing you can do to make it better."

They stood in silence until Shelley had to grab a tissue and wipe her eyes. Straighten herself up and do the next thing. Which meant facing an Alpha she didn't want to deal with yet, and the shifter she'd been fooling around with.

Both rather inconveniently camped out in her living room.

Chapter Seven

Evan watched with growing concern and annoyance as the women closed themselves in the back bedroom. "Gee, that went peachy, didn't it?"

The visitor to town across from him stretched out his legs and sipped his drink. "Don't know. You in the habit of interrupting your pack members whenever the hell you feel like it? If so, well done."

Cheeky devil. "Yeah, sorry about that, but what was I supposed to think?"

Chase shrugged. "I understand. Just don't expect me to have much sympathy for you if your mate rips you a new one when you get home."

"She's not my mate."

The shifter's brows went way up.

"She's not, and if you don't have a broken sniffer, you'd know that."

A piece of pizza disappeared before Chase spoke again, his slow drawl so different from the shifters Evan hung out with in the Takhini pack.

"Fine, your partner. Because sure as hell, you're together."

"For now."

Chase took another bite. Chewed. Then grinned. "Feisty."

Evan snorted. "Seems to run in the family from what I can see. I thought you were just passing through town..."

The shifter rose to his feet, languid and smooth as he strolled to the kitchen and reloaded his plate. When the dude had managed to inhale the enormous pile of grub he'd loaded up, Evan had no idea. He was still working on his first serving.

When Chase returned, he balanced his plate on his knee and stared thoughtfully across the room. "Yeah. One thing led to another, you know how it goes."

Oh, he knew all right, and if this had been a typical shifter-to-shifter conversation, Evan would have been encouraging the other man all the way. But with it being Caroline's sister caught in the act, so to speak, that changed things a whole lot.

"I'm surprised." Evan caught Chase's gaze and didn't let go. "I don't think Shelley's a good option for a one-night stand."

"Thanks for your opinion."

Chase deliberately broke eye contact and resumed eating, and Evan got a little pissed. "No, I mean it. I don't think you should be here."

"She in your pack?"

Chase's question stopped Evan from blustering on about protecting his own. "Well, not yet, but soon, I expect."

"Seems then, if you don't mind a person speaking bluntly, this is none of your concern." Chase raised a hand before Evan could blast him. "I'm not saying you aren't right in caring for all the wolves passing through or settling in the area, even the ones that haven't given you allegiance yet. I understand that more than you think. Only I'm not causing harm. She's happy. You do the math."

It was the longest speech Evan had heard from the other man. If his concerns had merely been about protecting his position, the mini-lecture would have been enough to convince him to back off. But there was more to the story. "Shelley's never been triggered."

Tension swooshed into the room like an icy wind. Chase sat far more rigidly in his seat than the second before. "You're shitting me."

Evan lowered his voice. "Caroline thinks I don't know, but hell, I've been Alpha for the past year. I've heard every rumor that's gone down the pike a dozen times. People especially love to share the horror stories."

"Horror stories—there's more to it than she's a virgin?"

Damn. At what point was it no longer his business telling tales? Half-blood wolves like Shelley were triggered as adults by the exchange of hormones during sex. It was a pleasurable way to finally be able to let the animal side come out to play, and not usually an issue.

Except in this case.

Evan examined the other man carefully. Didn't seem like an asshole. Seemed more the type to want the gritty details of what was wrong with Shelley simply in the hopes they could return to what they'd been doing before being rudely interrupted.

Nope. Evan still couldn't do it. Not the least of reasons that Caroline would probably rip off his balls if she caught him talking about things she didn't approve of.

The realization made him laugh. Great. Feared Alpha of the Takhini pack, hopeful amalgamator of the divided packs of the north, and he was seriously intimidated by the human he was sleeping with.

At least it kept life interesting.

"You need to ask her the details. I'm just suggesting, again, that you shouldn't consider Shelley a good one-time event." Evan looked around the room, pointing at the knapsack on the floor. "Looks as if you were planning an overnighter."

Chase placed his plate on the coffee table then sat back and rubbed his hands up and down his thighs. "She asked me to stay in town until she has test results for me tomorrow. The hostel is full—I already checked out."

"Easily solved." Evan nabbed his phone and waved it in the air before texting a message to the front desk. "I understand the pack house is out, but I own a flipping hotel. Room for the night on me. Only, you need to find a way to make this look like it's your idea."

The stare from across the room was impressive. The slow smile that followed far too comprehending. Evan was a strong wolf, but this Métis was no slouch. "You don't want them to know I've been warned off."

"Exactly. I like keeping body parts intact, thank you."

Chase nodded. "Fooling around isn't supposed to be this big a deal. I accept."

He rose to his feet and picked up his bag, slinging it carefully over his shoulder.

Evan joined him, heading toward the door. "You need a ride?"

"Nah. Moonshine Inn isn't that far. Nice night for a walk."

Chase's hand was on the door, and hot damn, they were nearly scot-free when a cough sounded behind them.

"Leaving so soon?" Shelley stepped forward, her gaze lingering on the backpack draped over Chase's back. "Sleeping on the street?"

Chase shrugged. "Remembered a place I can crash. Thanks for the meal—I left my contribution to the party on the table."

He had the door open. Was stepping through.

There was no reaction from the women, and for one glorious moment Evan thought they'd gotten away with it.

"Chase..."

The man turned slowly. Looked Shelley up and down with a slow, heated gaze. "It's for the best, darling. I'll see you in the morning."

Caroline grabbed Evan's arm and tugged him into the apartment as Shelley moved to say farewell and close the door.

"You hungry?" he asked Caroline, passing her a plate. "If it's cold we can—"

"Evan Stone, what did you say to him to make him leave?" Caroline plopped her plate on the counter and crossed her arms.

Shelley stepped beside her and suddenly there were two very pissed-off females staring him down. "Whoa. Let's get this clear. I didn't do anything. Man thought it best to go." He turned to Shelley. "You really think he would leave if he didn't want to?"

Caroline's jaw dropped.

Shit.

"I mean, if he didn't think it was for the best?"

Caroline scowled harder, leaning her head toward her sister.

Dammit. That was slightly insulting as well.

Evan opened his mouth and nothing came out. He'd gone totally and completely brain-dead. "Jeez, Caroline give a fellow a break. I'm damned if I do, and damned if I don't."

"It's okay, Caro. I get the idea." Shelley pushed her sister toward the couch. "Let's eat. I'm starving, and if I'm going to be bossed around by people I don't even know, I'm not doing it on an empty stomach."

Shit again. He could organize the slickest takeover of a multimillion dollar corporation and still be floored by two women in their twenties.

"Look—"

Shelley cut him off. "No, you look. You're obviously the big cheese around here, and whatever you've got going with Caroline..." she glanced between the two of them and damn near rolled her eyes, "...well, that's your business."

Caroline wiggled uncomfortably on the arm of the chair where she'd found a perch. "I'm sorry for not telling you. Really, I am."

"I know. And I get it." Shelley nearly growled out the words. "But you need to understand as well. This is on my terms. Moving forward, rejoining the pack or not rejoining the pack. Lord, even fooling around with someone—it's my decision. It's my bloody life and, no disrespect intended, I want you both to butt the hell out."

Evan stepped behind Caroline and rested his hands lightly on her shoulders. She wasn't wolf that he could sense her completely like a pack member. In fact, her sister was far clearer to read, but he'd been around the human and cared enough for her to know she was upset. Upset with herself for hurting someone she cared about deeply. He leaned over to brush his cheek against hers, giving a light soothing touch to let her know he was there.

Caroline sighed, but his trick worked. She breathed out slowly and relaxed, as if letting him take control.

Evan considered. Yeah, even half the crap Shelley had been through over the years would have explained the size of the chip on her shoulder.

But never having experienced full acceptance as a wolf had made her forget a few key components.

He released Caroline with a final squeeze before taking a step toward Shelley. He let out a portion of his power. Not in a rush, but a slow trickle. Almost a caress, but intended as more of a hug.

"You're right. It is your life, and I have every intention of letting you make your own decisions." He stood in front of her, arms at his sides, body at ease. Making sure there was nothing in his body language to say she needed to fear him, and he hoped that would help the real message get through loud and clear. "But Shelley—I am an Alpha, and that means I can't turn off parts of myself just because you tell me to butt out. It might look like interfering, but it's built into me. It's instinctive that I care for you, in a way you've never known before."

He increased that part of him that was *other* and enveloped her with it.

She snapped her head up to stare into his eyes. Her mouth hung open slightly, jaw trembling.

"That emotion I can't help feeling is there, constant, huge. It isn't sexual, it's not because we're family. It's deeper and more real than any passion you've felt before."

The room pooled with his power now. Her eyes had widened as he spoke, either from the words or the sensation of him tangling himself around her. Caroline sat motionless—in itself a bloody miracle as she must have sensed some wolfie thing going down.

In front of him, Shelley shook.

He had to finish it. "So you make the decisions you have to, and I'll support you one hundred percent. Period."

Her words snuck out in a whisper. "I've been so alone."

God. Pain rippled through him in sympathy. "I know."

Evan opened his arms, and she stepped into them, resting her head against his chest and weeping like a child. He soothed her as best he could, but mainly he just held her. Held her with his arms and that other part of himself that called to the faint bit hidden deep inside her that refused to break free and become real.

Caroline joined them, hesitant at first until Shelley sniffled and grabbed her into the hug. The three of them stood for the longest time.

"Oh Lord, I'm not usually such a weepy mess. I'm not," Shelley complained, wiggling free and snatching up the napkins from the pizza order.

"Big changes means a lot of stress, hon, and you've been pushing yourself like crazy." Shelley tucked her sister back into a hug and smoothed her hair. "But I'll second Evan's words, the part about supporting you one hundred percent. I swear I'll do anything for you, but from now on, I'll try not to do things for you until you ask." She stared over her sister's head at Evan, and he smiled at her, dipping his head slightly in approval.

Shelley had a lot of baggage to carry, but she didn't have to carry it alone.

One night of frustration completed, and Chase was that much closer to being able to retreat to the bush where things were simpler, in so damn many ways he couldn't even begin to count them.

Not even the lingering scent of Shelley's attraction could make him change his mind. Hands-off was much better for both of them. Freaking logic put the brakes on his libido.

He reported to the office at eight a.m. as she'd requested, hopped up on the examining table and didn't glance her way as she poked and prodded his sliced shoulder again. He didn't visibly react when she leaned in and her hair fell over his arm and sent a rush of desire straight to his groin.

The sooner he was back in the bush, with ready access to the icy cold waters of his lake, the better.

"So, will I live?" The horrified expression that crossed her face stopped his chuckle before it started. "Or...not?"

"I've never seen anything like this, and neither has my mentor." She looked up from where she'd been rumbling through notes, scratching new information on the mess of papers before her. "Okay, maybe that wasn't the most doctor-ly to share, but Chase, are you sure there's nothing else you can tell me about the shifter who gave you the cuts? Was he sick? Did you go around any other animals afterward?"

He shook his head. "Just tell me. I'm a big boy."

Shelley slipped a paper in front of him. She pointed to the top image. "This is what the culture looked like last night, before I gave you the booster. The center image is after the shot. Small reaction, not what I'd hoped. Usually if I gave that serum to a shifter the results would be far different."

"You'd said that."

She poked at the bottom picture, and even to his untrained eye it looked weird. "This morning. It's as if I took a culture of a completely different wound. Different shifter, different...everything."

It had to be his mind playing games, but suddenly his shoulder hurt a lot more than it had a moment before. "Plain English now?"

"The infection, whatever it is, is mutating."

Chase coughed. *Hell.*

She hurried on, laying her hand on his arm. "And that's not always a bad thing. I mean, think of white blood cells rushing to fight an infection. They adapt, you build up immunity to the disease, and you get better. That's how it basically works in humans. Our shifter bodies are more complex because of the transfer between forms. That's why we usually heal a little faster, the movement of the tissue from one shape to the other leaving a trace of healthier...I don't know, call it memory if you'd like. As if the muscle that was bruised in your cat changes to human and heals a bit, then doesn't feel right going back to being badly hurt in your cat."

"But it's not working. The shifter healing, or my human body."

She shook her head. "I need more information."

"I can't think of anything else to tell you."

She waved a hand and moved off to a cupboard, pulling things from inside and piling them on the counter. "You did what you could. And I've gotten all I can from your body."

Not really, but he wasn't going down that path again.

"What do you suggest?"

She grabbed a bag off the wall. "I need to see the man who attacked you."

Chase snorted. "Sorry. Chances of getting his butt into Whitehorse are slim to none. He hasn't been out of the bush for a decade."

She twisted to face him, chin lifted high. "That's what I figured you would say. But this isn't an option. I sent all the information I had this morning to the lab in Calgary, and my mentor already looked it over and gave me walking orders. I need you to take me to see your attacker."

Oh hell, no. "You want to go bush with me?"

She nodded. "It's the only way I can get the information I need."

Chase buttoned up his shirt. "You can give me the...doodads you need from him and I'll get them."

It was his turn to get a dirty look. "You're going to take medical samples and get them out in time for me to register results? Won't work."

"You going bush won't work either."

"Why not?"

Chase looked her over, deliberately slow in his perusal. "You know who lives back there? You know how long it's been since some of them have seen a woman?"

"Then you'll have to protect me."

He stood and shrugged. "I could also just put up with the scratches. They'll heal eventually. Thanks for everything. I'll be on my way."

She blocked his retreat. "Look, buster. You started this by coming in here. You're the one who presented me with this mystery, and you can't expect me to simply allow you to traipse off into the bush. What if the wounds don't get better? You could lose the arm. What if it festers enough you get sick out there and..."

Chase stared at her. "Get sick and die? Darling, we're all going to kick the bucket sometime. While I'd prefer it not be for a good long time, I also don't want to have to fight off or kill any of my friends because you're stubborn enough to intrude where you don't belong."

The flash of anger in her eyes made him take a step backward. "I know a hell of a lot more about not belonging than you think. This isn't some whim or random urge here. This is important to me."

He gazed around the room at her still-unfinished office. He'd be crazy to even consider this. It made no sense, to take the kind of risks the trip would involve. Especially with her no-sex rules.

Explaining to men who were mateless that an attractive, unattached female was off limits? Even his tenuous hold over them might not be enough.

"Is it really that important to you?" he asked. He interrupted before she could respond. "Think about it before you blurt out an answer. Maybe your mentor suggested something for you to try, but he doesn't understand the situation he's throwing you into. You might be curious to find the solution to something new and unusual, but if it's simply that, you can play here with the cultures for a bit longer and I'll get you the information. I promise I will, but this isn't just a simple romp in the woods. Of all the areas we could head, the Keno bush is one of the worst. No matter how hard I've worked to make it safer. You're an outsider. You will be considered suspicious and..."

And she was a female.

She nodded, slower now. As if really considering her actions. "I do know what it's like not to fit in. I would listen to you completely and follow your lead. I'm also not incompetent in the bush—my father often took us camping when we were growing up, and I mean rustic shifter camping—no tent, no pots and pans."

Shit. "Still one thing stopping me. It's fine for you to say you'll listen to me. That you want to find out what's wrong. You want it enough—"

Damn if he could say it. Damn if he could tell her she had better be scented to him before they went, or he'd be fighting to keep her from being claimed by others. That would require him asking if she really was a virgin, and while most shifters were fine talking about sex, this wasn't a typical situation in any way, shape or form.

Damn, damn, *damn.*

She waited.

He scrambled for other possible deterrents. "What about your business? You got things to finish here before you open. We'll be gone minimum of ten days, and that's if we find our target right off the bat."

Enthusiasm rushed from her. "My sister volunteered to find people to finish the renovations, and I've decided to take her up on the offer. Other than that, I'm waiting for forms and documents. Nothing holding me here."

The kitten sitting in the window chose that moment to stretch, its tiny mouth opening in a yawn. "Enigma?"

"I'm sure Caroline will watch him. And I can be packed and ready to go by lunchtime." She drew out her wallet and attempted to hand him cash. "You can get us supplies and—"

He pushed her money aside. "We can settle up later. Gather what you need here, and we'll go to your apartment to finish packing. And we need to be on the road by ten. It's a six-hour drive to the trailhead."

She nodded and turned away, hurriedly pulling supplies together, that constant rumble of noise as she talked to herself rising up.

Chase paced to the window and scooped up the fluff ball of cat. He absently petted the creature as Shelley packed. "You know what, little guy? Seems I'm far more a glutton for punishment than I expected."

And in spite of the dangers waiting ahead of them, he couldn't really find any reason to be upset. Sick bastard that he was.

It sounded a little exciting.

Part Two

We are the fated serfs to freedom—sky and sea;
We have failed where slummy cities overflow;
But the stranger ways of earth know our pride and know our
worth,
And we go into the dark as fighters go.

Yes, we go into the night as brave men go,
Though our faces they be often streaked with woe;
Yet we're hard as cats to kill, and our hearts are reckless still,
And we've danced with death a dozen times or so.

"The Rhyme of the Restless Ones"—Robert Service

Chapter Eight

Shelley pulled another branch forward to camouflage the car she'd backed into the thick brush at the side of the highway.

Chase shook his head. "Still say we should have hitchhiked the last part of the trip. Left your car in civilization."

"If we need to get away quickly, I don't want to have to rely on sticking out my thumb, thank you." She squeezed her eyes shut for a moment before facing him sheepishly. "Sorry. I'm off to a great start on the 'listen to what you tell me to do' part."

He held up the backpack he'd prepped for her and waited as she slipped her arms into the straps. "I didn't really expect anything different."

She smiled at his dry tone as she snugged up straps and adjusted the waist belt, settling the pack a little easier on her shoulders. It wasn't as comfortable as her own pack, but for some reason Chase had insisted he take hers and she use his. She supposed his pack was slightly smaller—she'd bought a brand-new expandable bag at MEC before leaving the south, and Chase had used every bit of extra space to pack all her medical supplies.

"Keys?"

She handed them over and watched in confusion as he dropped to his knees and reached under the vehicle. "What are you doing?"

He pulled back and grinned. "You lose all your gear, a hidden car isn't going to do much good. I stuck the key on top of the rear leaf-springs."

Chase looked her up and down, checked her pack by tugging a few straps. Eyed her footwear. Then without another word, he turned and headed down a narrow trail heading into the wilderness.

Shelley took a deep breath, squared her shoulders and followed.

The forest around them darkened under the towering lodge-pole pine and green aspens in full foliage. The lush underbrush was overgrown with new grasses and saplings all giving off the fresh scent of summer as they reached to grab a tiny allotment of the sunshine breaking through gaps in the canopy. Every step took them farther from the low rattle of vehicle noise—not that there'd been much activity on the remote highway, but even the occasional rumble faded until there were only the sounds of the backcountry. Intermittent birdsong, the rustle of little creatures scurrying through the low-lying brush. The high-pitched chattering of a squirrel as it clung to a tree trunk and scolded them as they walked past.

Twigs and fallen branches crunched underfoot as Shelley matched speed with the silent man in front of her. A rhythm developed in their steady gait. Lift. Lower. Extend and bend. She could have gone faster, but decided as part of the "follow his lead" she should just shut up with her bright ideas for a while and actually *follow*.

Besides, not having to worry about where they were going gave her time to mull over all the other things she'd been obsessing about.

Returning to the north had been her decision. She'd chosen to come back and fight to find a place. The unconditional acceptance she'd received from Evan the night before had changed many of her previous expectations. Her concerns weren't gone. He might be the Alpha, large and in charge, but even the most docile of packs could find ways to undermine a strong Alpha's wishes when they wanted to be cruel. Within a pack mentality, it only took one bad apple to swing into tormenting mode and others would follow.

Having Caroline and Evan firmly on her side was a start. It wasn't the destination.

And this trip was exactly what she needed right now. A chance to prove to herself that she belonged—that she mattered—in a way that counted.

Everything heated up as they stepped into a clearing, the full sun beating on their heads as the trail meandered along the side of a tiny creek. The pleasant freshness of the surroundings changed slightly, and she had no trouble identifying the other aroma—it was definitely Chase. The sharp, distinctive and mouthwatering version of his scent that she'd already become familiar with clung to his pack. As the day progressed, she was encircled until it soaked into her skin.

Having his fragrance constantly surround her was like lingering temptation. Both distracting and annoying because, while being turned on around the man had become the norm, an additional shot of out-sourced lust was not needed on top of everything else.

She wrinkled her nose and carried on, ignoring the disruption as best she could.

Up ahead Chase had stopped and removed his pack, lowering it to the ground. He reached to help her as she stepped beside him.

"Break already?"

Chase nodded, leaning her pack against a nearby tree before pulling out a granola bar from his supplies and passing it over. "We've walked for fifty minutes. Ten-minute break, then we'll go again."

He lifted his water bottle and drank in a steady stream, his throat moving smoothly. Shelley chewed absently on the sticky bar, far too fascinated with watching him. She caught herself in time to look away before he noticed, but she still felt it. A deep and undeniable attraction to this unusual man.

She'd bitten off a lot more than she should have in some ways, but she couldn't regret it. Full-on ahead, take charge and take chances.

"How long will we walk today?"

"Until we get to Rachel's."

Shelley waited for more details, but Chase's gaze lingered over the meadow as he enjoyed his break. "And…that should be how long?"

"Depends how fast we walk."

She snorted. "You going to be this talkative the entire time we're out here?"

Chase blinked. "Sorry. Didn't mean to be a chatterbox." They stared at each other for a moment before he cracked a grin. "Kidding."

Shelley shook her head and squatted by the creek to wash her hands. "Joker. There's one in every crowd. Let me be more specific. If we keep walking at the rate we're going, how long should it take to get where we're going today?"

"Five hours."

Whoa. She sat on the ground and gawked at him as she considered. "Okay. I can do that. And tomorrow? We head to your place, right?"

"If the river isn't in flood, four more hours. That will take us to my cabin."

Shelley knew he lived remote, but man, this was serious business. "You do like your places wild."

Chase shrugged. "I'm on the edge of the extreme area, really. The man we're looking for will be two more days' travel if he's still where I found him before. They were mining, so he should be at one of two places I know they staked claims."

She was doing the math, and suddenly this adventure was the big deal he'd warned her about. "That makes a minimum eight days' walking."

His brows rose. "Tell me now if you want to change your mind. It's only an hour back to the car."

"I'm not changing my mind, just making an observation." Although feeling a touch uncomfortable she'd been so flippant when Caroline had asked if she'd really thought this through.

Enigma was safely ensconced with her sister for the duration, and she wasn't worried about the final renovations to her shop. Caroline had promised to look after it, and that meant the job was as good as done.

Chase had told her they would be gone for at least ten days. She'd heard him. She had.

No, it was none of the big events involved in the trip that were currently making her head spin. Somehow during the time it had taken to pack and prepare, throughout the six-hour drive where she'd ended up reading and making research notes using her 3G phone, Shelley had managed to avoid considering one vital truth.

She was going to be in constant contact with this man for over a week.

He might be short on words, but long on allure. Something about him called to her. The sexual attraction between them was real. Shelley drank some of her water and pretended not to be checking him out as he stretched his arms.

Biceps that didn't bulge so much as just scream competency and power. The curls of hair visible at the top button of his shirt—memories of dragging her fingers through that thick mat were far too clear.

And with shifter senses, there was no way he was unaware of her involuntary physical response.

His habitual silence became a blessing as he grabbed her pack and lifted it for her, that damn grin saying more than words could have.

The fourth time they stopped the scent lingering around her was making her ache. The heat of the sun had increased as they rose above the tree line, crossing through the low point of a mountain pass, and everything around them became more intense. The fragrance of her own body. The potent aroma that screamed Chase, which constantly poked and prodded her. Shelley kept moving forward in the hope she could stay ahead of the fragrance and remove the dire need to drool.

"Last stop," Chase called.

He had chosen a clearing by the edge of a small pond, a pristine waterfall trickling down the mountain face into the rockbound pool. Shelley removed her pack with relief, holding in the groans she'd have liked to utter.

She was far from out of shape, but doing an hour-long workout a day was nothing compared to the nonstop marathon they'd nearly completed.

Still, she couldn't complain about the scenery. The verdant green around them was a part of the northern colour-scape for such a short time of the year. It was incredible to be right out in the middle of the crisp newness. They munched yet another small, high-calorie snack while silently examining the view around them. The constant murmur of the water synchronized with the constant pulse of her blood as her heart rate slowed, and she returned to a state of tranquility.

Then Chase pulled off his shirt, and she wasn't nearly as serene anymore. And when he rose and stepped behind her, pressing his hands onto her shoulders, the groan she'd managed to withhold earlier burst free.

Chase laughed. "You've done well. Nearly there."

He massaged a little harder, manipulating the muscles until they relaxed.

Shelley squeezed out the words. "You do that for too long, and I won't be able to bear putting the pack on again."

His hands kept moving, but he paused before he spoke. "You done in? Want to camp here?"

Tempting and yet not. "I can do one more hour, but it's up to you. Whatever you think is best."

He didn't answer with anything other than five more minutes of rubbing. She was too busy enjoying every second to worry about how turned on she was, with his half-naked body right behind her, pressing so close at moments that his chest brushed her. She wished she were half-naked again herself, to feel the caress of his heat, the slick of skin on skin.

Bad Shelley. Bad idea.

Chase squeezed one final time then tugged her arm to help her rise. Now that her shoulders weren't screaming in pain, her thighs and calves loudly called out their protests. Mixing in the instant images she got of Chase massaging those aches away?

Her face must have been beet-red, but there was nothing she could do about it or the very apparent scent of her aroused body.

Damn wolf senses, anyway.

Shelley made it to her feet and smiled sheepishly at Chase. "Thank you."

He nodded, his expression unreadable, although she didn't think he was mad. Maybe she was driving him as crazy as he was making her.

She turned and bent to gather the few items she'd dropped to the ground. Chase moved forward at the same moment, and somehow they bumped and she lost her balance, tipping backward, arms flailing. There was a blur of limbs, a moment of being suspended in midair, then an icy-cold sensation enveloped her as she landed squarely in the tiny pond.

Shelley screamed as she landed, and Chase rushed forward to help her. It was terrible that his first thought was less about how horrible it was that she'd fallen, or about how shockingly cold she must be, but more a sense of relief that he had another opportunity to work the system to their advantage.

Guilt rushed in.

That particular emotion and him had never been close bed partners. You did what you needed in the north, did what was required to survive. He'd never been a deceitful man, but it seemed deception wasn't a trait that needed much training to become instinctive.

Chase offered a hand to Shelley. "Did I bump you?"

She accepted his help and scrambled out as quickly as possible. "Not your fault, it's fine. But holy cow, that water is cold."

Her shirt clung to her, the gentle swells of her body clearer than before, and Chase swallowed hard.

This trip was going to be the death of him. He was the one who needed to fall into the pond and sit there for a few hours in the hopes his dick would smarten up. Or freeze. Or something. Sweet mercy, the woman was fine.

But untriggered. Damn and hell and...

He opened his pack and passed over a small cloth. "Chamois. Dry yourself off. Leave the pants—you'll need the layer for the last part of the hike to go through the bramble bushes, but take off your top and dry down. I'll get you something to wear."

She must have been cold enough, or just trying really hard to do as she'd promised—the *listening to him* part. Shelley turned her back and pulled off her shirt, drying herself rapidly with the super-absorbent fabric, wringing it out a few times and carrying on to sop up her hair as well.

"If you pass me my backpack, I can grab another top," she suggested.

Nope. While it wasn't his fault she was soaking and cold, he had to take advantage of her misfortune. Fingers crossed it would work, Chase handed over his outer button-down shirt. "Why don't you wear this until you can wash up for the night? We're nearly there, hate to get something clean all sweaty."

A gust of wind hit at the perfect moment, the rush of cooler air making goose bumps rise on her arms. She clutched his shirt tightly then slipped it on. "Thanks."

Chase pulled back on his T-shirt. It wasn't that cold out, even at nine in the evening. They could easily walk in shirtsleeves without needing protection, although the longer sleeves would help keep the bugs off her.

The bonus was that when he showed up at the cabin with Shelley in tow, she'd smell as if he'd been all over her. The fact he'd sneakily insisted she wear his pack all day would also have surrounded her with his scent as they walked.

It was a tangled web he was spinning, attempting to save her butt without letting her know what he was doing.

They grabbed packs and loaded up, Shelley squirming a little in her wet pants. "You'll dry as we walk," he reassured her.

One brow rose as she stared at him. "It's not the most comfortable of situations, Chase, but I'll live. Lead on."

The final distance disappeared quicker than he'd expected. Maybe the short dip had refreshed Shelley, or maybe the thought of getting to their stop for the night increased her energy. Either way, he had to step quickly to stop her from dogging his heels.

"Want to tell me about the place we're overnighting?"

Now it began.

"Was a regular cabin at one time. Family lived there for years before shipping out. Mom, Dad, couple kids and a cow—the works."

"Ahh, that's the Rachel you mentioned. So there's no woman still living there?"

Oh hell, no. But he wasn't going to even begin to tell Shelley about the last woman who lived there on a regular basis. He was sure she knew what a hooker was, but on the whole, not a conversation he wanted to have.

"It's a gathering point. The men in the backcountry use the cabin as a convenient rest place. Not everyone stops if they're close enough to simply find their way to Keno or Elsa. The folks out real far need the place though. There's a stove. A roof. A few places to sleep."

Shelley fell silent again. He wasn't sure if he was wearing her out or if she was naturally reticent. It was nice listening to her, but not having her chatter constantly—man, he'd been damn glad when she'd kept herself pretty much occupied the entire car trip.

She'd been distracted enough to not notice he had to adjust position a number of times to release the pressure on his dick.

He needed relief, and it didn't seem likely that he was going to get any. Now he couldn't figure out if he wanted the cabin to be empty or full. Empty would mean less trouble in terms of defending Shelley, but would also mean they would be alone. Overnight. With beds.

Sometimes he figured he was being punished, but damn if he knew what for.

The scent of wood smoke answered one question while they were still at least thirty minutes out.

"We'll have company tonight."

"I figured," Shelley answered. "Anything...well, you seem a little tense. Anything I need to know?"

Great opening. Perfect chance for him to share his concerns.

Right.

Like that was going to happen. *You might want to stick close to my side. If you pretend I'm fucking your brains out that would also make life easier.* Sure, he was totally going to say that to her.

Still, she couldn't be stupid. "I don't know who's there. Stay close. Most of them aren't going to be trouble at Rachel's. It's considered neutral territory in some ways. But don't assume."

"I'll follow your lead."

She would—which was the only reason he wasn't ready to completely panic. He did have more influence back here than most, even with the men who didn't take to authority well.

The cabin came into sight, halfway around the edge of a tiny lake, and Chase decided that he must be a touch crazy to be looking forward to finally facing the first of the challenges of his wonderful home territory.

Ahh, shifters. Death threats, potential dismemberment... So entertaining, in so many ways.

Chapter Nine

There was a bear sitting on the front porch. Or more correctly, a bear sprawled in the rocking chair on the front porch. The oversized rocker that had been reinforced to hold shifter weight barely contained the grizzly's massive bulk.

A wolf uncurled from his position in the sun at the base of the wide stairs. Another trotted up from the lake, and Chase slowed until Shelley was directly behind him, close enough to touch.

"Come on."

To anyone not versed in shifter protocol, his actions would have appeared suicidal. He grabbed her hand and boldly led her to the front door, the wolves brushing past their knees to enter at their side, the bear lumbering to his feet. Chase suspected the man would shift before joining them.

The layers of dust on the glass panes dimmed the light beating against the windows. Lanterns hung in two spots, but even their warm yellow glow wasn't enough to make things truly visible inside the dark cavern-like room. The wood-burning stove was lit, the shades of red, gold and orange reflecting through the glass front on the door lending a flickering Hades-like touch to the ambiance.

Inside four more pairs of eyes took him in, swung to spot Shelley, and remained fixed in place.

She pressed against his back, her fingers in his tightening.

He recognized three of the men, and both the wolves who'd shifted and rose to their feet. Six against one, seven counting the naked and very hairy male in the doorway who had to be the grizzly coming in to check out the situation.

Great, this got better and better. But if he'd stopped outside that would have lost him the advantage in the first place.

"Boys." Chase nodded toward the familiar faces. "Good to see you again."

He pulled off his pack and dropped it on the bench by the table. Shelley copied him before slipping against his side, torso pressed tight, those perfect breasts nudging his chest.

He didn't plan it. The growl of lust that escaped was purely instinctive after being tormented for over twenty-four hours with images of what he wanted to do with the woman.

Fortunately, his reaction was exactly the right one. Shelley's eyes widened but she kept her mouth shut, not protesting when his arm slipped around her back and dragged her close enough there wasn't room to slip a playing card between their bodies.

The shoulders on one of the wolves drooped in disappointment. "Well hell, Silver, thanks for getting my hopes up. You bastard."

"You been slumming it in the city, Silver?" the other asked. "You smell like civilization and death."

"Just taking care of business," Chase responded, ignoring the heat of Shelley's body best he could.

"So that's what they're calling it now." The bear leered, and the men laughed.

The conversation went downhill from there for a few minutes, and Chase let them have the dirt out. He glanced around the cabin and identified the best bed in the place. He pulled Shelley along with him and tossed the personal items strewn on the bed to the side, claiming territory as it were.

Rude? Probably, but it had to be done.

"Hey, stow it. That's my spot, you asshole."

Shelley slipped behind him as he turned to face the walking fur rug of a bear shifter. "The lady and I need the room."

"Really." Massive arms crossed, biceps bulging. The man was the picture definition of *brick shithouse.* "Maybe me and the lady need the room."

Silence fell.

Chase stared at the man's bushy brows. Face to face they were the same height, only the bear had to outweigh him by a good hundred pounds. Tension built, the floorboards creaking as one of the watchers shifted his weight.

"Taylor, you don't want to challenge Silver." It was one of the wolves.

Taylor's nostrils flared as he took in a deep breath. "He don't look so dangerous. And he's brought a woman. Ain't had a woman in a long time."

"If you bathed more often, that might not be the case," Shelley muttered.

Chase froze his expression to stop from grinning at her quip. "She's with me, and you want to step back."

"What if I don't?"

Tension continued to rise. In the background, the other men were finding safer spots, away from the potential brawl. At least they seemed to have an idea of what could happen, and the anger inside Chase settled into a calm point of power. He wasn't doing this for any reason other than violence was the language these men spoke.

The fact he needed a bit of a physical release right now was beside the point.

The bear roared and Chase moved. His first action was to plant a hand on Shelley's chest and shove her backward. She tumbled onto the relative safety of the bed. Then he ignored her and faced his opponent.

In typical bear fashion the man lunged, opening his arms as he stepped forward. He'd want to get a solid hold and crush Chase in an embrace. Chase ducked under the outspread arms and spun behind the man. He concentrated and let the shift to his animal form come, but only to his left hand. A shocked gasp rose from one of the strangers pinned to the far wall as Chase's entire left arm turned into his cougar paw, wicked claws extended with a shimmering gleam. He swung low before the bear could turn, swiping sharply across the lower edge of the man's legs and neatly hamstringing him.

The bear's scream echoed off the wooden walls as he fell to the floor. Chase stayed light on his feet, human right hand balled into a fist to be used if necessary, the powerful cougar claw hanging relaxed on the left.

Behind him, the rest of the crowd moved forward, commenting freely as they found their way to the bear moaning in pain on the floor.

"Not much warning there, Silver," one wolf complained.

"Hell, he could have waited five seconds and let Taylor turn about. Bet that paw could have scooped off Taylor's nuts with one shot."

"True." The wolf shifter squatted at Taylor's side. "Oh, quit your belly aching. We'll help get your ass outside so you can shift. You should be okay by the morning if you're done being an idiot to Long John here. Or you want to fight some more?"

Taylor was curled up in pain on the floor, jammed between the wooden bedframe and a couple of chairs that had fallen with him. The bear lifted his head and leaned it on the wall.

"How the hell you do that?" he moaned.

Chase pulled back the shift until his arm was human again and ignored the question. "You give the lady the respect she deserves."

Taylor grimaced as the wolves dragged him to a sitting position. "Bed's yours, woman's yours. I'm not stupid."

Chase ignored the men as they manhandled Taylor out of the cabin. He turned to face Shelley for the first time since the altercation had begun, a little concerned what he was going to discover.

She'd wiggled back on the mattress until she was plastered against the wall. Her eyes were wide, but not with fear. She was staring at his arm with something close to delight.

Shit. "Oh hell, no. Don't you start getting any ideas now."

She bounced forward and knelt, jerking him to the side and forcing up his T-shirt sleeve. "That was the single most fascinating thing I've ever seen in my life. Can you do it again? I wanted to see how the musculature of your cat combines with—"

He twisted as he planted a hand over her mouth and sat on the bed. That brought her halfway into his lap, basically into an embrace. "Shhh."

She froze, then as realization hit she turned her head toward the door. Luckily, the cabin was empty, at least temporarily, as the entire group had helped drag Taylor out. Chase let his hand fall away, but damn if he could willingly remove her from his lap.

"Sorry. I'll save the questions for later when we don't have an audience." Shelley wiggled until he set her free. "Why'd you make a big deal out of kicking him out of the bed? In fact, why come here at all when it looks as if you expected we would have troubles?"

She spoke in a hushed whisper and he answered the same way. "Because at some point we're going to meet people. Here I had more control over who and how I showed them to back off. Word will spread. We'll be safer traveling if they're wary of us than attempting to stay hidden the entire time."

Shelley nodded slowly. She took a deep breath before looking him in the eye. "I'm sorry."

Chase frowned. "For what?"

"For making trouble in the... Well, I don't suppose it's a pack, is it? Not with all the different kinds of shifters."

He reached over and, more carefully than before, pulled Taylor's possessions into a bundle and tied them up. "We are a pack or a clan or a coven of sorts. And they're good folk, Shelley. Even ol' Taylor there was just acting like a typical outcast. Trying to find his place in the scheme of things. Scrambling for what he wanted."

She moved off and picked up chairs, setting the insides of the cabin back to rights without any further questions. He had to make sure she knew. "Shell?"

She turned those eerily beautiful eyes his direction. "Yes?"

"You understand we'll be sharing this bed."

She took a quick glance toward the door to make sure no one had returned. "I figured that bit out. I hope you're not terribly upset."

Oh hell. Upset was not the word that had sprung to mind. "It's for your protection."

One smooth brow rose. "Oh, is it now? I think that's the first time I've heard that excuse used as an attempt to get into my pants."

"If I'm in your pants, the last thing you'll be doing is thinking." The words slipped out. His control had evaporated. Her face flushed, and he shook himself. "Forget I said that."

He pulled out his sleeping bag, spread it on the bed. Basically ignored her and got their spot together.

She moved silently to his side, bringing her pack. She accepted the food he handed her and headed to the tiny kitchen area.

Chase watched her walk away and wondered just how much more hellish this day could get.

One by one the men returned to the cabin, giving her a wide berth as she placed the food bag in the cupboard to keep their supplies safe from the mice. There was so much more she wanted to ask. To find out. Their names, who they were, what they did in the bush.

She itched to go check the injury on the bear, but figured heading outside alone to accost him wasn't the smartest idea at the moment.

All her thoughts and concerns muddled together into a blur as fatigue overtook her. It had been an incredibly long day, and she was spent.

Chase was at her elbow, her clothing bag in his hand. "Come on, I'll take you to wash up."

She used the outhouse then followed him wearily to the edge of the lake where someone had built a dock. There was just enough of a platform to allow a person to be past the grasses and mud at the edge of the water and access the deeper part. She sank happily to her knees and pulled off the shirt he'd loaned her. The water she scooped up was icy cold against her face, the cloth she soaked and brushed over her skin refreshing but in that lazy *had enough and ready to collapse* kind of way.

A splash sounded to her left, and she snapped her head that direction to watch the ripples circle outward from where Chase had plunged into the deeper section off the end of the dock. His head broke the surface, silvery brush cut glistening with water droplets in the setting sun.

Eleven thirty and the sky was finally beginning to darken, the blue fading to a deep indigo highlighted by streaks of gold and red against the clouds.

Naked.

Strange how that thought filled her brain more and more, distracting from the beauty of their surroundings. Chase was in the water, and his clothing lay discarded on the dock beside her. Ergo, the man was naked, and she was in so much trouble.

She glanced back toward the cabin, but everyone was out of sight. Taylor must have lumbered into the bush before she and Chase had come outside. It was possible he was watching them, but she didn't really care.

Naked.

Chase was naked, and he was swimming back to the dock, and he'd probably push himself upright and step up and he'd be naked beside her and she didn't really think she could handle that right now.

So she stripped off her own things as rapidly as possible, waited until his hand touched the edge of the dock, then took a flying leap over his head to land in frigid water for the second time that day.

This was way worse than the first time. Worse and better, because it was so shockingly cold she couldn't breathe. Which was good because then she didn't inhale while her head was underwater. Bad, because parts of her body that she really enjoyed having, like toes and fingers, went instantly numb.

She surfaced and opened her eyes to find she was facing away from the dock. Hallelujah, no distracting delicious Métis shifters—*naked* Métis shifters—to stare at.

Washing in water this cold was like rapidly running a hand of ice over her skin in the hopes she'd remove at least the sweat of the day's exertions. She turned to face her upcoming bed partner.

He was staring at her with an expression of hopelessness.

She snorted. Okay, she wasn't the only one feeling the heat.

Chase growled, his frustration clear in the tone. "Damn it, woman. Get your ass in here and put some clothes on. You want me to have to fight the lot of them?"

Oops. "Sorry, that wasn't what I was thinking about."

She swam in closer, getting ready to pull herself out of the water.

"Wait."

Chase grumbled a few times then put himself between the cabin and her body. "Get out and get dressed quick."

She obeyed, accepting the chamois he handed her. She slid the soft cloth over her skin rapidly to gather the water best she could. Then she pulled on the T-shirt and the pants he'd readied. She wasn't about to mention that he'd forgotten to grab her underwear.

The T-shirt got stuck for a moment on her wet skin and he helped her, his touch brief and fleeting, but she swore that his fingers were heated brands against her skin. Her breasts ached, and between her legs she was hotter than she had any right to be considering she'd just bathed in ice water.

Finally covered, she looked up and got caught by his gaze. By the large dark circles of his pupils as he all but ate her up. He stood with his fists clenched at his sides as if fighting to keep from grabbing her.

He cleared his throat then snarled the words. "You're damn lucky I'm a gentleman. Ready for bed?"

Maybe I don't want you to be a gentleman rushed through her brain. Which was not what she should be considering. Pondering. Imagining or otherwise adding to her thought patterns.

"Wait. They're going to think…" Oh, she was pathetic.

Chase drew a slow breath in, almost vibrating with tension. "Think what?"

Shelley lowered her chin. "Nothing."

He sighed, a heavy lost sound, a second before his fingers brushed her cheek and cupped her face, lifting her to look at him. "You're getting on my last nerve, darling. Now hold still."

She waited for him to kiss her senseless. To haul her against all those rock-solid muscles and tightly bound energy. What she got was a tender caress, his lips briefly connecting with hers. The skim of his tongue over her bottom lip too rapid to allow her to open in response and let him in.

Because she was totally going to. Totally ready to give back and let them at least mark each other with the scent of a few mostly chaste kisses.

He pulled back and stared, his gaze darting over her as if he were attempting to read her mind. "We need to hit the sack. Tomorrow's gonna come soon enough."

He slid his fingers down her arm, and a shiver raced ahead of his touch. When he linked their fingers together and led her back to the cabin, her heart pounded and her palms got sweaty.

Inside, the men had all settled into quiet activities, or crawled onto one of the platforms that created bunk space on the far side of the room from where her and Chase's bed sat.

Bed. Chase. *Oh boy.*

Quiet, except for the crackle of the fire in the wood stove and the beginning rumbles of snoring from one of the berths. Shelley slipped off her shoes and crawled into the sleeping bags that he'd joined together. She rolled onto her side, faced the wall and braced herself.

There wasn't enough time to truly prepare as Chase followed her a moment later, spooning around her. He slipped an arm over her waist and unapologetically tugged her against his body.

He was hard all over, and one specific part of the hardness nestled too intimately in the dip between her butt cheeks. She could barely breathe.

A light kiss landed on her nape, his lips whisper soft. "Shhh. It's okay. I've got you."

Oh yeah, he did. Any way he wanted her, he had her. Forget the no-sex sex, she was ready to change her mind and let him go all the way.

A loud rumble sounded somewhere beyond their feet, and Shelley considered swearing. A room full of chaperones. How marvelous.

Yet, the situation was exactly what they needed. She and Chase obviously weren't going to do anything about the tension between them, not with a room full of witnesses. Shifters might be upfront about sex, but this kind of setup had more kink-show potential than most.

The knowledge they weren't going to do anything helped her relax, and bit-by-bit her tension slipped away. The fatigue of the day rose and she closed her eyes. His warmth enveloped her tighter than his embrace, and the last thing she remembered was the tickle of his slowing breath against the back of her neck as he fell asleep.

Chapter Ten

A finger stroked across her stomach, and Shelley rolled slightly to let it tickle her gently, the heat of her body so perfect she figured she was still dreaming. Had to be a dream—the last time she had someone touch her like this in a soft, drowsy wake-up-sex kind of way she'd been back in university and...oh, wait.

She had never done the slow morning after the wild sex the night before. She left. Enjoyed herself then hit the road so there would be none of the awkward morning-after stuff.

Although this wasn't awkward, which meant it had to be a dream, and when that mysterious hand rose and circled her nipple with a firm fingertip, she moaned happily.

Had to be a dream. Her breasts weren't playboy-bunny style so were usually ignored by the guys she'd taken into her bed. Her wolf had never cared about the lack of attention to small details of foreplay. When she was looking for release, hot and sweaty and fast was just fine. But—oooh, another reason she was sure this was a dream—she actually liked having her nipples played with. Only a fantasy lover would know to pinch lightly and send shivers through her body. Only the imaginary male in her life would scratch his nails over the rigid tip and draw another gasp from her lips.

She should have gone in for a different field of science than animal husbandry. Maybe a psych department, one with a research facility where she could have signed up to be an experimental subject in dream seduction.

That oh-so-talented hand left her breasts and trailed over her belly. She held her breath in anticipation. And right about the time he cupped her mound, middle finger pressing on the perfect section to wake up her clitoris...

Her brain woke as well.

The hand doing magical things stilled as she involuntarily sucked in a shocked gasp. There was a very aroused crossbreed shifter lying pressed up against her naked body—naked? When had she lost her clothes?—and this was no dream.

He kissed her neck. "Relax, I won't do anything you don't like."

Well, there was a problem. She pretty much liked it all. Except the *in a cabin with an audience* bit.

"Trust me," whispered past her ear a second before his tongue began tracing the edge of her earlobe, and she was lost. Even more gone when he slipped his tongue into her ear briefly. She would have jumped a good foot off the bed if he hadn't had her pinned in place.

Trust him? Oh boy. Everything blurred together as he touched her slowly, fingers slipping through her curls and dipping inside.

She was such a dirty girl. He didn't ask, but she did it anyway. Running her foot along his calf where it lay next to hers, she lifted her thigh and draped her limb over his, effectively opening her core to his touch.

If he didn't get that as a clear invitation, she wasn't sure what would. Fireworks going off? A radio announcement? A sky writer?

Chase tilted his hips, and his erection pressed more firmly against her lower back as he rolled them both slightly, using her leg as a lever to drape her over his lower body. He brought up moisture from her core and teased her clit. Once. Again.

She was so sensitized from the dream and the past days longing for this man's touch, she was liable to have the fastest orgasm of her life. That couldn't be good.

One thick digit pressed deep inside as he rubbed the heel of his hand against her clit, and she was gone, passage clutching his finger as her climax blew. Her ears rang and there was this tingling aftershock racing over her skin, and it wasn't going away because he didn't stop. He touched her and teased her, playing her perfectly again and again until she had to bite her lips to stop from screaming.

Chase rocked against her as he worked his fingers in and out of her slick passage. It was somewhat surreal, to have the light sneaking in the windows, the continued rumble of snoring from at least a few of the men, and Chase doing dirty and wonderful things to her. And when he pressed his mouth against her neck and sucked?

White lights in front of her eyes, deer-in-the-headlight type, total out-of-control response as she orgasmed again. The sensation was nearly eclipsed by the bite of his teeth on her neck muscle, almost as if he was holding her in place as he continued to rut against her. He pulled his fingers from her body and grasped her hip, stickiness ignored as he held on tight.

Wetness spread over her back as he grunted, and the scent of his release mixed with hers and, oh Lordy, there was another reason why shifters shouldn't have even non-sex sex in the same room as other shifters.

He pushed her onto her belly and levered away the sleeping bags, probably to keep from getting stickiness all over them. She buried her face deeper into the pillow and enjoyed all the little happy pheromones racing through her. The wet patch on her back somehow added to her contentment, as relaxed as she'd been in days. Maybe months.

Amazing what an orgasm by someone's hand other than your own could do.

When Chase pressed his big warm palm against her back she didn't move. When he slipped his fingers through the seed he'd left on her skin, she rumbled with happiness before forcing herself to stop. Okay, not a human thing, or maybe not a human thing all the time, but having him rub his semen into her skin like he was painting her was so utterly wolfish she was floored.

Yes, he was probably doing it as an extra step for her own safety, creating a clear marking to warn off other shifters, but her brain didn't care. It was so. Freaking. Cool.

And if her friends back at vet school saw this, they'd need therapy.

The snoring in the room had lessened, and at least one person exited the cabin. Shelley stared at the wall and wondered if they could stay in bed until the place was empty. Chase continued to touch her, only now his talented fingers were massaging her tight calves.

If she groaned again, would the guys in the room think they were still at it? And did she really care? Because this felt so very, very good.

Chase adjusted position, crawling over her, and she flushed at the vivid images racing through her brain. Pictures of him lifting her hips and taking her from behind.

Seems once she'd let the sex fiend out there was no holding her back. Chase dug his thumbs into her hamstrings and dragged upward to press deep into her butt cheeks, and she gasped.

Yeah, a virtual orchestra of grunts and groans. She was so classy.

Chase leaned over her, the heavy weight of his groin resting against her ass as he covered her back and kissed her neck. "Time to get up, lazy bones."

Up. Like that thing between his legs was once again up, if she was any judge of male anatomy. Shelley tried to roll out from under him. He merely trapped her once she rotated halfway, and then she was in real trouble because now they were face to face and... Yeah, that naked thing and the *up* stuff were a definite reality.

As hot as the situation was, she fought for control. "This is so not fair," she complained, lifting her hands with the intention of pushing him away.

Hmm, palms to hairy chest.

She was a goner.

Chase smiled. "Just wanted to be sure you were okay."

The unspoken rest of the sentence was there in his laughing eyes. The...*make sure you're okay and not going to kick me for being too forward and smearing my jism all over you.*

"Oh, move it, Chase. We've got a long way to go."

But not nearly as far as she'd thought before this little escapade. As in, she really and truly was ready for a romp with another shifter which, after so long of doing without, was about the most wonderful thing she could imagine.

Chase got them breakfast. Packed. Said goodbye to the two shifters still hanging out at the cabin, and led Shelley into their second day of the wilderness.

He had to slow his pace three times before he finally hit a section of trail that was clear enough for Shelley to take the lead and go her own speed. It wasn't that he was in a hurry to get anywhere—

Liar.

First he'd justified his rapid tempo on feeling great after making Shelley come. Plus, coating her with his seed had been so damn hot he could be expected to have a little more vim in his vigor. Neither was the real reason he was marching like a crazy man.

Somewhere inside he'd realized that today's destination was his cabin, and there they were guaranteed privacy. Didn't matter if Delton was still in the area. The man would hightail it out soon enough. Even if Jones were around, the boy would be fine in a hammock in the bush for the night.

He and Shelley were going to have a night alone with a bed and no snoring shifters keeping an anxious ear and eye on them.

Deciding what to do to her first was driving him mad because there was no longer any doubt where this was going to end. Whatever had kept her from wanting sex with him before was gone.

And if he was at all familiar with female anatomy, Evan had been wrong about one thing. Shelley was either no virgin, or she'd at least played with some toys over the years.

He tripped and barely caught himself from tumbling to the ground.

Okay. Thinking about Shelley playing with sex toys was not allowed while hiking along the ridge of a mountain.

They followed the same routine as the previous day. Forward motion, break for a snack, hike again, repeat. They didn't talk about much. Certainly not about the cabin and him waking her up. But she smiled and fluttered her lashes at times, and he caught her staring when he stripped off his shirt to dip his head in a creek to cool off.

The last section of the trail opened up enough they could walk side by side, and Shelley fell into step with him.

"So, one thing, Chase. What's with the *Silver* business?"

"I wondered if you'd catch that." He grinned. "Yeah, it's easier sometimes, since a few Mikes or Daves in the area can mean having to say 'the Dave that lives by the bend in the creek'. I got the handle Silver a few years back—the hair and my last name, I guess."

She frowned, hands clutching the backpack straps at chest level as she concentrated. "Last name. Johnson. How does that turn into Silver?"

He sighed. This part made him a touch insane. "Arghh, avast ye maties."

Shelley laughed. "No. Long John Silver?"

"Never said they weren't a creative lot up here."

She matched his speed. "They're good people, aren't they? On the whole?"

"They are. Misunderstood, kicked around. Some of them are out of touch with reality, but whether that's from being in the bush or what drove them into the wilderness in the first place, I'm not sure."

"Why'd you end up here? If you don't mind me asking."

He shrugged. "Told you I can't control the shift. Which group is going to welcome me in? The wolves or the cats?"

She sighed. "Yeah. Shifters aren't always the most forgiving of differences."

It was the perfect opportunity, again, and this time he couldn't allow the chance to slip past. "What's your story? You live in Whitehorse but you aren't a part of the pack? That's not wolf."

"That's the type of wolf you know up here." She said it with a bit of attitude, as if daring him to prove her unsuitable for his part of the world.

He wasn't about to fight her. "You do fit in up here. More than I expected. But that doesn't answer my question. Why did you not know the Alpha?"

"Just moved." She paused. "Well, that's not the entire truth. I did just move back, but I left Whitehorse years ago almost as much of an outcast as you would be."

He waited. Didn't need to fill the air with noise when she obviously had more to say.

"Funny how some thoughts drag you back to being twelve years old again and sad that people don't like you." Shelley took a deep breath. "I promised myself I wouldn't complain anymore, so just the facts. I can't shift. Not sure why."

Impossibly, Chase felt his cheeks heat. "You ever try to trigger your wolf?"

She coughed. "Yes. Didn't work."

His tongue tangled in his mouth. He wanted to say something meaningful like *Damn shame.* Or, *Sorry to hear that,* but the only thing his thick skull fixated on was if she'd tried to trigger her wolf, she was most definitely not a virgin. Suddenly the nice firm mattress waiting in his cabin was more important to reach quickly than before.

"Chase?"

"Yeah?"

He slowed his step and she stared at him as they walked. He was sure she was going to ask him if they were going to have sex.

"How...I mean...do you think? If it's not any trouble..."

Trouble? His dick woke up and paid attention. "What, Shell?"

She grabbed him by the arm and pulled him to a full stop. "Can you show me how you changed just a part of you like that?"

He snorted. Then laughed. And as her face brightened at his response, he laughed even harder.

Oh, Chase, this is what you get for having sex on the brain. The woman didn't want in his pants, she wanted to further her education.

He forced his lustful thoughts into line and gestured her down the path. "I don't mind."

"How is your shoulder? Any better? Worse?"

Her tone indicated the doctor was in the house. Chase had to stop from imaging her in a short little white skirt wearing nothing up top but a stethoscope. He rotated his arm thoughtfully. "About the same. A little hot, a little achy. Just not getting any better."

"I have an idea I want to try when we get to your cabin."

"Sure."

"And I want to see you change only partway."

Bossy thing. He liked it. "Yeah."

Shelley looked up at him. "One other request, if you don't mind."

"What?"

"Next time you plan on us hitting a dangerous situation, warn me ahead of time. I don't mind thinking on my feet, but I'd prefer a little head's up."

She was right; he'd been a jerk. "Sorry. And I will."

They topped the hill that overlooked his cabin. He watched her face instead of glancing over the familiar panorama he'd witnessed a million times. For some reason he felt a deep need to see her response. To have her excited about the place he'd built for himself in the bush. He tried to explain away the longing as the normal anticipation of bringing a stranger home, but the desire was more than that.

She was getting under his skin in a way that wasn't very smart.

Her eyes lit up then a crease folded her brow. "Chase? Is that your place?"

"Yeah."

She turned those mesmerizing dark eyes to meet his. "Why are there dozens of people gathered on the front porch?"

He snapped around to look. There was no denying it. His usually tranquil home was swarming with men. Pouring in and out the door, some sitting on the front clearing he liked to call a lawn. Some were pitching tents.

He'd been invaded.

Chapter Eleven

Caroline turned over another set of records and forced herself to concentrate. Her least favourite part of the job. Paperwork sucked, but she refused to let herself get behind when it looked as if the hotel would be overrun in the next couple weeks once the full contingent of bears arrived in town.

Enigma wrapped himself around her ankles, and she scooped him up mindlessly, the soft fur ball an amazing balm to her tight nerves. She flipped one-handed through pages as he settled in her lap. Stroking her fingers through his soft fur again and again was like playing with a worry stone. Relaxation rose.

He seemed to enjoy her attention as well. By the time she made it to the bottom of the pile, the kitten was purring like a train.

"How can a little thing like you make so much noise?"

His ears twitched, but other than that, he didn't move.

Behind her the door opened and closed. "Caro? You here?"

"In the office."

Evan's footfalls came closer. "I need the contact numbers for the Miles Canyon—*achoo. Achoo.*" He stopped in front of her desk, wrinkling his nose. "Don't tell me. Let me guess. That furry thing is in—"

He sneezed toward his elbow another couple times before groaning in frustration.

She rose to her feet, tucking a protesting Enigma against her body. "I'm so sorry. When I promised Shelley I'd babysit her cat, I had no idea you were allergic."

Evan grabbed a handful of tissues from the box on the desk then backed toward the window. "No reason for—*achoo*—you to expect this."

He propped the window open, stepped in front of the fresh breeze that rushed in and breathed deeply.

"I can find someone else to look after him." Caroline felt horrible, but couldn't stop a small smile from escaping.

Evan's eyes narrowed. "What?"

"Nothing." She straightened up and wiped her expression clean of all amusement.

He stepped forward menacingly then stopped as Enigma meowed. "Tell me what's got you smirking, or I will get revenge."

Caroline snickered. "Fine. I never expected such a great and mighty Alpha to be floored by a teeny little thing like this."

He sneezed again.

And again.

She giggled.

"It's not—*achoo*—funny."

Caroline tried to stop, she really did, but by now just the thought of giggling made her laugh. Add in Evan's terrified expression as Enigma escaped from her arms to land on the desk and stalk toward him.

She was dying.

Evan tossed her a dirty look as he stripped off his shirt. "I will get you later."

"Me and my little dog too? I mean kitten?" Caroline squeezed out the words. "So, you need contact numbers. I can do that. Well, sort of do. I still haven't been able to figure out who the current leader is over there."

Evan tossed his shirt on the desktop, and the kitten dropped to a crouch. His tail twitched as he stalked forward to pounce on Evan's shirt and bury himself in the fabric. "How can an entire pack keep their Alpha undercover? It's just not very typical wolf behavior."

"Because most packs like to brag on their leader?" Caroline watched in fascination as he continued to strip. "Is there a reason you're getting naked in the middle of the afternoon? Not that I'm complaining, not really."

Evan finished a sneezing jaunt before being able to speak. "Experimentation. I want to see if I react to the fur ball in my wolf. In the meantime, find the file on the Miles Canyon pack and read me the parts about any activity they've had in the city over the past ten years. Oh, and that information you found about the last bear territorial settlement. If we're about to be— *achoo*—invaded I want to know possible troubles to be ready for."

He shifted in the middle of sneeze, the human *achoo* changing to a wolfish one, and Caroline had to grab a tissue to wipe her eyes.

He sat on the floor, a simply enormous black wolf with streaks of grey starting to show on his muzzle and ears. As a human who had grown up with half-sibling wolves, the entire family regularly visiting the local packhouse, Caroline had pretty much been around people who popped to wolf form her entire life.

It still gave her goose bumps to witness.

"Gathering information. Make yourself comfortable. Let me grab a coffee. If I'm going to be talking at you for the next hour."

She scooted out of the room, returning in time to witness the moment Enigma discovered he wasn't the only beast in the room.

Evan wasn't sneezing anymore, which Caroline figured was a good sign. He'd placed his paws up on the desktop and took an experimental sniff of the moving pile of fabric. Enigma was still playing happily in Evan's shirt.

The pile stopped moving, and the tiny black head popped out a bit at a time. The little pink nose wiggled furiously. Then the muzzle, and the rest of the creature appeared as he crawled out the neckline of Evan's shirt.

Evan sniffed.

Enigma meowed.

The kitten pounced, his tiny body landing on top of Evan's forehead, legs wrapping around the wolf's muzzle. For a moment Caroline thought Evan was going to toss his head to throw the offending creature into the air, but the big bad Alpha remained absolutely still and allowed the tiny thing to scramble to a more solid perch.

Directly on top of his head.

If a wolf could sigh with exasperation? That was the noise Evan made as he cautiously made his way to the couch and crawled onto it without disturbing his passenger. Caroline grabbed the files she needed and sat in the easy chair to the side, going through the information Evan had requested. All the while he was pinned in place by Enigma, who found a spot of sunshine on Evan's neck, curled up and promptly fell asleep.

Caroline focused on the task at hand to stop from losing control again. One thing she had to admit, though.

Living with shifters was never boring.

Chase eyed the mass of humanity that surrounded his homestead with disgust, concern and more than a little trepidation. He was a leader to these people, but there was only one of him, and dropping into a volatile situation with Shelley in tow? This was more than either of them had signed up for.

He sorted through and discarded solutions rapidly.

"Chase?" Shelley nodded toward his cabin. "You obviously didn't expect this."

"Normally it's me and the birds. Maybe a visitor or two, but that's it." *Hell.* "You're here too, so let's see what you think. Give me ideas."

"Head back to the highway?"

"Nope. Retreat is a sign of weakness. They have to know we're coming by now. I bet at least one of our cabin mates from last night ran ahead in shifted form to let them know."

She was probably unaware she stepped closer to him. "You think this gathering is trouble?"

"It's not normal, that's for sure." Chase tried to spot familiar figures, but at this distance, individuals were mere blobs.

Her breath passed his ear as she leaned in even closer. "You said they aren't bad people. What if we assume they're here for a good reason?"

He rolled through possibilities and couldn't think of one that would make the outcasts willingly gather in one place. "Men who crave privacy don't give it up on a whim. It's not a carnival or something like that, if that's what you mean."

"No, I'm not suggesting anything that frivolous, but they also wouldn't come together to do something...bad. If they safeguard their solitude?"

Bingo. "Probably not. They take their mischief the same way they like their pleasures—alone."

Even the word *pleasures* couldn't cross his lips without him thinking a whole lot harder about touching her and feeling her body's response.

Concentrate. He turned her to face him. "I will protect you."

She nodded. "I know you will. But I'm not defenseless."

She pulled out a switchblade. Fancy one, looked like an out the front with the instant pop-up. Illegal in Canada, and extremely dangerous.

"You know how to use it?" He wasn't trying to be insulting, but there was nothing worse than a knife being pulled during a fight by a person who was afraid to draw blood.

Shelley gave him a dirty look. "I can not only use it, I know exactly where on both human and animal anatomy to do the most damage with the least effort. Though I probably can't hold off more than two people at a time."

Which was more than long enough for him to get to her side if needed. "Good. Here's the plan. We head in. Don't cling, don't look down. You belong here."

"Right." She nodded, but a quiver in her voice warned him to dig deeper.

Chase shook his head. She had to buy in all the way. Had to show that strength he'd seen in her up to now and make it obvious to others. "I mean it. See that cabin? It's yours. Consider this place yours. You told me you understood about not fitting in and being made to feel an outsider, right?"

Shelley waited, her gaze darting back to the distant crowd. "Right."

"You like how that feels? Being on the outside? Think about. Own it."

She might not be able to shift, but she was still a wolf. The growl of disgust and anger that escaped her pleased him with its intensity.

Surprised her, if her expression was any indication.

"There. That. The way you feel right now. Take that and turn it around. You have the right to belong. Maybe not everywhere, but here? Oh, darling, you belong here."

She caught his arm, strength growing in her response. "You're saying these people are good people."

"Most are. Some aren't. But they're my people. Your people." Chase tugged her to him and pointed down again. "We're going to walk in there and find out what we need to do. Because it's our place, and they must have some rational reason to talk to us."

And if he was wrong, he'd take out as many of them as possible before he died.

Shelley's grin stretched wide. "You know what, Silver? For a man who doesn't talk much, you sure have a way with words."

She grabbed hold of him and slammed their bodies together. Lips meeting in a rush of passion and fear. Fear that gave an edge to the sexual desire haunting them. She was kissing him, then he was kissing her, and hell if stripping down on the side of the hill and going for it right there didn't sound like the most marvelous idea in the world.

She slipped her hands under his T-shirt, her fingertips digging into his chest and massaging. Skimming around to his back for an instant, avoiding his cuts, before she dragged forward hard enough to mark him with her nails.

His control wavered on a thread. He dragged his mouth off hers and panted. "You should save that fire for facing them."

"I've got more than enough fire for both now and later, thank you." She caught his head in her hands and took one more kiss.

One more, it had to be the last one because he was seriously going to lose control and flip her to her knees and— good Lord, she wrecked his mind.

He caught hold of her wrists, taking control of the kiss, his lips and tongue dancing with hers, their breaths mingling. It was crazy, insane. He manoeuvred them just below the ridge of the hillside so they weren't in plain view anymore, then tugged her hands until they dropped from his face. He didn't let go, though. Couldn't. Somehow this raging heat pouring through him had to be dealt with, and while the thought of what might be a couple dozen pissed-off shifters should have been all the ice he needed, her reaction, the little show of bloodthirsty female?

He was so fucking hard right now he could barely walk. Screw going into the middle of a battlefield with that kind of a handicap.

He brought her hands down until he could press them against his groin, and she gasped into his mouth. Shelley took over exactly how he hoped she would. She unzipped him, reaching in to pull out his length. Her fingers wrapped around his heated shaft, and she squeezed so exactly right he wasn't going to last.

Now that the frantic moment of wondering if she would follow through had passed, he could work on pleasing her. He slid his fingers into her hair. Cupped her neck and held her in place so he could pepper her face with kisses. He worked his way along her jaw to her ear to nuzzle that spot that when he licked, she whimpered, and her stroke on his cock faltered.

He was happy he'd made her react, but sad she'd stopped. Hell—what to do?

He tugged her shirt up, followed by one more jerk that yanked her sports bra over her breasts. Hmm, wide-open access that allowed him to play with her tight little nipples to his heart's content. He would have bent over and licked them, but he was selfish enough to want to have her hands continue the wicked motion she'd resumed on his shaft.

When she released him and stepped away, he nearly tripped following after her. Panting hard, aching for completion.

But following her cues. "We need to stop, right?"

She shook her head. "I'm not cruel enough to call it quits right now. Just wanted to be sure you were okay with me doing something else. Since this is kind of the wrong place and the wrong time."

"What else you thinking of doing?" He caught himself stroking his shaft, his hand a miserable substitute for the pleasure she'd been giving him.

"Are we safe?" She rolled her eyes as she stepped closer. "Stupid question. This is insane."

He laughed. "Animalistic passion seems to have got the best of us. No, you're right, we probably shouldn't be doing this on the side of the hill, but damn if you aren't the most tempting creature."

Shelley stalked forward, a gleam of heat in her eyes that nearly buckled his knees. "Probably shouldn't isn't a no, correct?"

If he had more brainpower, he could have answered that tongue twister. As it was, he backed away awkwardly, his erection hard in his hand as she crowded him toward a rocky outcrop. She brought a hand to his shoulder and pushed him until his back was against the rock wall. She replaced his hand with hers, and he groaned in gratitude. A couple more minutes and he would have finished. A few more strokes with her directing his pleasure—he'd be toast in no time.

Obviously pleased with her organizing, she smiled mischievously. "If it's not a no, it's a yes."

She dropped to her knees and took him into her mouth, and forget about lasting a couple minutes. He was no longer a marshmallow being slowly roasted over the fire, he was a gas-soaked cloth being tossed in the direct line of a blow torch, and the heat of her mouth and the slick wetness took hold of his balls and dragged him onto a dangerous ledge.

She moved enthusiastically. Her head bobbed over him three, four times at the most, and he exploded, the suction of her lips triggering his response, dragging his brains out his cock. The intensity of his attraction grew by the minute, but right now, there was nothing left in him to give. Until she looked up at him and winked, and *oh hell*, if his cock didn't twitch again.

Sometime in the last minute, if it had even taken that long, he'd woven his fingers into her hair and clutched her head. Now she smiled as he lifted her and propped her against his body, shamelessly using her weight to hold himself in place.

"That was about the kinkiest thing I've ever done," Shelley confessed.

He still couldn't draw a full breath. "Our timing sucks, but damn, I'm not complaining. You want to do other kinkier things to me down the road, you just go right ahead."

He closed his eyes and leaned his head back on the rock. She laughed softly, her body shaking against his. "We should have waited."

"I'm leaving you hanging."

Shelley stroked his cheek, resting against him. "I'll survive. And, not that I gave you the blowjob for any reason other than I wanted to, but you and me being a little more connected scent-wise is not a bad thing. I understand how this backcountry situation goes. More now than when we set out."

Had it been only yesterday? "You're a smart woman, Shelley. Smart and desirable. And I promise to return the favour as soon as possible."

She kissed his cheek. "I'll let you deal with straightening up."

Good idea. If she put her hands on him again, he might just start all over, and this time she'd be pinned to the rock face with his cock buried inside her.

Even the thought of it made him harden. He tucked himself away and straightened clothing, Shelley doing the same to his side.

They returned to where they'd abandoned their packs.

"Forward, full steam ahead, right?" Shelley asked.

"Where we belong. To see what's going on."

He offered his hand, and she took it, squeezing their fingers together for a moment before releasing. They turned and headed down the trail.

Chapter Twelve

What a weird day. Weird, as in out of the normal. Out of conceivable normal. As in, totally and in no way could she in a million years have imagined this.

Hiking in the wilderness. An impromptu blowjob on the side of a mountain. A...regal procession into the midst of a mob?

They marched through the crowd at the bottom of the hill, heads pivoting to face them, men stepping out of their way or stopping their work to stare with wide eyes. Some looked her up and down a few times, but they always finished by glancing at Chase with a little trepidation before returning to their tasks.

"Silver. Finally." An older man eased out the door of the cabin, two or three others rising from where they'd been sitting in the sunshine. "You got company."

Chase spoke quietly. "Delton. You been cooking for everyone?"

The grizzled-haired man grinned. "Thought of setting up a restaurant, but figured you might take exception."

Chase paused at the foot of the stairs. "Am I welcome home?"

"No troubles, Silver. Not for you." The man to the left of the door glanced Shelley's way. "Or for your lady."

Shelley remembered Chase's admonition from the hillside. When he motioned her forward, she lifted her chin and boldly looked the men in the eye as she marched past.

The cabin was totally unlike the last place they'd stayed. Sun shone through the sparkling clean windows. The hurricane-lantern-style wall sconces were decorated with bits of coloured glass. There was a comfortable sitting room with a couch and easy chairs. One leg of the couch was scratched, but the rest gleamed with a simple, rustic beauty.

Sturdy logs made up the furniture. More supported the open room and created crossbeams overhead. The fireplace on the sidewall was built of river rock, smooth and even, with a log plank for a mantle that had to be six inches thick.

Chase laid a hand on her shoulder and directed her farther in. "You been sleeping in my room, Delton?"

"Cleared out this morning when I got word you were on your way home. Jones did up the bed with clean sheets."

Chase chuckled. "The boy's still around?"

"Some. He's been alright."

The door to the bedroom was open and Chase pointed her in. "Make yourself at home. You hungry?"

She took off her pack, still looking around in awe. "Yes, I could eat. Chase, your place is gorgeous."

He shut the door to the outside room and drew close, foreheads touching. "Talk quiet. Shifter hearing."

She nodded.

"You okay?"

Shelley returned his grin and nodded again. That had felt pretty damn good, marching through a sea of strangers and pretending to belong. The men hadn't reacted like the pack in Whitehorse at all, even though they had to be able to tell what she was. They had noses, as well as shifter hearing.

Chase stepped back and opened his pack. "You can use the inside bathroom. There's a composting toilet, and a shower I'll set up later. But we need to sit down with the men and find out what's happening."

"I was surprised they didn't start filling you in right away."

He shrugged. "It's my house and I've been gone. It's only polite to let me get settled for a couple minutes before they jump me with their concerns."

Shelley stopped in the middle of pulling clean clothes from her pack. Chase continued to move methodically, emptying his pack, putting things away. He didn't seem in the least concerned about the mass of company outside.

It hit her. This was his place. He'd insisted she belonged here, and in a way it was true. She was as much an outcast as any of these men could ever be, but Chase truly belonged.

He belonged to these men.

He'd affirmed she belonged pretty much the way Evan had welcomed her into the fold of the Takhini pack.

"Holy cow, you're their Alpha." She breathed the words as quietly as she could, but someone in the other room still must have heard her because there was a snort of laughter, and the murmur of male voices talking about clueless women.

Chase rubbed his forehead, then twisted to face her. He put his finger to his lips.

She shook her hands in the air, asking for an answer.

He shrugged and wiggled his fingers.

Maybe? *Maybe* he was the Alpha to the misfits and outcasts?

She wasn't sure if she should hit him or hug him. This was probably one of the items on that list of things he should have told her about back before they started the trip.

She folded her arms in front of her, to make sure he knew she wasn't happy. He silently crossed the room to stare at her wordlessly. He didn't look the least bit guilty about deceiving her. Well, not deceiving, but keeping her in the dark.

He brushed the back of his knuckles over her cheek. Lowered his hand and nicked the tip of her nipple just as softly.

She jerked at his touch.

He grinned. "I like you in that position. Can think of all kinds of things to do to them pretty breasts."

Her face heated, and she was ready to pull her knife and teach him some manners.

Chase leaned one arm against the wall behind her head and dipped his head so he could speak right next to her ear. "You should look in the mirror to see how beautiful you are when you're riled up. Makes me want to tie you to my bed and do all sorts of things to you."

Instinctively she looked around the room for a mirror. That's when she noticed the window was open, and there were faces peering in at them.

The temptation to growl was huge. No wonder he was acting like an ass. He was putting on a bit of a show for the boys. Although, after their time out on the hillside, and this morning, if he didn't think they were going to be sleeping together for real seemed odd.

There had to be something else on his mind. Something else he wasn't telling her.

Again.

Damn Alpha shifters.

"I'm so going to do...*things*...to you later, as well," she threatened sweetly.

He winked, obviously happy she'd finally got the message. At some point she would write him a scathing note, or it might be simpler to just rip his head off, but for now, he was Alpha and she'd play along.

And try to ignore the tingling in her breasts he'd initiated with a single touch.

Delton had put on a full spread of food, and Chase was more than ready to dive in. His shoulder throbbed terribly, but the relief of still being in charge—*ha!*—of his own place at least let him relax enough to consume the first plate of food with barely a pause for breath.

It was two in the damn afternoon, he'd hiked for kilometers, gotten manhandled most wonderfully by an incredible woman and faced down a group of unpredictable outcast shifters.

He reached for the bowl of noodles and took a second helping.

There were three others at the table with him and Shelley. Delton, who was probably there by right of being found house-sitting when the others arrived, since the old-timer wasn't usually much for politics. Frank, whose shifted form was an enormous grizzly, sat to his right, easing away from the table and leaning back his chair. The wolverine Mark was on his second helping as well, his gaze constantly darting around the room. Those two, Frank and Mark, were about the closest thing to rational men that could be found in the bush.

It was clear there was no dire emergency. Not with the way they'd all sat down to feed instead of getting to business when he and Shelley emerged from their room.

And if he didn't stop thinking things like that, he was going to be in huge trouble.

His room. *His* cabin.

He glanced up to see her looking his way as her tongue flicked out to lap up a spot of gravy at the corner of her mouth.

His woman flashed through his brain, damn it all. They stared at each other, and his body responded.

Enough. Distraction was needed before he kicked them all out and took her again and again, on every piece of furniture in his cabin, just so when she went back to civilization he'd have memories of her left to drive himself crazy.

"Why the gathering, boys?"

"Rumors. Dreams." Frank leaned forward and the legs of his chair landed with a thump. "There's a few men gone missing, and people are getting spooked."

Mark nodded. "Clancy's crew showed up at my place with their hats in hand. Wanted an introduction to you. Said they figured if the rumors were true you'd be the best one to take care of them."

Jeez. "On account of rumors?"

Mark screwed up his face. "I ain't going to apologize. I didn't know what else to do, and if you say it's all a piece of crock I'll kick them off your land myself. And stand still while you kick my ass."

"We thought hard before gathering, Silver." Frank shrugged with a deceptive slowness that probably had deceived a fool or two.

Chase was no fool. But hell— "I don't know what to say. It's bad enough to have to deal with a flood or a mine collapse. Fires or ice storms. Real solid disasters a man can sink his teeth into."

Mark rushed on. "There's something real out there, Silver. The natural wolves are howling with it. There's a shaking in the wild that don't feel right."

"But dreams?"

Delton cleared his throat. "That there one is my fault."

Oh double hell. "You, old man?"

He tilted his head. "Weren't what I planned, but it's the truth. I'll tell you later."

"Tell me now." Chase dragged a hand through his hair then pointed at the front door. "There's a shitload of men setting up camp on my lawn for God knows how long, and you want to wait to tell me what visions you've seen. Looking for the right ambience or what?"

Delton glanced toward Shelley. "You brought a guest."

"She's just fine to hear whatever you've got to share."

"Don't want to spook nobody if I don't have to."

Oh.

Chase must have been partly asleep because he finally clued in on what Delton was saying. If shifters who weren't scared of shit, all were cowering in fear on his lawn, maybe he'd better hear the details before sharing with Shelley.

She pulled back her plate. "Um, if you don't mind, I think I'll go...get my things together for tomorrow's trip. Delton, thank you for the wonderful meal."

Four pairs of eyes watched her duck into the backroom.

"She can still hear us, you know," Mark pointed out.

"Not if I escort her to the lake to take a walk," Frank offered.

The fur on the back of Chase's neck stood up at the suggestion. Which was both really uncomfortable and shocking since he was still mostly in human form. Mostly, except for a wild swatch of fur that had instantly sprouted at Frank's suggestion. Along with a wickedly sharp set of cougar incisors.

And claws.

Ah, hell. Partially shifting portions of his anatomy when he wanted to was convenient. This? Not so much.

Fortunately him going wild in only bits and pieces didn't freak out his friends. Frank held up his hands slow and reassuringly. "She's your woman. I know. Trust me. I'll keep her safe. Let her take a peek around. You get caught up and figure out what the hell we're gonna do."

Chase breathed out slowly and wondered exactly how much more insane this situation could get. He willed his animal parts into obedience, made the change back to full human and settled into his chair.

Shelley going off with the big bear shifter made his temper rise and every protective bone in his body ache...but it wasn't a bad idea. Only he was going to learn from her little flash of fire in the bedroom. "If she's okay with it, I am."

Frank nodded.

"Shell," he called as he rose to his feet and marched across the room to meet her as she rejoined them in the living room. "I need to talk to the boys and..."

"You don't want me to hear." She rolled her eyes dramatically. "Fine, yes, I'd love to go for a walk with Frank."

He didn't think about it, just did. Leaned forward and kissed her briefly.

It surprised them both, but her hesitant smile in response was a lot friendlier than she'd been a moment before.

"I'll tell you what's up as soon as I can."

"No worries." She stepped to Frank's side. "Oh, wait. Chase, if anyone tries to pull a fast one on me, what's the limit? Death? Dismemberment?"

She'd gotten her knife out and against Frank's groin faster than any of them could react.

Hell of a woman.

Frank chuckled, deep and low, staring down with amazing unconcern at the woman holding a very sharp blade to his gonads. "I like her, Silver. She fits in just fine."

Shelley retracted her blade carefully and grinned at the towering bear. "Thank you, sir. Now you said something about a walk?"

Chase watched them go. There was a ton of details he needed to discover, but there was one truth that Frank was perfectly correct about.

Shelley fit in just fine, and that was a dangerous thing for them all.

Chapter Thirteen

She wasn't some stupid little female to be tucked off to the side and protected, but in light of the men's hesitancy to talk freely in front of her, Shelley had decided that her best course of action was to play along and head outdoors.

Chase would get her caught up later, but in the meantime she would take the opportunity to examine what she could of the area and the men. She grabbed her medical kit and hauled it with her because she was fairly certain that most of the outcasts hadn't seen a doctor in years.

The crowd was far more silent than any pack gathering she'd ever attended. Muted conversations only, some men sitting side by side with only the occasional word passing between them.

"You want to walk away from the men or through them?" Frank asked.

"Through." It was the best way to find out what was happening. She glanced up at the big man as he moved at her side, protective yet giving her enough space she didn't feel threatened. Probably simple, direct questions were the best way to get the information she wanted. "How many days ago did you arrive?"

"Four. Most of the men showed up the day after that, and they've been trickling in since."

A quick head count showed there could be close to thirty in the area. "You think more are coming?"

"Depends."

"On what?" One of the shifters was in wolf, rubbing his paw over his muzzle in a repetitive motion as if he was in pain. She pointed his way. "I want to check him."

"Sure. Just don't try to pet him."

"I'm a wolf who can't shift, I'm not an idiot," Shelley muttered under her breath.

Frank chuckled. "Tobias doesn't shift out of his wolf too often. Let me make sure he's got some brains operating today."

He called out the man's name, and the wolf lifted his head for a moment from where he'd been worrying at it.

"You up for a visitor, wolf? She's the Alpha's woman, so you be nice."

Shelley stared ahead and ignored that *Alpha's woman* comment, because that was what she was for the moment, for all intents and purposes. She was honest enough to admit hearing the words caused some interesting sensations inside.

Tobias twisted to face her as she squatted by his side.

"You having troubles? Muzzle? Or your teeth? I'm a...doctor." It still felt weird to say that as a profession, even though it was true according to shifter rules.

Aged gums and worn molars came into view as he opened his jaw wide. The source of his pain was clear—a broken tooth partly lodged in the swollen flesh of his gum line. The wolf was old enough that even shifting wouldn't fix this kind of deterioration anymore.

"Hell, man," Frank whistled. "That's got to hurt. You want the lady to take it out for you?"

Tobias looked her up and down then sniffed, long and low. Shelley held her hidden blade at the ready. Just because she was the *Alpha's woman* didn't mean that old prejudices weren't liable to pop up. If a group of wolves back in the relative civilization of Whitehorse had found her unsavoury and suitable to be attacked without warning, how much more danger was she in at this moment? If he made any rapid move, she was prepared.

The wolf rolled and opened his mouth, a position of servitude and surrender.

Shelley was so shocked she didn't move for a moment. Just took it in, the sight of another wolf submitting to her, the lowest of the low.

It was hard to breathe.

Frank grunted behind her. "You need anything? I can hold him."

She shook herself into action. "No, I should be good."

This was different from a lab setting and someone's pet retriever. Shelley grabbed the small pair of needle-nose pliers she had in her bag, rested the wolf's head in her lap and with a couple experienced moves had the offending piece of tooth out.

She resisted patting his flank like she normally would have soothed a visitor to her clinic. He rolled away to allow her to stand.

Frank grunted again. "That was simple."

"It would have worked loose eventually. Tobias nearly had it out," Shelley explained. She faced the wolf and bowed politely. "You're welcome, though."

Tobias dipped his head in response before wandering off in the opposite direction. Shelley watched him for a moment before joining her bear escort on the trail that circled the small mountain lake. They walked just far enough they could look back toward the cabin and the tents without having to dodge strangers. From here the setting looked even lonelier, the low swell and fall of the Patterson Mountain Range around them creating an impressive backdrop behind the cabin. Not the ragged towering mountains of farther to the west, where the Tombstones and Ogilvie ranges thrust skyward. Here the land rose and fell constantly, but over a large flatter plateau.

It meant the land around them felt endless. Nothing to close them in, to contain them. If she could shift, she could turn toward the north and run until she hit the Arctic Ocean.

This was so vast a land her worries and concerns shrank to things of lesser consequence. If she could tame this land? Survive here?

She could do anything.

"You want to walk a little longer?" Frank asked.

She laughed. "How long you think the guys need to talk before we head in?"

He snorted. "A walk to the point and back should do it."

The path was wide enough she didn't have to trail behind him, remaining at his side instead. "You never answered my question, about why more men would show up."

"Hoped you'd forget, but you aren't the stupid kind now, are you?"

"I hope not." A touch crazy, perhaps, as she looked around her and considered exactly what she'd jumped into without thinking. "Is it serious? You really worried?"

"Hell, yeah."

"Yet you deal with the unknown all the time. It's dangerous living out here."

"We can face just about anything if it makes sense. Men gone missing? Don't sit right."

"Could they have just left the north?"

Frank wandered to the edge of the woods where there was a fallen tree. He arranged himself on the smooth section where the bark had slipped off.

"Maybe. Even the loners usually tell someone they're cutting out." He stared at her. "You're not a typical wolf. You seem different."

She shook her head. "Can't turn furry. There's something wrong with my shifter, and the wolf's never come to the surface."

"Hell of a thing," he offered with a sympathetic headshake. "Bears don't have that trouble, you know. We're bears, no half-blood, no full. You got bear, you got bear. No needing to be triggered like you wolves, mother's milk or otherwise."

She'd never gotten a chance to talk to a bear shifter like this before. The bits and pieces she'd been taught by her mentor regarding bear shifters had tweaked her curiosity, but knowing how to patch someone up didn't require total knowledge of the species' secrets. This was a golden opportunity to learn more.

She dug for the most important tidbits. "Really? Doesn't matter how much blood, you can always shift?"

He wavered for a moment. "Always got the ability to shift. Whether they do or not is up to the person. You've got to talk your animal side to the surface then convince them it's okay to come out. Not everyone does. Not everyone wants to."

She couldn't believe that. "No way. Why would someone not want to shift?"

"Family lives in the city, wants to leave behind the wilderness. I don't know, but it happens. Also means there's none of this worry about leaving behind babies with a mixed family. You know, if a man gets someone pregnant, there's no 'surprise-you-can-turn-furry' when the kid becomes a teen.

Can't shift unless you decide to, and you sure can't decide to if you don't know you're a bear."

Shelley thought for a moment. "Your family units are different. You don't mate for life."

"We do, if we choose. It's not usually the bear side doing the bossing about like your wolves do."

"That seems so strange to me," Shelley admitted. "All I've ever heard and known about is the mating for life of the wolf."

And she'd always been devastated by that knowledge because she really didn't see any happily ever after in her future.

Frank shook his finger at her, his big thick beefy digit in her face. "Now you're going and letting your prejudices show. Wolves take life mates based on their wolf side, and make their human sides catch up. Bears use their human brains along with the attraction the animal side feels. Cats are the same way. Hell, most of the shifter breeds I know use their brains more than some *mate-mate-mate* thing. Sorry, wolves are the whacked-out fools of the shifter kingdom."

"Some would say they're the only ones that have it right."

"Because that *my mate* makes wolves all so accepting all the time?" Frank poked at a still-open wound, and Shelley cringed. "Yeah, that's what I figured."

He rose to the full height of his six-foot, seven-foot whatever.

"You ever have a girl, Frank? Or a family?" Maybe it was a dangerous topic, but she wanted to know.

He looked her over for a moment. "Yeah. Had a girl. She passed away and I came out here. Didn't like to stay where there were too many reminders of her."

Shelley laid her hand on his arm. It wasn't sympathy; it was just a touch of understanding. "I have so many bad memories of Whitehorse. But I'm being stupid and running right back to the same place. There's a saying about that. Insanity is doing the same thing over and over again, and expecting different results."

"It's also brave."

She shrugged. "I don't feel brave."

Frank gestured her down the path back toward the cabin. Obviously figured they'd given enough time for the serious business to be discussed. "You got family there?"

"My older half-sister. She's human."

"Whoa, that's different. She know about shifters?"

Shelley bit her lip to stop from snorting. Sharing that her sis was sleeping with the wolf pack Alpha—*nahh*, she'd keep it general.

"She knows. Manages the Moonshine Inn for the Takhini Pack. She's rather good around shifters. Probably better than me." The last confession snuck out grudgingly. Then she reconsidered. Caroline did do well. More than well. "Actually she's the reason it's worthwhile coming back to face the memories. She's strong and accepting. And giving. I need people like that in my life, and the fact she's my sister makes it even more vital."

"Sounds like she's important to you."

"I guess you could say she's one of my heroes," Shelley confessed.

Frank escorted her back up the steps of the cabin and knocked on the door. "She's got to be damn cool, because you're pretty impressive yourself. For a wolf."

Shelley laughed. He tweaked her nose before swinging the door open and gesturing her into the cabin. He rambled easily down the stairs then disappeared between a couple of tents.

Watching Shelley leave with the big bear appeased Chase's discomfort a little. He knew she would be safe with Frank.

The question still remained if Frank would be safe with Shelley.

He turned to face his remaining friends. "Spit it out. Details, dreams. I want to know fast."

"Don't think it's an immediate thing, Silver, just—"

"Fast because I've promised to take Shelley out again in the morning to gather information, and if you're going to go all mystical and hairy on me, I want to know now what to expect when we get back in a few days."

Mark nodded. "There's men from out Townsend way who ain't been seen for a couple months. Someone found a collapsed mine opening and the smell of death around it. Plus there's a cabin, well more of a lean-to, that burned to the ground, but that would only account for a few of the missing."

"There's that bear gathering in Dawson. Their once-in-a-while redistribution of territory, or some such nonsense. We figured it wouldn't affect any of the crew out in the bush. Frank ignored the summons when it came, as did most of the other bear shifters." Delton pushed back his chair.

Chase frowned. "How do they get all the bears to gather in one spot? Send out mail? How do they even know where to look?"

Delton cleared the plates off the table as he talked, seemingly unable to sit and stop working. "Hell, you know the

Pony Express wouldn't work up here. No, it's freakier than that. They got some kind of connection that they set off, and the bears get the urge to gather. Don't ask me for more than that. Frank said it felt as if someone tapped him on the shoulder. He ignored it."

Freaky indeed. "Glad we don't have that with wolves."

"Or cats," Delton agreed. "But if I remember correctly, the last time there was a call like this they didn't stop at the polite shoulder tapping. They tried to round them up."

"You remembering correctly, old-timer?" Mark asked. "How long ago was the last?"

"Who you calling old? The last call was only thirty-five years ago or thereabouts, so, hell yes, I remember correctly."

Chase scrubbed his fingers over his brush cut. "If they're going to try to round up outcasts and haul them into Whitehorse, they're stupider than we need to worry about. You seriously think Frank could be herded anywhere he didn't want to go?"

"Maybe Frank won't, but he's about the biggest and sanest of the bunch. There's going to be isolated killing happening all over the north if the bears try to make someone involuntarily move—and it could be either side dying, ours or theirs."

Their men.

And that was the truth. These men were his, in some strange and undefined way. Part of the pack of outcasts.

"It's not just the bears, Silver." Mark shook his head, worry in his every move. "Something's off. The wolves are howling with it. The regular animals are making scarce like there's a snowstorm ready to descend. You add the two things together, hell. I wasn't able to convince the men to just relax. They wanted to see you."

Chase sighed. "I understand why they gathered. You're right, Mark. You did the right thing. I won't be doing any ass kicking, not of the men who banded together here for protection. Bears or whatever the hell."

Mark tilted his head in respect.

Chase looked up at his oldest friend. "But you. What're you bringing to the mix, old man? Dreams to scare little children in their cozy beds at night?"

Delton waved the cast-iron pan in his hand as if it were a feather. "You've never discounted my dreams before."

Which was more the pity. Under the midnight sun, there were more unusual and unexplainable situations and things than Chase was willing to try to explain away. "And you see death?"

The old man nodded. "Shifter deaths."

"Maybe it's the bears fighting, like Mark talked about."

Delton hesitated. "No. Yes. Both."

It was still early, but hell if Chase didn't need a drink. His shoulder ached, his head ached, and if Shelley didn't get back soon he was going outside to find her because his body ached from maintaining his composure with her away from his protection.

He rose and poured three tumblers of alcohol, gesturing for the men to join him in the living room. "If we're going to talk about death and dying we may as well do it like real Yukoners."

They clinked glasses and tossed back the first round. The alcohol burned as it went down before smoothing into a heated ball in his gut. He poured a second round before making himself comfortable on the couch. His friends settled and the room grew quiet. Peaceful. Chase took a deep breath. Now he was ready for this conversation.

"Other than the bears, what kind of death, Delton?"

His friend hesitated. "Yours."

Chapter Fourteen

The inside of the cabin smelt like shifters and booze. Shelley wandered in cautiously, but there were only the three men sprawled on the furniture in the main open area, glasses in their hands and a nearly empty bottle on the low coffee table.

Chase grinned at her sheepishly. "We left you a little."

Oh boy. "I think I'll be designated driver tonight. You all done talking about scary things without little ol' me around?"

Mark nodded twice. Huge head motions that threatened to topple him to the floor. "You sure a right smart woman. How the hell did Chase manage to snag the likes of you?" The wolverine hiccupped then slid to the floor. "'Cuse me."

Delton shook his head. "Don't mind him. He's an ass."

"Am not. Am a wolfer. Wol-*ver.*" Mark straightened up best he could and pawed the air with his fingers spread wide. "Scary dude with sharp claws. Only I got much better hair."

He hiccupped again.

Delton sniggered.

Shelley glanced in disbelief at Chase. "Mark knows about X-Men? And what did you give them to drink to get them so wasted in the half hour I've been gone?"

"Sourdough thermometer." Chase blinked innocently. "Perry Davis's Patented Painkiller."

She sucked in a quick, shocked breath. The old-timer's method of knowing how cold it was. The glasses of liquid set outside the window of their trappers' cabin would freeze in sequence. The mercury would be the first to go at minus forty, then the coal oil, then the Jamaican Ginger extract. By the time the Perry's turned to slush, they knew it was time to stay indoors or freeze their lungs just breathing. "I'm so glad you're all taking your responsibilities to the pack seriously."

Mark snorted. "Lady, I think I love you. You said I was pack." He lifted his head and pursed his lips in her direction.

Chase kicked out a foot, knocking the leg of the chair Mark was propped against, which sent it flying. Mark collapsed to the ground and lay there smiling at the ceiling for about ten seconds before he started seriously snoring.

Shelley rested her fists on her hips and stared down at where Chase sprawled on the couch. "Well, that wasn't very nice."

"No one kisses you."

A snort escaped. "Air kisses? You're nuts."

"No one." Chase raised his glass in the air. "You sure you don't want some?"

She laughed as she stepped over the motionless body of the wolverine. "I should have at least one shot or you guys are going to be too ridiculous for me to handle."

Delton nodded. "Serious business being Alpha. Chase needs a little fun and frolics every now and then."

He drained his glass and rose unsteadily. With deceptive strength, the old cougar grabbed the wolverine by the foot and dragged him toward the front door. "I'll find a berth outside. You two have a good night. If you like, I'll make you breakfast in the morning before you leave."

He vanished out the front door. Shelley cringed as Mark's head thumped over the doorsill.

Something smooth and cool brushed her arm, and she grasped the glass to stop Chase from bumping it into her. "Are you three sheets to the wind, Chase?"

He shook his head, leaning back to relax against the cushions. His voice was clear when he spoke. "No. They drank more than I did. They were upset. It was one way to settle them down."

She sat on the coffee table directly across from him, enjoying the way his gaze slipped over her. Protective and admiring all at the same time. "They have a reason to be upset? Frank said he figured there would be more men showing up. Afraid they'll go missing as well if they don't band together."

Chase stopped staring at her one piece at a time as if deciding which bit to dine on first, and his gaze snapped up. "I thought he was taking you away to save you from all the grizzly details."

"Oh, he didn't tell me much. Just that he figured this was the safest place to be the next while."

Chase nodded. "And you probably still want to head into the bush tomorrow, right?"

"Well, let's see."

She curled her finger at him to motion him forward. When she took hold of his buttons, he grinned. "We've got the entire place to ourselves."

A shiver took her that she ignored as she opened his shirt to reveal that magnificent chest of his. "I've been trying not to notice, thank you. First things first."

"Getting naked sounds like a good first thing."

Pushing the fabric off his shoulders just meant more muscles to admire, and a thicker scent rising to her nostrils. He was turned on by her touch.

She was feeling the same draw. Damn it, she might have tossed all professionalism out the window by getting intimate with him, but she'd at least check his injury before they fell into bed.

He reached forward and slid his hands up her thighs. Determinedly driving her crazy.

"Chase Johnson, you sure you didn't have a few too many swigs of that rot gut?" Shelley stood so his hands would fall away, and clamped a firm grip on his shoulder to remove the bandages. "Now stay still."

She snapped her lips together when the claw marks came into view. The protective covering had stopped the blood from staining his shirt. If possible, the cuts looked fresher than before, instead of closing in and forming a protective scab. This time she managed to keep her head about her and not blurt out horrible things like *holy shit, what is going on?*

He leaned his head against her nearest arm and nuzzled. "You just patch that up fresh for me. Don't think there's much else you can do."

"It hurts, doesn't it?" she asked.

He stroked his hand up the inside of her thigh. "It does, but I know what can make me feel better."

In spite of the mess on his shoulder, Shelley had to smile. "You are such a cat. I'm pretty sure that after bandaging you up I should give you a shot of antibiotics and make you sleep in the hope that helps you recover."

He continued to run his hand up and down the inside of her thigh as she bandaged him, taping the gauze into place. "You didn't answer me. We're heading bush, right? That's what I told the boys."

"I need to talk to the puma who attacked you, now more than ever. There's got to be a reason you're not healing."

"That's fine. We'll go. We'll have to be extra careful of meeting anyone—Mark offered to travel as an escort. Delton did too, but I'd prefer to have him back here to help deal with any newcomers. Frank is good, but he lacks a little..."

Shelley put aside her supply bag and squatted in front of him. "Frank lacks a little *knowing when to keep his mouth shut-ism.*"

Chase slid his hand around her neck, threading his fingers into her hair. "Frank who?"

He pulled her forward and their lips met, and she gave in. All the things she'd been holding off, all the reasons she'd avoided fooling around with shifters? None of them applied to Chase, and if they could have a night of enjoying each other before heading into the wilds?

No objections at all.

Especially when he kissed as if he was craving her. Fingers tight on the back of her head to hold her exactly how he wanted. His other hand returned to her thigh, thumb teasing, compelling. Dangerously slow. Like a trickle of a narcotic into her veins, his touch built a hunger inside.

He worked their lips together, brought his tongue into play. She met his exploration with her own, sighing with happiness at letting go of the restraints she'd maintained for so long.

Well, not including when she'd attacked him outside on the ridge.

But that had been her reacting to the jolt of adrenaline as much as her attraction to him. Responding to the animal side of the equation, because while her wolf never deemed it proper to rise any higher than her gut level, the beast was still there. Still influenced her decisions at some subconscious level.

But now was about the human side. The animal was interested, but only distantly. Not as if she were responding to a mate call, or anything.

Chase grabbed the bottom of her shirt and tugged on it, letting their lips separate for long enough to lift the fabric over her head and bare her.

He grumbled disapprovingly. "Sports bra."

Shelley laughed and removed the offending garment. She also took a peek at the windows. They had no audience yet, but there was nothing to say they wouldn't have one later. "Can we move this to the bedr—*ohh...*"

He'd swung her up in his arms and they were halfway across the room before she could finish her sentence. Chase lowered her to the mattress and stared intently, his gaze burning as he took her in. He twisted the blinds upward, sunshine hitting the ceiling and bouncing down to give them light and privacy.

"Nice."

Chase whirled back on her as if she were prey he'd let out of his sights for far too long. "Nice would be you removing the rest of your clothes."

Shelley kicked off her shoes and slipped out of her pants. "Only nice?"

"I'm a simple man. No need for fancy words."

She wiggled back on the bed until she was propped up against the headboard, massive pillows at her back. Chase was shirtless, shoeless and he'd undone his belt and the top button of his jeans.

Guh.

The mental image was going to stay with her for a long, long time. Delicious, powerful. He stalked forward and leaned a knee on the bed, and she was sure she was about to get pounced on.

"You want this?" Chase caught her foot in his hand, those talented thumbs instantly beginning to work magic on her skin.

Stupid question. "Don't you?"

"Hell, I've wanted you since I spotted you on the field in Whitehorse, and I know you're attracted to me. But do you really want this?"

Shelley scooted closer, drawing him over her and using him like a Chase blanket. His weight settled slowly, with his jeans and her panties separating their hips. Nothing between her and that gorgeous chest.

She groaned, not sure what was holding him back. "I want you. I don't understand the question."

"We don't have to have sex because the guys are calling you my woman. This isn't about needing to be marked."

Oh. Now she got it. "Chase?"

Resting on his elbows to keep his weight from crushing her, he was still close enough his answer fanned air over her face. "Yes?"

Actions spoke better than words. She caught his face in her hands and connected their lips again. At the same time she wrapped her legs around his hips, and that solid bit of him met the aching part of her.

By his enthusiastic response she figured he'd gotten her message, loud and clear.

Chase took a long taste of her mouth as he luxuriated in the feel of her under him. Willing woman, mostly naked?

It didn't get much better than that.

Except for the mostly part. Damn if he wanted to have anything between them. She'd said yes, now he was going to take and take and take, greedy for more than the touches he'd had.

Knowing that she was willing reduced the frantic panic inside. Let him concentrate on making this more than a quick rut up against the rocks like she'd have gotten from him earlier in the day. Chase licked along the tendon of her neck. Her skin, so soft, hint of salt, desire-laced. Her want for him poured out and flowed around them, and he nibbled along her collarbone hungrily.

It took him a good five minutes to finish laving her skin on the right side. Small tastes of her shoulder, her neck. Teasing the sensitive spot where her arm and torso met. He alternated between licking and sucking, biting and kissing until she squirmed under him.

His animal sides rumbled with approval. They weren't even to the good parts yet, and she was making wonderful noises.

Shelley grabbed his head and tugged him toward her breasts. Pretty things. Just small mounds with rosy tips now that she was lying on her back. He resisted her pull and smiled at the treat.

Shelley whimpered. "Chase?"

"I'm anticipating."

Her laugh slipped at the moment he covered her areola with his mouth, the happy sound shifting into something deeper and far rawer. He played with the tip, using his tongue, pulsing his lips to draw her flesh into his mouth. He traced around and around, pulling off and blowing on her wet skin to watch the sensitive tip pucker to a tight nub so he could feel it better against his tongue on the next pass.

167

Shelley still had her fingers laced around his head. His hair wasn't long enough for her to grab, or she'd have torn it out with her frantic grabs as he switched from one side and back to the other.

"So good." She moaned out her satisfaction, and Chase's cat purred in response.

"So tasty," Chase noted, sadly abandoning her breasts, but looking forward to his next course.

He skimmed her belly, unable to maintain his slow pace. Especially when he got a peek at the lacy thing covering her mound. "Sweet mercy, woman. Now that's a pretty surprise."

Shelley opened her thighs wider, allowing him to slip between her legs. "Girlie bras aren't good for hiking, but my panties can always be fancy."

"Like you better with no bra anyway, but these I approve of."

He pressed a kiss to the tiny bow at the top of the sheer fabric. So sheer he could already see her dark curls under the material. He could smell her arousal. Could barely wait to taste her on his tongue.

But those panties? *Damn.*

Chase sat back. "Roll over."

Shelley struggled up on her elbows and frowned in confusion. "What?"

He forced the words out again. "Roll over."

Even in his ears his voice sounded harsh and rough. But hell if he wasn't about to lose it. And when she drew in her legs from where they'd been spread around him, tucked herself into a ball and rolled to present her ass, he held on by a thread.

The thin lace ribbons wrapped around her hips like tiny delicate tattoos. Barely there pencil marks on a page. There was a teeny triangle of fabric just at the small of her back then the thin ribbon dropped to disappear between her ass cheeks.

"Oh God." Chase caressed her skin as gently as he could, but his hands trembled as he fought for control.

Shelley twisted her head to stare at him, her upper body supported on her arms, ass higher than her shoulders. Her eyes flashed with fire. "You don't have to wait, Chase. I want you. Need you."

He clutched the edges of the ribbon but managed to stop from snapping the material off her. She wouldn't have a lot of clothes in that bag. He couldn't trash them. He couldn't.

She somehow grabbed hold of one side, pulling the fabric free from his fingers and tugging the lace down her thighs.

He was trapped. Caught in a place between giving to her and just bloody well taking. "Sorry, darling, I can't..."

She left the panties bunched around one knee and resumed position in front of him. That position that turned his mind to mush. "Don't stop. Please."

Chase rubbed her ass cheeks, wondering at his incredible luck. "Shell..."

"Fuck me, dammit. You need a written invitation?"

The forceful command nearly broke his final restraint. Only hell if he'd fuck her now. Yet. He slipped to the floor, grabbed those soft hips and yanked her to his mouth.

Shelley screamed as he pressed his tongue into her depths, tasting and taking her into his system. He licked and teased, circling her clit, swiping along her labia. Returning again and again to her wet opening and fucking her with his tongue.

She couldn't move, couldn't resist. He had her suspended in the air, and all she could do was accept the pleasure.

"Chase. Oh yes, there. Right *there*."

Chase smiled against her body as he flicked her clit with his tongue, lapping her up like a full meal. Only this was better because food didn't wiggle and quiver with happiness. Didn't sigh and moan. Didn't scream as it was consumed.

She climaxed, a rush of wetness meeting his tongue as her passage attempted to grasp hold. He had something much better for her to be squeezing, and Chase dropped her hips in near desperation. Unzipped and hauled out his cock.

He forced her farther onto the bed and levered himself over her in a flash. His shaft lined up, his hands wrapped around her hips. Instead of slamming into her like he wanted, he moved slowly. Used her hips to drag her backward as he tilted forward.

The sight of her body wrapping around his dick and taking him in blew what little was left of his mind.

She was still squeezing inside, whether her climax or intentionally, and he swore at the incredible sensation. His groin met her ass and they both froze for a split second.

Then there was nothing left to restrain him. Chase drew back and thrust forward, her wetness easing his passage. He kept his hips going but skimmed his hands upward, leaning over to press a kiss to the center of her back. She turned her head to rest her cheek on the bedspread, a smile lighting her face.

He rocked again, harder this time, and she closed her eyes and took a deep breath. "So, so good."

So, so close to exploding. Chase couldn't decide what to look at. Her content expression, the point where his cock slid into her body. A gentle brush of fingers hit his balls, and he gritted his teeth.

"That's it, darling. Play with that pretty clit. Make yourself come again."

She nodded. Continued. Grew tighter and wetter, and between the moans and heat and sight, Chase toppled off the cliff of control. He slammed into her hard enough to shake his sturdy wood bed. Leaned over and grabbed her shoulder with his teeth. Nipped and bit and chewed on her as his hips pistoned, and she writhed under him.

She cried out a second before he'd been about to give up and come first. Chase buried himself as deep as possible, then it was impossible to tell if it was him losing his load or her dragging it from him. Connected and yet independent, like two miniature tornados impacting and blowing each other apart.

His arms and legs shook, and when she collapsed to the mattress he followed, unwilling to leave the warmth of her body. He kissed the spots he'd left on her skin. The bites and teeth marks, small bruises on her upper body. "Damn, I worked you over hard."

She laughed, shaking under him. "I don't mind. Really. Holy moly that was good."

He tilted them onto their sides, still connected. He stroked his fingers over her back, gently. Unable to stop touching.

They had a long way to walk in the morning, but it was early still. He figured at least once more before dinner was possible. Probable.

"Again?" he asked.

She squirmed until she faced him, the mischief in her expression all the answer he needed.

Again.

Chapter Fifteen

The taste of bacon, eggs and what was possibly the strongest coffee she'd ever had in her life lingered on her tongue as they hiked into the bush.

Chase had woken her at five, his head buried between her legs. It wasn't a bad way to face the dawn, even if she'd sworn they only turned out the light fifteen minutes earlier after he'd fucked her on top of the back of the couch.

If she kept smiling this hard all day, her cheeks were going to ache. For whatever reason there had been none of the usual shifter mind-games dancing through her brain as they'd worked each other over. And over. And over again.

Maybe she'd totally given up on ever triggering her wolf. Maybe knowing Chase's mixed ancestry had allowed her to subconsciously cross him off the list of potential people to help trigger her wolf. Either way, all she knew was by the time the lust had run its course, or they were both so sated they couldn't move, they also couldn't stop grinning at each other like fools.

Now if she could just figure out what was wrong with him, things would be awesome.

Other than that part inside that wondered how this one-night stand they'd begun would end.

"Stream ahead," Chase warned. "Hop on my back and I'll carry you across."

Like hell he would. "You forget you've got a mess on your shoulder, mister? I'm not going to cling to your back and make it worse."

Chase stared her down as she stepped to his side. "Didn't seem to stop you from clinging hard last night."

Wolves don't blush at the mention of sex. She reminded herself of that, but it didn't seem to help. "I avoided touching your injury. Not possible if you've got—*oh...*"

He did it again. Snatched her up as if she weighed two pounds and settled her and her pack into his arms. "There we go. Now don't wiggle."

They were already five feet into the creek, and while she wouldn't have minded wet feet, she didn't want a wet ass again. "Bastard. You had planned that all along."

"Arguing takes too much time."

"It's called discussing, not arguing," Shelley protested.

He snorted and kept walking, swaying as he found footholds on the bottom of the rocky streambed.

Shelley wrapped one hand around his neck carefully to try to help balance them. "Spring flood waters done for the year?"

"Late. This area doesn't see much change, and the one river we need to worry about has a cable car to use for the crossing, so we'll be fine for this stretch of the journey."

"Cable car? How's our shadow going to use that?"

Mark in his wolverine form had been keeping pretty much out of sight. She'd only spotted him one time because Chase had silently lifted an arm and pointed. Mark sat along the hillside in full view, probably a deliberate announcement of his presence.

"He can swim. Or he'll shift, and go hand over hand. We don't have to worry about him. Pretend he's not even there."

Shelley nodded, instead looking into Chase's face.

His square jaw had thicker stubble on it now. Darker than the hair on his head, it emphasized his strength yet made his lips seem softer and fuller than any man had a right to own.

The corners of his mouth tilted upward. "You looking for something, darling?"

Her grin matched his. "Not at this minute, but eventually, yeah."

He took his focus off the shoreline for a brief second to wink at her. "You're addictive. Can't tell you how much I enjoyed last night."

"And this morning," Shelley teased. "I'm not complaining either. You're a generous lover, Chase. Thank you."

He lowered her to the ground, making sure she'd gotten her balance on the round river rocks before releasing her. He stroked her cheek again, that totally soft motion with the back of his knuckles over her skin. It felt like a kiss with his fingers.

He coughed lightly. "Mind if I ask a couple personal questions?"

Shelley joined him as they headed up the riverbank toward a section of open grassland where it would be easier to walk. "Let me guess. You want to know if I can play the piano."

Chase snorted. "If that's a polite way of telling me to mind my own business, we can talk about other things. I just wondered about your wolf. I understand about things not working right—I offer my contrary cross-natures as an example."

She didn't really know where to start. "I'm half-blood. My dad is full wolf and fell in love with a human woman in Whitehorse. Mom already had a little girl who was two when they got hitched."

"That's Caroline?"

"Right. I was born a couple years later, so there's four years between us, and neither my dad nor mom had any troubles with the pack until I arrived. It was as if I...was wrong, and all the wolves could sense it."

Chase pointed to a rock outcrop, and they moved together to have their first break of the day.

Shelley drank some water and nibbled on chocolate as she considered what she wanted to tell him. Chase waited patiently, the silence between them far more comfortable than it should have been. Then again, that was part of Chase's charm. He didn't seem to need to fill the air with noise.

She stared at the creek not far from them, its low rumble a soothing sound that carried clearly on the still air.

It was time to leave some burdens behind. As often as possible, she wanted to drop and discard the things that were holding her back.

Bitterness was the first that needed to go.

"There's one more in our family. Kent arrived three years later, and he's fine. But I got picked on by the pack kids. As a half-blood there was no way I could shift until I became an adult anyway, but even back then they all seemed to sense I wasn't right."

Chase growled. "Nothing wrong with you. People who would pick on a kid for something that's not their fault—they're the ones that ain't right."

Shelley nodded. "I know that now, but try telling that to an eight-year-old who doesn't get invited to any birthday parties. And the kicker was it didn't matter that there were humans in my class who shouldn't have had any reason to hate me. They picked up on the clues of the pack kids and followed their lead."

She reached down and grasped a handful of small stones, tossing them as she continued to speak. "Our pack had lost our

175

Omega, so there was no one looking out to keep the emotional side of the pack in check. When I turned eighteen I guess everyone figured I'd be so grateful to be triggered, all kinds of offers came forward."

Chase sat beside her, thigh touching hers. "After years of ignoring or hurting you, they offered to have sex with you?"

She shrugged. "They're wolves. You know the whole shifter attitude toward sex is a lot more casual, other than between mates. They couldn't understand why I didn't want to accept their oh-so-generous offers."

He breathed out slowly, his body rigid beside her. "Fucking bastards."

Shelley snorted. "Yeah, that's pretty much what I said to them. The son of the then-current Alpha didn't like it much."

"Shit."

She sighed. "That was the beginning of a lot of chaos. I ran as soon as I could. Headed south and got myself registered for vet school, working and taking classes part-time. The rest of the family stuck around for a few years, until my dad found a job outside the north and moved them all. After I left there was a huge uprising in the pack, and someone took out the Alpha. Pretty sure that made me the most notorious girl in the territory for a while."

He threaded his fingers through hers and hung on. "By 'took out' I hope you mean slit the asshole's throat."

"Well, aren't you the most lovely bloodthirsty fellow? I don't know. There was a change of leadership, and from what my sister said, there's been another. Evan isn't that kind of Alpha. Not at all."

"How a shithead like that got into power and let you suffer..." Chase rose to his feet and stomped away, dragging a hand wildly over his head.

176

"Hey. It happened. It passed. I'm fully of the look-forward mentality now. Which is why I came back."

Chase eyed her from a distance. "But you tried to trigger your wolf when you were down south?"

Sheesh. Cheeks flaming hot, she forced herself to answer. "Yes, Chase. I had sex with shifters when I was in school. And they all hoped they would 'be the one' to magically flip my switch, but it always failed. After a while I stopped letting them sniff around because, frankly, having someone constantly checking how you feel while you're doing the deed kills the mood."

He nodded once before grinning. "I'd feel sorrier for the bastards, but their loss. You're a hell of a package in bed."

Shelley laughed. "And you, Chase, are not like any shifter I've ever met. Last night did you even think once that maybe you'd be the one to push the right button for me?"

"I thought about it the entire time."

What?

Chase leered at her. "Oh *that* button. No. Sorry. Thought you were talking about that sensitive button between your legs. Too interested in fucking your brains out otherwise."

It was impossible to hold on to the hurt of the past when he stared at her with that fire in his eyes. Even if this relationship between them was only for the next couple days, Chase had already pushed a few right things for her, and Shelley was so grateful.

Chase ignored his desire to call it an early night, continuing to hike long after he'd liked to have stopped. Caving to the urge to set up the tent would mean he could explore Shelley all over again.

One night hadn't been enough.

But they might be able to find the puma who had sliced and diced him with a single night out if they kept moving for a little longer, especially if the man had switched camps, which was highly likely. The idea of heading back to his comfortable bed and his cabin tomorrow for more romping motivated him in part.

His aching shoulder provided the rest of the incentive.

He'd had cuts and bruises before—all shifters had, especially an outcast like himself. Shifter metabolism didn't mean instantaneous healing, but more rapid than the average human. Complications like his were extremely rare. The kind of pain he was experiencing was unique, something similar to the descriptions of blood poisoning he'd heard. Strings of heat and the occasional sharp dagger-like blows he felt made him more concerned now than he'd initially been when Shelley expressed confusion over his injury.

So he marched them across the deserted territory with brief stops for lunch, snacks and a dinner that left a lot to be desired.

One more hour and he'd give in. Maybe two. If they hadn't found the miner by then, they'd break for the night before swinging around to the second camp in the morning.

"Chase? I need to stop," Shelley called.

He stepped to the side of the trail, eyeing the terrain. It wasn't the best place she could have selected. "Now?"

"Unless you want me to pee my pants."

She was getting blunter, which was a good thing, he supposed. "Now is fine."

She dropped her backpack before giving him a dirty look and heading off the trail toward the bush.

"What's that for?" he shouted after her.

"Damn boys and their bladders. You think we can all drink two liters of fluid and keep it in."

He turned his back as she found a bush to squat behind. He had been forcing the liquids on her as they hiked to make sure she didn't get dehydrated. "You forgot to mention the bit about how unfair it is that we can pee standing up."

"Bastard," she muttered.

Chase grinned, enjoying how much he'd been smiling since he met Shelley. "Don't wipe with poison ivy."

"I'm going to—"

Her mocking response was lost under the snarl of an animal. Chase twirled and raced toward her, vibrating with adrenaline.

Mere seconds had passed, yet she was already on her back with a full-grown puma on top of her. Chase fought the spontaneous urge to shift that rolled over him. He screamed, the cougar shriek escaping from his human vocal cords nearly as terrifying as the real thing.

Shelley called out as well, her insistent *no, no, no* echoing off the nearby tree line. Chase's heartbeat pounded in his ears, dimming the volume of her cries as he focused on the big cat.

He shifted one hand to cougar, claws at the ready, and swiped it over the beast's shoulder in a wound eerily reminiscent of his own injury. The cat lifted its head and snarled, but otherwise didn't budge from where it loomed over Shelley. Muscles flexed as it lifted a paw, head twisting back toward his prey. There was that sense of *other* about the creature—and recognition and horror slammed simultaneously into Chase.

It was a shifter attacking Shelley.

A second later the animal roared, this time in pain, not fury. Its body jerked once, then again, blood spurting out to coat the ground, Shelley, Chase's shoes.

He snatched at the animal's shaking body, the knowledge it was a man inside this beast forced down as his concern for Shelley washed away all hesitation. He made ready to reach around and slit the cat's throat with his claws. Only the creature wasn't mauling her anymore, it was quivering slightly as it lay draped like a thick skin rug.

"I'm sorry. I'm so sorry. Chase, oh my God, help me."

Shelley's shouts were the only thing that kept him in human form. He grabbed the heavy beast and dragged it aside, ignoring the horrible agony that ripped through his shoulder as he manhandled two hundred pounds of puma to the ground.

Her face was streaked with tears, and there was blood everywhere. It only took a glance to double-check that the puma was dead. The animal's limbs still twitched, but it was the long open wound across its neck and a very familiar knife handle protruding from its chest that caught Chase's eye.

He dropped to his knees and gathered Shelley close, looking for claw wounds, for bite marks.

"Chase, I killed him. I didn't mean to, but he just—"

"Did he bite you? Cut you? Tell me."

She lifted her arm in the air and held it out for inspection. There were a couple slashes in her skin, deep enough she'd need stitches. "Shit."

"Grab hold of your arm and squeeze. We need to get you bandaged before you bleed into trouble."

"I killed him. Killed a shifter." Her voice trembled.

Chase carried her back to the trail. She dropped her head on his shoulder and all the fight went out of her, and he was damn sure she'd fainted. Only when he lowered her to the ground, she dragged herself upright and leaned against the pack.

Tears marked their tracks on her face through the dirt and dust. He wiped one cheek tenderly. "You killed him because you had to."

Shelley hesitated. "I didn't want to. Oh God, what have I done?"

Chase cupped her chin in his hand and locked their gazes together. "He attacked. You responded. Nothing more—there was no ill intent on your part."

"I could have—"

"Could have what?" Chase refused to let her start second-guessing. "He attacked you, Shell. It wasn't a conversation where you could consider your responses. Instinct kicked in and you defended yourself, and that's what you're supposed to do. Accept it."

She nodded slowly, her fingers clenched tight around her arm. He stroked her cheek, willing her to accept the truth. The back of his neck tingled as he attempted to stay alert to the dangers around them even as he gave her the attention she needed.

She breathed around the pain. She was afraid, but she wasn't going to pass out.

And when she spoke, he couldn't have been any prouder— the strong, capable woman he'd come to know shining through as he expected. "Get my red medical kit out of the backpack. And...I need you to get my knife."

He nodded and rose to his feet, all senses on high.

He'd recognized the puma. The shifter was a sometimes partner with the man who'd initially clawed him. Chase grabbed the medical supplies for Shelley then made his way to the body to recover her knife.

Chase stared down at the body, another jolt of admiration hitting alongside sorrow at the shifter's death. She'd done exactly what she said she could. The slice to the throat should have been enough to warn off an opponent—it wasn't that cut that killed the man. It was the perfectly executed thrust that had stopped the puma's heart cold.

Chase needed two hands to pull her blade free.

He cleaned the knife, watching the bushes, staying vigilant for any further disturbances. By the time he returned to Shelley's side, she'd wiggled out of her shirt and wiped most of the blood from her torso. She'd single-handedly gotten out a needle and thread, and was preparing to stitch herself together.

He laid a hand on her shoulder and kissed her temple. "Let me do that. Did you take a painkiller?"

She nodded. "Numbed the area I need to stitch."

He grabbed the water bottle lying at her side and picked up the remains of her bloody shirt. The one she'd obviously been using to clean herself up.

Shelley protested as he dabbed the cloth over her skin. "You have to stand look-out in case there are any more mad men out there. Last thing we need is to be caught with our pants down."

There was so much wisdom in her words, and so much anguish in his heart for putting her into this situation in the first place. That she was joking about it didn't reduce his guilt.

"I can watch *and* help."

It took time. Him pulling off her bloody pants, washing her clean and helping her dress. All the while she clutched her arm, the cloth he'd torn from his shirt staunching the wound.

The instant she was clothed, she dropped to the ground and applied the needle to her arm. Chase had done a lot of bleeding in his life, but never sewed himself up. Offering to help didn't seem the right thing to do—not with her clearly in control. He pressed her cleaned and closed knife against her thigh. She glanced from her bloody task to grimace then nod.

Chase stood and eyed their surroundings, wondering where Mark was. If ever they needed their backup, it was now. "Do you have something to take for when the freezing wears off?"

"Once I'm done. I need a clear head to make sure I'm doing this right."

The thought anyone had considered this woman worthy of being tormented made his blood boil. "I'm going to shift. Check out—"

"No."

Her shouted denial of his plan stopped him in the middle of removing his shirt. "No?"

She shook her head. "Don't change. I need you..." Shelley swallowed hard and continued stitching, her voice amazingly level. Controlled, as if she'd reached deep inside and flipped a switch. "I need you human. I need to be able to talk to you, and I need you to not go anywhere. If that's crazy and selfish, then so be it. Please?"

Crazy, maybe. Selfish? He'd never call it that. "I'll wait until Mark arrives. Let me know when you need help."

In the end, she let him complete the final stitches once she discovered she couldn't cut the thread left-handed. Instead, she kept lookout as he wiped her clean and applied a bandage.

Followed her directions and found the bottle of painkillers so she could swallow a couple pills.

He arranged their packs as if he were circling the wagons. Made sure she had her knife. Then he pulled her into his lap and held her as they waited for Mark to find them.

Part Three

This is the Law of the Yukon,
that only the Strong shall thrive;
That surely the Weak shall perish,
and only the Fit survive.

Dissolute, damned and despairful,
crippled and palsied and slain,
This is the Will of the Yukon,—
Lo, how she makes it plain!

"The Law of the Yukon"—Robert Service

Chapter Sixteen

The puma was dead.

Not the one she'd personally sent to his grave, but the one they were looking for.

It had taken at least thirty minutes before Mark found them, his pulled-back lips revealing razor-sharp teeth as he prowled the perimeter before returning to their side.

The wild-looking creature gently bumped her arm, offering comfort. Her world whirled as someone who she barely knew, who was on the *more likely to rip off a hand than shake it* list, gave her tender attention.

Misfits and outcasts they might be, but damn the men of the Keno bush had soul. She wasn't going to forget that.

And she was going to do whatever she could to help their leader.

Mark led them unerringly past the still body of the shifter she'd killed, guiding them into a clearing not far away. A small rustic lean-to, barely standing, teetered where the sunshine met the shadows. Rachel's cabin had been a luxury resort compared to this.

The broken door half-hanging off its hinges was the first indicator something was dreadfully wrong. The second was the smell, which shifter senses brought to a high-pitch gag-level before they stepped within throwing distance of the hovel.

The third and most obvious proof was the naked body sprawled just inside the doorframe.

Chase touched the body with a toe, ready to roll the corpse over when she stopped him.

"No. Don't. Not without gloves."

Chase gave her a look she recognized too well.

"Look, Mr. Indestructible, humour me."

He shrugged. "Not as if I can catch anything from him I ain't already got."

A shiver shook her from head to toe. She barely contained it, forcing herself to pull on a mask and protective gloves. After being stomped on by a crazed puma, she had reached the breaking point. "Great, so why don't you just give him a cuddle, and when we bury him you can crawl into the pit at his side." She snapped out a spare set of gloves, ignoring Chase's expression as she waved them in his face.

If he wanted to be nonchalant about what they'd found, fine. She wouldn't be a wimp and fall apart. She was more than ready to poke back.

Chase followed her directions. He pulled on the gloves, grabbed the man's arm and carefully tugged.

Rigour mortis had set in, and the entire body rotated as if the shifter had turned to stone. An eerie and horrible statue designed by Picasso on one of his less lucid days.

It wasn't the body of a man they gazed down on. It wasn't a puma. The shifter had died in the middle of a change, arms and legs not quite human, not quite animal. Shelley took a deep breath through her mouth, swallowing hard to stop the bile from rising.

She'd seen death before. She could cut and slice and stitch and repair the bodies of both forms. But this was worse than trying to stitch together flesh that had been torn apart in a fight.

It just wasn't right, in all the ways that a person could possibly be wrong.

She took a peek at the man's face, needing clues to his death. If he'd been in pain, if it had come upon him unaware.

His face was worse than the rest of him, that mixture of man and beast creating something out of a horror novel, and she totally understood how the stories of terrifying werewolves and Sasquatch could have developed. If anyone from vet school had seen something like this on an autopsy slab, they would have been convinced that the world of the gothic nightmare existed.

"Shelley."

Chase gazed at her, his nonchalance from earlier gone, replaced by concern. She shook herself alert. "I'm okay."

"I know you are. But I want to get out of here as soon as possible. Mark is standing lookout, but I don't want to camp anywhere near this site."

She nodded and braced herself, stepping forward to begin to gather the samples she needed. "Will we hike back to your cabin tonight?"

"Partway."

"I can walk. I'm tired, but I can go for a while."

He hummed noncommittally. "How's your arm feel?"

"How's your shoulder?" she snapped back.

Chase snorted. "Woman, you are so not good at the *do everything you're told* thing."

Carrying on a conversation made it easier to ignore exactly what she was doing to the body in front of her. "You'd have been bored. Admit it."

"I would have been completely bored," he drawled.

Shelley slipped samples into a small hard-covered case and broke the vial inside the cooling pack. She squished the chemicals together until the reaction began, turning the container into a miniaturized refrigerated carrying case for the tissue and blood samples.

She rose and stepped away from the shifter, managing at the last to see him inside the twisted layers. "Poor fellow. I'm sorry we couldn't talk to him, though. Find out where he'd been, what he'd been exposed to. If only..."

Chase came to her side and turned her away from the sight. "I'm going to take care of the body. You rest for a minute. We'll be hiking shortly."

She didn't waste energy arguing. She sat on the rock he led her to. Glanced around to see Mark patrolling the area, his nose visibly twitching even at a distance. Then she closed her eyes for a moment and breathed out slowly.

There was something horrible happening, and she still had no idea how to save Chase. The puma who'd attacked her? Chase had said the man was a partner with the horribly malformed man.

If she did the basic logic equation that meant whatever the dead man had succumbed to was contagious, potentially deadly, and both Chase and she had been exposed.

A loud crash brought her gaze back up to where Chase worked, piling combustibles over the body. He methodically cleared a space around the collapsed lean-to, separating the wilderness from his stack. Then he lit a corner and stepped back.

Flames licked inward in a slow trickle, swallowing the wood and leaves. The thick white clusters of old man's moss clinging to the branches sparkled as it was consumed. Chase watched intently, his body strong and straight as he stood vigil.

Shelley wanted to go to him, but this wasn't the place. There wasn't any time. But Chase's expression? It looked as if he was considering his own funeral pyre.

In all his years of living in the bush, he'd never faced this before. Ahead of him Shelley was barely keeping herself vertical as he pushed her to walk one more section of the return trail before allowing them to collapse in exhaustion.

It wasn't the smartest of moves—with potential dangers growing around them, he should have bunkered down and found a place to rest that was defensible. But the fear running through his veins motivated him far more than he wanted to admit.

There was death in the wilderness, and this time it was calling his name.

The thought of dying wasn't what kept him walking the uneven path. The bright sky lit their way—the midnight trail was daylight clear. And the same clarity filled his mind. His arm was weaker than before, pain radiating out and stealing his strength at times.

He'd seen what had happened to the men. The loss of their humanity, the change into monstrous beasts.

If he'd been alone he would have turned and headed north, retreating as far into the bush as possible. He would have dug a pit or found an abandoned mine. Ended his life to protect others from whatever it was that had him in its grip.

Shelley stumbled, and he raced forward to steady her. She pressed off his assistance and resumed her mindless march, nothing but sheer determination keeping her going.

If he'd been alone he would have done all sorts of things differently, but he wasn't alone.

Shelley.

Injured and the only person who had a chance of finding a solution to whatever was happening.

The rumors Delton and the others had shared were true. The men had known. Had listened to the voices on the wind and from the wild creatures that cried out that disease and death were coming. He'd already been marked, but damn if he wouldn't see Shelley safely back to civilization where she'd have a chance at a cure.

She stopped, feet coming together as she rested a hand on the nearest tree. "Chase? Break. Please."

He surrounded her and leaned her head on his shoulder. "Soon. This spot is too contained. Five more minutes and we should be at a clearing."

She nodded, her fingers finding his arm and squeezing for a moment. "You're a harsh taskmaster."

"I know, a slave driver. Pirate. Why do you think they call me Silver?"

Her laugh, weary as it was, lightened his step. "I'm going to offer to walk the plank in a few minutes, just keep that in mind."

"You're too damn tough to make that offer, Shelley. Now come on, tell me what you'd really do if you were on a pirate ship?"

They'd resumed walking. Slower, but still covering distance. "I'd probably get sick. Can't stand the motion."

Her confession surprised a tired snort from him. "Really?"

"Even canoes do it to me. You should have seen Johnny the first time he tried to take me fishing."

"Your dad?"

"Yeah. Poor man. I spent the entire trip with my head hanging over the side. I swear I was green."

He kept her talking about good times—and they were all about family. Chase caught himself smiling as she shared another tale. She really was a healer. As he listened to her smooth voice, the tight knot of pain inside that had threatened to drive him to his knees eased.

For this woman? He could hold on and accomplish great things.

Time passed in a blur. Chase finally brought them to a halt and set up camp. Shelley collapsed still fully clothed onto their hastily assembled bed. Mark prowled the area around the tent, constantly sniffing the air, his bristled nose wiggling and twitching.

"You call if there's even a hint of trouble."

The wolverine motioned his agreement.

Chase crawled in beside Shelley and curled himself protectively around her. Passing out in exhaustion wasn't what he'd originally planned for this evening, but it was the best thing for them both at the moment.

He fell asleep with her warm breath fanning his neck, lips pressed up against his throat as she rooted in closer.

Daylight, or more properly the next day, was going to come a whole lot quicker than either of them wanted.

Chapter Seventeen

Shelley had never felt more grateful for the sight of a rustic log cabin in her life. "You said you'd ordered more pizza."

Chase chuckled, stepping forward to slip his arm around her waist and escort her toward his home. "For you? One with the works. Anchovies, shrimp, extra-spicy sausage."

"Oh Lord, stop that. I'm drooling as it is. I can't stand this kind of teasing."

He squeezed her. "You did incredibly well out there. And you deserve pizza."

She nodded briskly, ignoring his compliment. "We all did what we had to."

Every step her legs went more rubbery, and if she slept for a week, she might get caught up. Unfortunately, that luxury was out of the question. "When do we head back to Whitehorse?"

Chase smiled. "How about I arrange transport?"

Oh Lord. "Really? I don't have to walk?"

He shook his head. "Maybe not. Don't get your hopes up too much until I confirm a flight, but if you want to shower, I'll use the ham radio and make a few calls. We should be able to get a chopper out here so you can take those samples to a lab as soon as possible and get your arm looked at."

The idea of skimming effortlessly over all the terrain between here and Whitehorse made her whimper with want. "I would kiss you if you can arrange that."

He laughed. "Motivation. Come on."

Shelley glanced at the men they walked past with a whole new admiration. For their way of life and just how remote, dangerous and free it truly was. Their courage made her even more determined to find a cure for what could be coming to destroy their world.

The fact they looked at her now with respect instead of suspicion made something inside her very happy. Acceptance had never come easily, and each time it came, it felt more incredible than before.

Delton barely glanced up from where he stood by the kitchen stove. "You two smell like shit, begging your pardon, ma'am."

"So nice to see you again, Delton," Shelley responded.

He grunted. "I'll feed you after you wash off the stink. Won't be able to keep my food down otherwise."

Shelley had been avoiding taking a deep breath. She knew what he was taking about.

"Shelley wants pizza," Chase deadpanned.

Delton whistled. "Whoa now, good thing I love a challenge."

"Oh stop, I'll eat anything, Delton, don't fuss."

"'Don't fuss, don't fuss'. That's what you say to old grannies. Who you telling not to fuss?" The old man glared for a moment before dropping one lid and winking.

She was so tired she didn't know which way was up. So tired if she started giggling she was bound to not be able to stop.

Chase had removed her pack without her even being aware he had undone the straps. Shelley reluctantly reached for it. Lifting the heavy object was the last thing she wanted to do at that moment.

"Don't worry about your stuff," Chase soothed her.

"I need to put the samples somewhere safe."

"Shit, okay, fine. In the bedroom."

Shelley nodded.

Chase squeezed her shoulder. "I'll be with you in a second. I need to call Whitehorse."

She made her way into the back and stood beside the bed with its rustic quilt, the soft pillows. The blinds at the window were still turned upward just as they'd left them. If she didn't stink as bad as she did, she would bet the scent of their lovemaking lingered in the air.

Had it really been not much more than twenty-four hours?

All that she'd seen and done floated in her brain, jumbled and confusing. Pain and fatigue turned the mental movie into a chaotic rollercoaster of flashing images. She wasn't sure how long she stood there, too dazed to even collapse.

Chase's arms closed around her. A sign of just how exhausted she was, she hadn't heard him approach.

"I'll get you set up. This way." His voice had that rough, scratchy tone that made her think of sweaty sex. Not good, considering her knees were already on the verge of buckling.

Chase led her into the tiny bathroom in the corner of his cabin. The composting toilet was more convenient than an outhouse, and that's about all that could be said in its favour. "So surprised you have a shower."

"Yep. Makes me a greenhorn son of gun, according to Delton and the other men. Shoulda just kept throwing myself in the lake for a bath like they do, but damn if I want to do that all winter when I've got to break the ice before I even hop in."

The thought made her body tighten up. "Shower is good."

Chase filled the holding tank. "Stay in as long as you want—I'll keep the tank topped up."

She was exhausted, stinky and scared to death. It was the least logical thing for her to suggest, but the words spilled out anyway as she grasped his forearm. "Join me."

Chase cupped her chin in his hand, his thumb rubbing gently on her cheek. "Shelley..."

"Please. We don't have to fool around, I just want to touch you." And more than that she couldn't explain.

He stared at her for a moment then nodded. "I'd be an idiot if I turned down a lady's request to scrub her back. And I ain't never been accused of being stupid. I left messages with my contacts, and they're supposed to call me back about flights. I'd love to join you."

She slipped out of her clothes and abandoned them on the floor, his mixing in with hers as he stripped as well. There was barely any room in the teeny stall for them both, and only seconds later they were skin to skin under the heated liquid.

She didn't want sex. Didn't need him to get her turned on. She honest-to-God just wanted to have him there beside her so she could figure out what the heck was going on, and his warm body was the only rock-solid base she had to center herself on.

"Our bandages?" Chase asked. He had leaned back on the wall and draped her up against him.

"Let them get soaked. We'll need to put on fresh ones anyway." She ignored the part inside that dryly commented about how much good her doctoring had done for him up to now.

Chase grabbed soap and slowly ran his hands over her skin. Top to bottom, he worked her over. Removing the dust and the stench of death from her body. Letting the blood and the tears swirl down the tiny drain.

197

The heat was a little bit of heaven, but it was the touch of his hands that were like ministering angels taking away the pain and refreshing her. He pressed his lips to her temple and stepped out to refill the holding tank.

"Where does the water from the shower go if you don't have regular plumbing?"

Chase laughed as he stepped back to her side and tucked her against his chest. "Now that's a strange change of topic."

"It's a gift. Minds turned to mush jump from topic to topic with ease."

She dug her fingers into his chest muscles, smoothing and cleaning him as best she could with the limited space he allowed her.

"Simplest is always the easiest. There's a funnel under the cabin that leads to a pipe. In the summer the water just flows out and away until it hits the garden patch. In the winter I catch the water in a bucket and drop it in the bush."

There was a light ringing in her ears. Shelley glanced at her arm, peeking at the cut and the stitches. "I should take up embroidery this winter."

Chase snorted. "You jumping topics again?"

The cut hurt more than it looked like it should. "What?"

He lifted her chin. "And that answers my question. Come on, darling. I'll get you tucked into bed."

"It's only lunchtime," she protested.

He wrapped a towel around her, careful of her arm. "And you can sleep until supper. I'm pretty damn sure of that."

She could sleep until supper the day after tomorrow if allowed. "Let me see to your cuts first."

He nodded. Patted her arm and stuck on the gauze. She was sure she'd reached for the medical kit to care for him, but something wasn't right anymore and the soft pillow under her cheek was too delightful to fight.

Chase's warm lips touched hers. That was nice.

"I think you're the sweetest shifter I've ever met, Silver Chase Johnson."

His chuckle faded away far too quickly.

She was out before he could straighten up from kissing her.

Chase stared for the longest time, the water droplets clinging to him forgotten, ignoring how his body chilled in the air. Definitely ignoring the heat in his arm and shoulder.

Her lashes rested against her cheek. All the tension in her expression was gone, leaving nothing but peace behind, the whisper of a smile around her lips where he'd touched her. So different from the chaos and terror he'd witnessed in her eyes out in the bush. Different than the strength and determination she'd pulled on like armour. He absently dried off, staying in the room and watching her, not wanting to be away any longer than he had to.

Not wanting to say goodbye a second before it had to happen.

"You gonna build a pedestal and swing her up on it?" Delton rumbled softly from the doorway.

"Going to pin your smart ass to the wall if you wake her," Chase returned.

Delton snorted. "Come on, Silver, I'll take care of your shoulder. Sleeping Beauty ain't going anywhere without you for the next ten minutes."

Chase quickly pulled on some clothes. He drew the blinds open to allow fresh air into the room and closed the door carefully to let her sleep for at least a few hours. Frank and Mark were back at the dining room table, pretty much the same position they'd all been in two days ago, except for the missing liquor bottle.

"What's the plan, boss?" Frank asked.

Chase motioned Delton over and handed him the first aid kit. "I'm going to get Shelley choppered out of here with her stuff. We'll wait on alert to see what happens with the bears. Maybe it'll all be pissing in the wind, and we can go back to enjoying the summer."

Frank and Mark exchanged glances.

Behind his back, Delton cussed lightly at the sight of Chase's injury, but he was Yukon enough not to say anything. Probably not much he could say anyway other than *damn, that looks like hell.*

Mark cleared his throat. "She ain't going to like that very much."

"What? Getting a ride out? I already told her I would arrange it. She was pleased as punch."

"Pleased because she thought you were going with her, I think," Mark muttered.

"Ten to one she puts up a fight and gets him onto the heli with her," Frank offered.

"Oh, I ain't taking that wager. That would be like betting on black flies to bite your ass in the evenings."

Delton pressed a little harder than necessary and Chase swore. "What's your problem, old man? Fingers losing their ability to stay steady?"

"What's yours? Brain not able to figure out what you got happening in front of you? Eyes too dull to see what you got slapping you in the goddamn face?"

Chase looked around the room in disbelief. "What the hell are you guys talking about? You didn't think she was going stay, did you?"

Three pairs of eyes refused to meet his, bodies wiggling uncomfortably in their chairs, Delton swaying on his feet.

The bear shifter cleared his throat. "If you don't mind, boss, could you turn down the volume a notch or two? You're making me want to crawl on my belly, and I always heard it ain't good for the digestion to crawl less than an hour after eating."

It was a good sign of how far he'd lost control, that he hadn't been aware he was sending off shifter power. With them all different kinds of shifters, he couldn't use the unusual sensation to boss them around, but with his mixed heritage he was strong enough he could make them damn uncomfortable. "Shit. Sorry, boys."

He collapsed onto the couch, ignoring the smarting from his back as it hit the cushions. He dragged his hands over his scalp before sighing and leaning back to stare at the ceiling. "I don't want her to go," he confessed.

"Then don't let her." Delton's instant answer cut and burned.

"She needs medical help right away. Besides, there's nothing for her here. She's got a life out there in Whitehorse. A life she's determined to face." Chase's stomach was in knots. He wanted her to stay, once she was healthy, but he couldn't even guarantee he'd be around for the rest of the summer.

What kind of selfish bastard would ask a woman to stay somewhere that could end up being a deathtrap?

The ham radio sounded and he jumped to his feet. Ignored the other men as he took the call.

"Whitehorse transport transferring you to Maxwell's Silver Hammer. Go ahead, please."

201

The coincidence with his nickname was amusing enough to make his lips twitch. "This is Chase Johnson. I'm up in the bush past Keno, and I've got an emergency medical pickup ASAP."

A somewhat familiar voice carried over the line. "You got landing space, and lat and longitude for me, buddy?"

"Tons of room, and yes. Ready?"

Chase snapped off the cabin's coordinates and acknowledged them back. "How soon can you get away?"

There was a moment's pause. "I'm double-checking clearance as we speak, but if everything is a go, I should be able to fuel and be in the air within the next two hours. You're lucky the bird is parked here in Whitehorse instead of out in Haines Junction."

Chase did the mental math. "You leave by two, you'll be landing by four at the latest."

"You're good. Yeah, about that. Mark out a perimeter for the set-down point so I'm not in a bog. And what kind of medical am I looking at? Do I need a stretcher on the landing struts or should I bring a paramedic?"

The smooth competency of the pilot eased Chase's nerves. "She'll be a walk-on. Ambulatory, carrying medical tests."

"Shit. *She?*" A few crashes resounded in the background. "Fuck, you're in the Keno area. You talking about Shelley Bradley by any chance?"

Crap. "Who am I speaking with?"

"Shaun Stevens. You that dude who took her north?"

Double crap. That was the Takhini Beta. "I am, but—"

"You are so going to get your ass kicked if she's hurt. What the hell were you thinking taking her out in the bush in the first place?"

Chase wiggled the wires to the receiver and listened to the slight crackle of interference. "Sorry. Breaking up. You got our position?"

"Asshole. Don't you dare try to pull a fast one. I'm the freaking king of fast ones. You're playing with the receiver wires."

Crackle, crackle.

"Chase, you bastard. Just tell me. How bad is she hurt?"

Chase relented. He didn't need to have a revengeful wolf pack on his back every year when he went to town. "She's got a couple scratches and she's exhausted. Had a bad shock, but overall she's strong. She'll be fine. She needs to hit her office to do some tests ASAP. Can I trust you to make sure that happens?"

"You aren't coming with her?"

Chase didn't even stop to reconsider. "No, but she doesn't know that."

"Shit. You're pulling a double-cross on an injured female wolf? Wear a cup, man."

It wasn't a bad idea. "We'll have the landing pad marked."

"Whitehorse out."

Chase hung up the phone slowly, resting the receiver in the cradle with an almost delicate touch. He'd done it. He'd organized everything that was needed to fly Shelley to safety.

And out of his life.

Boo-fucking-hoo for him.

Chapter Eighteen

If things had gone according to plan, Chase would have let Shelley sleep until three. Woken her slowly then fed her before slipping her and the samples onto the helicopter. He would have shut the door and watched her swear at him through the window as the chopper lifted her into the sky and returned her to the safety of Whitehorse.

Then he would have sat down and drank, followed by a shift to whichever of his beasts arrived to tear the fuck out of the forest trails. A few fights, a little violence to finish?

It had all the makings of a lovely Yukon evening.

So of course things went dreadfully wrong.

He couldn't wait until three. Instead, he stood with his hand on the doorknob at two. He wasn't going to *wake* wake her early. Just sit and stare for a while, take deep breaths and try not to think about how creepy it was that he would be perched on the dresser watching a woman sleep.

If he happened to slip into bed with her for one final session of sweet lovemaking, who could blame him?

Opening the door and discovering the bed was empty put a crimp in his plans. Chase peeked in the bathroom, uncertain how she might have gotten past him without him knowing.

No one there.

He returned to the bedroom and took a deep breath. Anger bubbled up faster than he knew how to control.

"Delton," he roared, stomping to the open window.

"What do you want?" Delton grumbled.

Chase didn't give a damn if Delton and the others were acting all girlie upset with him for planning to trick Shelley into leaving. "She's gone and I smell that bastard Jones. Have you seen him lately?"

Delton cursed and spun on his heel, heading for the front door. "You want me to find us a wolf to track them?"

Chase examined the room. There were no signs of a struggle, so Shelley had to have gone willingly.

Why?

Her backpack was gone. So were the medical samples.

He followed Delton into the living room. "Get a wolf. Get an entire damn pack of them. I want to know where she is, and right now. That chopper arrives in two hours, and if we haven't found her, we're going to have more than some mystical forest fairies breathing down our necks with the maybe scaries, we're going to have the entire Takhini pack calling for blood."

Chase stripped off his clothes and let his animal overtake his human. For once in his life he wanted his wolf like he'd never wanted the beast before. Cats could smell for shit compared to wolves.

Again, he was screwed. The transition rippled over his body, muscles and skin aching like he was being flayed to the bone. He stretched his cougar paws on the floor in front of him and released his claws.

Fine. The cat would hunt her down. And God help Jones if he didn't have a fucking good reason for abducting Chase's woman.

He bounded outside, Delton's call already sending three or four men scrambling to shift and respond. Chase would track her down, see what the hell was going on and then—

He was still on the porch, the light summer breeze ruffling his fur. The scents of the camp and the cabin filled his head. The chance of him actually catching her trail before the wolves did was slim. He waited, pacing back and forth in the six feet of space at the top of the wide staircase, his tail twitching as he moved, his body tense and ready to fly as soon as possible.

There was something uneasy on the air.

For the first time he sensed it, that *otherness* the men had reported. That strange foreboding that had brought them all into his backyard in the first place.

Chase snarled his displeasure at being tugged aside from his task and yet—

Damn it all, he wanted to go after Shelley. Needed to find her, but something was wrong. Something was headed their way.

He plopped his hindquarters onto the deck boards with more force than intended. Swear words filled his head as he fought with himself. Struggled with what he wanted to do, and what he needed to do.

She needed to be tracked down, yes. But these men, his pack, had gathered to be under his protection. His guidance. All the reasons he hadn't wanted to be Alpha in the first place made themselves abundantly clear.

Chase drew back his animal. Reined in the beast with every ounce of his energy, but it had to be done. The transformation to human left him sweaty and aching, legs shaking for a moment as he adjusted.

On top of his other complaints, that the shift no longer felt good totally sucked.

"Delton. Let me talk to them."

The old-timer had five wolves gathered on the lawn in front of the cabin. "I thought you'd be in the bush by now. What gives?"

Chase scrubbed a hand over his scalp. "Something's coming."

Delton swung toward the tree line, his sharp gaze examining the bush. "That does put a kink in the search plans."

Out from their resting spots, all the outcasts rose and stepped toward the cabin. There were more than Chase remembered from before he and Shelley had headed north the previous day. "I can't go. I have to stay."

Delton nodded. "You want me to go?"

Shelley wouldn't be as frightened if the kindly old cougar was with the wolves that chased her. Also, the man creaked in either form. Sending him away from what could be a deadly fight might be the best possible solution.

Chase stared at the wolf shifters. "You know the lady? Shelley? She's important to me. I don't know why Jones took her. Find her. Take Delton, find Shelley and Jones." At the last minute he reluctantly remembered one more warning. "Don't hurt the boy."

Delton stripped, his wiry muscles covered with snowy white hair. "Don't bring her back unless it's safe?"

"Right. The chopper should set down in the clearing. Stay out of sight if you can, but once you find her, try to get her on it."

The old man shifted, his cougar more grey than tan. Four of the wolves pranced around him, then they all went to the side of the house, sniffing eagerly below the windowsill.

They weren't bloodhounds, they were better. No one made a sound, but it was clear they'd caught the scent. Seconds later the group vanished into the bush behind the cabin, Delton hard on their heels.

Chase's fingers twitched. His body was on fire, and this time the ache had nothing to do with the injury to his shoulder, and everything to do with wanting to go after the woman he'd come to admire so very much.

He strode forward to meet the men left behind. The ones who didn't fit in, who had placed themselves into isolation. Yet, now when their lives and the lives of others might depend on solidarity, there were no boundaries between them. Bear, wolf, cat and all the variations thereof.

Together.

Chase stood and looked them over. Stared into faces. Saw the strain of years of loneliness. The power and determination they'd gained from surviving where others wouldn't last a week.

"Don't know what's coming, but be ready."

They stared back. No one moved. Waiting.

Chase nodded once, giving approval that they'd sorely lacked in their lives. Giving them a place to belong. "We fight only to keep what's ours."

They turned as one, scattering to their campsites, removing clothing and shifting into their animals.

Within five minutes Chase was surrounded again, this time by the strangest of menageries. Massive grizzlies, smaller black bears. Pumas and bobcats and a couple of lynx. There was a three-legged wolf and a dozen more lupines, their fur every variation of silver through black.

All of them sniffing the air warily.

Frank stood on his hind legs. The upright position placed him a good three feet taller than the rest of the group, but even he didn't respond.

Waiting sucked hugely.

"Keep to the clearing until we know what's up. Wolves. Patrol the tree line." Chase planned to stay in his human form as long as possible.

The breeze over his naked skin refreshed and cooled the burning. Whatever was out there was on the move—of that he had no doubt.

How he could tell? He wasn't human to require more reasons. It was enough he and all the others knew something was approaching, and all they could do was stay ready.

A wolf howled from the far right. For a moment he thought it was the search party returning already with Shelley, and he was ready to run and grab her and give her a piece of his mind, right after he kissed her senseless.

Instead it was one of the wolves he'd just sent out scouting, and his heart fell.

The silvery figure cut off in mid-howl and spun on his heels, returning to the center of the clearing as fast as possible.

Behind him the bush turned dark as a virtual avalanche of furry bodies emerged. Like a wall of oversized lemmings, bears of all sizes and colours emptied out of the woods.

There were nearly fifty of them, all headed directly for Chase's cabin.

Chapter Nineteen

Evan slammed his hand down on the stack of paperwork. "I'm coming with you, and that's the end of that."

Shaun glared back, but the fight wouldn't last long. "Fine. Go latch down everything in the bird. And don't blame me if you have to act as a nurse or some shit. I have no idea what I'm flying into."

"Which is why you want me along."

Shaun was too busy working through preflight protocol to respond, which was just as well from Evan's point of view.

It suddenly struck him that having one of the pack with flying abilities opened up all kinds of possibilities. Hmm, maybe after they'd completed this snatch and grab, they should have a long talk about organizing sightseeing tours based out of Whitehorse using Takhini resources rather than Shaun's old alliances.

Evan had gone up often enough to know what to do as he slipped into the storage space and ensured all the webbing and buckles were latched and secure. Up front, Shaun was flicking switches and swearing at the control tower—nothing unusual, not for Shaun at least.

Salty dog was a mild term for his Beta's language.

Evan's cell phone rang. *Shit.* He tucked the phone away without answering. The jaunty tune stopped then picked up again.

He closed the storage compartment door before crawling into the passenger seat, his phone still ringing.

When the ringing finally stopped for the fourth time, he had himself strapped in and was whistling lightly as he stared out the front window.

Shaun coughed.

Evan stared forward, refusing to meet his Beta's gaze.

"You really that big a wimp you're not going to answer Caroline's call?" Shaun asked.

Evan gave him the stink eye. "I'm not scared of her. Just being reasonable. I don't want her to worry while we're gone."

"Oh, because it'll be so much better when we get back and she greets us and her injured sister on the tarmac. You tell me she's not going to kick your ass then."

"Caroline will be completely rational."

Shaun snorted. "Which is why you're refusing to take her call."

"Shut up."

Evan's phone went off again and Shaun laughed loudly. It only took Evan a moment to flip the ringer off and set the damn thing to vibrate.

"Shit, you are pussy-whipped. You don't see me hiding what I'm up to from my mate."

"You and Gem are still in the honeymoon stage," Evan growled. "Just wait until she decides you need a little closer chaperoning. We'll see how you deal at that point."

A loud blast of pulsing music filled the cabin. Shaun slapped at his hip and pulled out his phone. He eyed it, a huge grin spreading across his face. "It's Caroline. Think I should answer?"

Evan had the phone out of his friend's hand, turned off and tucked into a travel bag in three seconds flat.

"Hey, that's mine."

"Trust me, you don't want to answer. I'm saving you from whatever interrogation we don't have time for right now." Evan glared harder as something clicked. "Hey, why the hell you got such a sexy song as Caroline's ring tone anyway?"

Shaun held up a hand for silence as he went through takeoff procedure. Evan slipped on his headset, the thick padding blocking the loud buzz of the overhead propellers. Only moments later they were clear and angling to the north, Shaun expertly manoeuvring them out of Whitehorse airspace and over the Yukon River, headed toward Keno.

Evan had just happened to be in the room when Shaun got the emergency call. No way he was going to let Caroline know Shelley was being medevaced out of the bush until they actually had something to tell. And whether she'd officially joined or not, Shelley was a part of his pack. There was no arguing that point, not in his mind. He wanted to be sure she was okay.

"We got two hours. What do you want to talk about?" Shaun asked.

Evan flicked the mic button to respond. "You mean a serious discussion, or is this going to be another one of those conversations that deteriorates into dissecting the latest pack foible and who got caught doing who?"

His friend grinned and shrugged. "Those can be fun. We could also rate the latest pack pranks."

"Thank you for reminding me to kick your ass for starting that damn *Top Ten* list at the pack house. Some of the high jinks are hilarious, I'll give you that, but good grief. Use your bloody brains more."

"What?" Shaun complained. "It's all good clean fun."

"Why does even the good clean fun seem to end up kicking me in the pocket book? It was oh-so-entertaining when Caroline and I had to come to the pound to pay fines for having unregistered animals roaming the streets."

Shaun held up his middle finger. "That was only one time, dude, and it wasn't my fault. One of the other guys ordered the dog tags. I didn't realize he'd actually put *Property of the Moonshine Inn* on them."

"You were wearing one of the tags, asshole. Read much?"

Shaun grinned at him. "We've got a fine life. I mean really, thousand-dollar fines at the pound aside, we got it good."

It was impossible to stay upset with Shaun. "Life with your mate suits you. Even though I hope someday to see you settled down and acting like a grownup."

"You sure you want to insult me while we're flying? There's another death spiral just waiting to happen. I'll totally do it." Shaun shook the control stick and the chopper swayed from side to side.

Evan chuckled. "You're such a bastard."

"You love me, you know you do."

"*Gag.*"

Spending time goofing off with Shaun was so much a part of what he'd come to expect from their friendship. Irrelevant and rowdy as he might be, the Beta was one of the best around. Evan glanced out the window. Life *was* good, other than worrying about Shelley, and considering Caroline and how well she fit into the pack. And didn't fit in.

It was the weirdest thing. They got along gangbusters in the bedroom. They liked similar movies and had the same taste in twisted jokes. She was as powerful as a woman could be without being a wolf.

213

And they were...just friends. Like they'd tried to be more and they cared about each other, but then it stopped. He wasn't sure why. Didn't think the barrier was because he was "looking for his mate" like most wolves. There didn't seem to be any rhyme or reason.

Shaun's voice crackled over the speakers. "I can bloody well hear you sighing without you clicking on your mic. What's got you moping like a teenager?"

Evan shrugged. "Caroline."

"*Duuude.*"

There was a world of understanding in Shaun's single response. Which cracked Evan up.

"You are such a shithead at times."

"I aim to please. Just, seriously. I get that she's got a hot bod, and I get that she's a cool person. I like her, I really do. But you two are the weirdest couple ever."

"Because she's human?" Maybe Shaun could help him figure this out.

Shaun made a rude noise. "It's not that. Hell, we all know human and wolf combinations. Some are mates, some are couples that decided to get together because they fell in love. It's all good."

"You are way too sappy now that you and Gem are together, have I mentioned that yet?" Evan growled.

"It's a mate thing. And...maybe that's the best I can do. You don't have to be mates to promise to stick together, but you guys are like the most perfect fuck buddies I've ever seen. Friends who fuck."

"Now you make me sound all mercenary and crude, only doing the girl because she's hot."

"Nah, that's not what I'm saying at all." Shaun glanced at him quickly. "It's also as if she's only doing you because you're hot."

Evan nodded. "Guess this just confirms we are one bloody inflammatory couple."

Shaun didn't respond for a moment. When he did, all his teasing was gone. "Evan? If someone mentioned to me that Gem was using me, I would bite their fucking head off. It didn't even register for you, did it? That you and Caroline are good together, but you aren't together. Period."

Evan sat and considered Shaun's evenly delivered message. It was true—the words didn't sting. Didn't annoy the hell out of him. It just was. Which was probably the strongest indication how fucked up the entire situation was.

Shelley was sweaty and dirty. Again. She probably smelt as well, but this time she didn't care.

She'd been woken up by a hand covering her mouth. A young man with the biggest green eyes stood beside her bed. As a shifter, his nakedness struck her as less peculiar than his face which, strangely enough, was missing both eyebrows. He placed a finger to his lips.

He stepped back, freeing her mouth and allowing her to call out for help if she wanted to.

Should she?

There was no reason she shouldn't. No reason except the small, usually silent part inside that for some inexplicable reason chose now of all moments to make itself heard.

Her wolf told her to trust him.

The stranger didn't give her a chance to ask any questions, which was probably a good thing or those in the other room would have heard. He shifted into a wolf, put his paws up on the windowsill and waited.

Shelley checked her watch. One thirty. She yawned as she pulled on her pants and silently shoved things into her pack. Her backpack this time, not Chase's.

Maybe following the youth was crazy, but it was the first time in forever that her wolf had nudged her this hard. What good was it to long to have her wolf more responsive if she was going to ignore the beast the rare times it did show up?

Besides, Shelley was pretty sure she could take the kid in a fight.

She grabbed the samples, dragged on her hiking boots and slipped out after him.

Walking into a trap was the last thing on her mind. Maybe it was from years of hanging out around animals and learning when they could be trusted and when not. How it was never the big scary-looking ones she had to watch out for. It was usually the sweet, innocent granny's poodle with that twinkle in its eye that would knock the needle to the floor a second before driving teeny razor-sharp teeth into her finger.

This wolf was one of the big, gentle ones. She bet she could crawl on his back, pull his ears, and he'd sit patiently and wait for her to finish tormenting him.

There was a chill in the air she'd felt earlier in the day that vanished as she followed him into the tress. Ahead of her his hindquarters bounced as he led her down a thin path back toward the main highway. The trail rose slightly as it moved toward the hills they'd crossed before hitting Chase's cabin.

He trotted slowly for a wolf, as if adjusting for her speed, and she was grateful. She didn't think she could keep up even the gentle pace for long though. When he walked straight into the middle of the creek she swore.

"Damn, you're hiding our trail."

He nodded, lupine head dipping regally.

"You'd better not be leading me wrong, or you and I are going to have words."

Words with her big knife. Still, she couldn't shake the instinctive urge to trust him.

Twenty minutes later they had broken free of the water and he led her up a heavily overgrown goat path toward the top of the ridge. She no longer had the energy to do anything but put one foot in front of another.

That pizza Chase had promised her was getting farther and farther away.

When she finally hit the top of the rise, she found the wolf had curled up in the lee of a tree on the side of the ridge that faced the cabin. They were high enough to have a good view of the surrounding area, but unless someone knew exactly where to look, she and the wolf would be nearly invisible.

She slipped off her backpack and joined him, wiggling until she'd found a comfortable spot against the dirt of the hillside. "Well, you're obviously not trying to take me away somewhere to hurt me. Thank you."

He circled a couple times before lying down nearly in her lap. He rested his chin on her knee and stared up at her with something close to puppy love in his eyes.

"Where were you when I was a little kid? I could have totally used a wolf to accept me back then."

He opened his mouth and grinned before yawning and getting cozy.

Shelley tucked her shirt around her and relaxed. So. Hiding in plain sight. She supposed from here she'd be able to see if there was a huge panic over her departure. If needed, she could stand up and shout, even take off her top and flap it to get attention until everyone down at the cabin knew where she was.

It salved her guilty conscience. Maybe crawling out that window hadn't been logical, but shifters were more about instinct than logic.

The heat of the sun washed over her and lulled her off into nearly sleeping.

Something crashed and Shelley jerked upright. There was a second staccato bang. Branches to her left smashed together in the gust of wind that played over the hillside. A quick glance at her watch showed she'd only slept a few minutes. The wolf was on his feet, growling as he stared down the hill toward the cabin. Shelley yawned and blinked the sleep from her eyes, attempting to focus.

But when she did, the view wasn't at all what she expected. On the lawn outside Chase's cabin, men and animals milled everywhere, all facing toward a line of rapidly approaching bears.

Chapter Twenty

From a distance there was barely any sound to accompany the fighting. It was as if she was witnessing everything on a teeny tiny screen, a newscast on her cell-phone. Only when a body was left behind on the lawn could she make out additional details. A bear went down, curled into a ball and was abandoned as his core group surged forward.

A wolf flew through the air, caught in the backswing of a massive paw.

Her young kidnapper wolf slipped under her hand and nudged her.

"I'm not leaving," Shelley insisted. "I'm safe enough watching from here. I have to see what's happening. Why are they doing this, I wonder?"

She double-checked her blade was in place. Just in case she needed it, although, please, no. She would fight if she had to, but a battlefield of shifters seemed a terrible place for a human woman. It had been bad enough killing the puma, even in self-defense.

Down to one side the bears were forcing their way forward. Chase's huge cougar body was easy enough for her to spot, or maybe it was because she was sure that had to be him. The biggest body headed into the worst of the trouble, slamming himself against a group of shifters and knocking them over like bowling pins.

A small bear rolled to his feet, and this one, instead of returning to the fight, hightailed it back toward the northern bush.

Shelley frowned in confusion. Now that she'd noticed one, there were clearly more of these runaways. One or two at a time, bears broke away and disappeared until there was only a small contingent still fighting.

She'd had enough. From what she could see, the good guys outnumbered the baddies two to one.

"Come on, wolf boy, escort me down."

He stepped in front of her, blocking her path.

Instinctively she growled at him, and he snapped back in obedience faster than she expected.

Hmm, that little sensation of power was a sweet thing for a lowest of the low to experience. "You are totally going to give me an ego if you keep doing that. I mean it. I think we need to head back. Sniff for me. Make sure there are no bears coming at us from the side, okay?"

The wolf waited for her to grab her pack then led her on a direct route down the hillside toward the cabin. They popped in and out of the trees, allowing her to check again and again how things were proceeding on the lawn.

If things turned ugly she wasn't sure if she'd run forward faster. It was damn tempting. She was concerned about Chase. She'd taken off because her wolf had insisted on it, but the entire time she'd wondered and worried what his reaction had been to her disappearance.

She was caught in the middle, and it was time to throw caution away and make sure he was okay.

Wolf boy stopped at the base of the hill and led her off the main trail. Shelley sighed as the branches closed in around them, scratching and tugging at her long sleeves. "I hope you know what you're doing," she complained.

He obviously did. Not even five minutes later they broke out at the edge of the lake, not far from where she'd walked with Frank. Which was only...two nights ago? Shelley shook her head in wonder.

There were a lot of shifters between her and the cabin, and she hesitated. Being brave was one thing. Being stupid was another. She watched and analyzed until she was confident what she saw were mainly Chase's men.

Now her role as a vet could be used. Unfortunately.

The wolf gave a low bark before slinking into the clearing. Shelley followed cautiously, but firm in her steps. Someone waved from the right, and she headed his direction.

Mark glared down, the hand slapped over his forehead partially covering a bloody gash. "Where the hell did you go?"

"Never mind that now. Where's Chase?"

Mark stared at her.

Shit. "Mark, you hear me? Where's Chase? I saw the fight from the hill. Where is he? And who the heck are those guys?"

She pointed toward the dozen bears all sitting on the lawn, surrounded by shifters. That's when she noticed one of the men stood over them with a rifle at the ready.

"We'll figure out who they are. Chase is in the cabin. Frank carried him in."

Carried? "He's hurt?"

"He was already hurt, lady."

She pushed past him and headed at a dead run for the front door. Her wolf guide sped past her, darting into the house long before she could reach it. All along the route the shifters in her path separated and stood aside, clearing space for her.

Chase. Dammit, she'd left and he'd gotten himself hurt again. She was going to kick his ass.

She was nearly through the front doors when her wolf boy blocked her again. Words exploded from her. "Move it, or I'll turn you into a eunuch."

He tilted his head to the side, the most puzzled expression on his wolfish face.

Delton's slow drawl carried over her shoulder. "Jones, the lady means she'll cut off your balls. It's okay, let her in."

So that was the boy's name. She gave Jones a dirty look as she pushed past him, frantically searching the cabin for a sign of Chase.

Frank hadn't carried him to the bedroom, and she understood why as soon as she got close enough. "Oh, Chase. What have you gone and done this time?"

The cougar on the floor of the kitchen was bleeding profusely from deep cuts. Bite marks and torn skin made a mess of his beautiful body. He opened his mouth to snarl softly.

She understood enough cat body language to answer that one.

"No, I won't go away. Now let me check you."

The bear tried to get in her way again. "You don't want to—"

It was certain stupidity, but she did it anyway. She slammed a hand against the man's huge chest and shoved him. "Shut up, Frank. I know what I want and don't want."

Of course, for all her shoving, he didn't move an inch, but at least he didn't try to block her when she slipped around to Chase's side.

She kept her touch light as she examined as much of his body as she could reach with him in an awkward position against the wall. He snorted and sniffed when she hit delicate sections, but there didn't seem to be enough damage for him to be lying there as if he were more seriously injured.

He had to be exhausted, but even that didn't explain his immobility.

She patted his flank gently. "Come on. It'll be easier to stitch you up if you shift to your human form."

Chase closed his eyes and ignored her.

Ignored her, or was going into shock? Damn. She scrambled to get in position to check his vitals, but Frank held her back with his big pawlike hand.

"Shelley?"

She looked up to find the bear shifter staring at her sadly.

He shook his head. "He's not going to change."

Frank pointed, and she moved in closer, following his lead. Chase had been hiding his back against the wall. He'd moved just enough she could finally see.

There was a hole where there shouldn't be one. Not only was he injured, either a bite or a huge claw wound, but the area around it had changed back to human, twisting his cat body to the side with the mismatch in size between his forms.

The puma in the bush, with its twisted mutated corpse, instantly flashed to mind, and she shuddered.

Panic hovered, but she fought off the fear. That horrifying conclusion wasn't inevitable. There had to be a way to stop it from happening, stop the disease from continuing. The shifter in front of her was impressively strong.

The fact he had captured her heart in their short time together only made it that much more important.

"Chase? Can you shift? Come on. Shift and give me a chance to fix you up. There's not that much damage, and I've got the samples. There's a chopper coming, and you can fly out with me and we'll find a way."

Chase opened his eyes and stared unblinking for a moment then rolled, blocking the wound completely from her sight. Ignoring her request, all but ignoring her. His eyes were glassy, and he had to be in pain, but right then she wanted him to keep on fighting. To not give in.

And the thought of him dying before they'd figured what the future could hold? Sucked so hard she couldn't stand it.

She scrambled for the words to encourage him. To poke him into doing everything he could.

"No. Damn it, Chase, do not give up. You have a whole field of men you need to take care of, and you are not allowed to just close your eyes and die. Do you hear me?"

She was dragged to her feet as she continued to rail at Chase.

Frank turned her toward him and held her tight, stopping her from facing Chase. Stopping her from seeing his still body. "Let him decide. It's only right."

She didn't care if it was the right thing because she wanted the selfish thing. "I don't want him to die."

The big bear patted her back kindly, but he wasn't Chase.

Shelley knew what she had to do. If Chase was going to die, she wasn't going to let him die alone. She squeezed Frank fiercely then slipped from his grasp to curl up at Chase's side on the hard wood planks of the kitchen floor.

"Looks as if you're stuck with me for a bit, Long John Silver. So why don't you make yourself comfortable, and I'll be here if you need anything, okay?" Shelley cupped his furry face and stroked his muzzle. She wrapped an arm around him carefully, hugging as much of his cougar body as she could.

He might have been rejected at times during his life, but damn if she'd let him feel anything but acceptance as he died.

There were layers to the pain, and layers to the confusion. Not like a multi-tiered cake where everything was visible all at once, but like in the winter, when pulling back the thin sheet of ice covering the pond would reveal what lingered beneath.

Chase hurt. That was his single, clear focal point at first. Then *she* came into the room, and at least that gave him something nicer to concentrate on than hurting. The cat and the human fought for a moment over which one of them would actually get to see her, but that was one of the layer things that seemed to be broken.

He really wanted to talk to her, which meant shifting to human. But the cat liked it when she got all riled up and started yelling. Her anger was kind of cute and invigorating, and if it didn't feel as if there were a three-foot dagger stuck in his side, Chase would have gotten up and kissed her, in either of his forms.

But that dagger was there, and it seemed to have him rather effectively pinned to the floor. He tried twisting, but that only made the pain increase, and now his heart felt strange as well.

She was a pretty woman. Beautiful, really, not just the outside bit. The wolf inside that refused to come out appealed to him, as did her human body. Yet those were surface things, they weren't who she really was. They weren't her strength of will or her caring heart.

Even his cat thought she was all right.

When Frank hugged her, the cat almost snarled his disapproval. Almost, until the stab of agony through his torso effectively stopped any complaining.

Chase closed his eyes. Dying was a lot more work than he thought it would be.

A rush of her scent washed over him, a hot body snuggled up tight, and he managed to crack open his eyes to enjoy the sensation of her hand on his face. He really wanted to kiss her goodbye, and since kissing was a human gig, he gathered his energy to attempt the shift.

And the strangest thing happened.

His wolf, who had been gone on some kind of weird sabbatical for the last three weeks, showed up. It hurt like the blazes for a moment, as if the creature were digging its way out of his skin instead of shifting. The skin-crawling sensation increased until finally his wolf was right there, ready to go. When the actual moment of the change came, it was the easiest shift he'd done in ages and glory hallelujah...

It felt *good*.

Body altering, limbs reforming, his vision changing from feline to lupine. Size adjustment, fur, teeth, muscles.

Chase didn't usually shift from one animal to the other, normally utilizing his human in-between, so it was an unusual sensation in the first place, but the overall mind-numbing difference to the entire process hit with incredible relief.

When he shifted, he left behind the pain.

He rose to his feet and shook out his fur, and was immediately trapped as a pair of arms wrapped around his neck so tight he could barely breathe.

"Chase, oh Lord, you're alive."

"Well, damn." Frank peered down at him. The big bear tilted his head to the side. "How the hell you do that?"

Shelley ran her fingers through his fur, laughing as she examined him. "Chase, I don't believe it. You have barely any damage to your wolf."

That was good. Very good. Except for the ringing in his ears that made his vision blur. His hind legs slipped out from under him, and he sat heavily on the floor.

"Chase?"

Shelley tried to catch him, but even his wolf was too heavy for her, and when his front legs gave out he landed in a heap on the ground.

"Chase. Stop. What's wrong? Damn, don't you go and do something stupid like die."

He chuckled, the sound escaping in a series of tiny barks. He'd get right on that. The not-dying part.

Shelley was far too fascinating to leave right now.

She shouted at him again, but the ringing had gotten worse, and if he didn't want to throw up or do something equally undignified, he had to lie still for a moment.

Wolves didn't like doing undignified things.

As he lay there, working on not dying, he suddenly remembered a vital fact.

She'd run away from him. Asking her the details was impossible in his wolf, so he made the effort to attempt another shift, not really expecting that it would work. Because everything else was broken.

Imagine his shock when his attempt succeeded.

Once again human, he groaned in pain. Damn, the hurting part wasn't supposed to return as well. What a weird day.

Shelley was at his side and examining him in seconds. "How did you...? Chase, you're so much better than you were only minutes ago. How did you do that?"

"I have no idea." The words rasped over a dry and scratchy throat. "I've just been lying here, innocently taking a nap, woman."

She tugged on his shoulder. "You were napping. Good timing. Way to scare me to death."

Chase struggled upright, sitting on the cold floor. "Way to scare me. Where the hell did you go, and where is Jones? I want to rip his ears off."

Shelley ran her fingers over his back, skimming the place where the original injury had been. He glanced over his shoulder to see the claw marks were still there, plus a new slash, ugly and wet and deep, but the pain was a lot more manageable.

"Poor Jones," she said. "I just threatened to rip off his balls."

"That's a good idea as well. Now where were you?"

She flushed. "He took me up the hill and we watched the fight. You were crazy."

"I thought you were gone."

"So that made you act crazy?"

Damn. He wasn't about to confess that the idea of her leaving had made him reckless.

She coughed lightly then the fussing began in earnest. She wiped him down. Stitched and closed his wounds.

"You should be checking the others," Chase complained.

Frank grunted. "We got a few wolves fixing them up. You're the only one stupid enough to get himself hurt this bad."

"That's what I said," Shelley muttered.

"I heard that." He'd closed his eyes because while the pain was much more manageable, it was still difficult to stay vertical as she wrapped a bandage around his chest.

"Good, means you're only stupid, not gone deaf. What were you thinking wading into a huge group of bears like that?"

"They were convenient."

And he snapped his mouth shut and refused to say anything more.

Her expression tightened, a hint of murderous intent in her eyes. "Well, I guess Frank and Mark will figure out what to do with the idiot bears while you're sleeping."

Chase grumbled. As if that was going to happen. If he wasn't wasting time being dead, he might as well go finish the job properly. The fight, not the dying. "I'm not sleeping. Help me up and I'll go talk to them."

"I think you'll be sleeping."

"Wanna bet?"

Shelley sighed, her frustration clear, but she scrambled to her feet and held down a hand. He needed it far more than he wanted to admit, and when she opened her arms and offered him a hug, he was willing to accept that as well.

The sharp stab in his right butt cheek hit a second after she'd wrapped herself around him.

The room grew blurry. "Shit, Shelley, a needle?"

She stepped back, and right about the time Frank grabbed him from behind she flashed a grin.

"What can I say? I like to win."

Chapter Twenty-One

If there was the equivalent of having a hangover, a marching band playing in your head and a sock wrapped around your tongue, Chase had found it. He wasn't sure why anyone would want to experience such a thing, but he most certainly had found it.

Other facts slowly filtered into his brain. He couldn't move. Well, not more than the straps holding him in place would allow, which was all of half to a quarter of an inch.

Hurrah, party time for sure.

He was naked, he hurt. He hurt all over. His toes, his nose. He swore his balls hurt, and not in a good way. Every inch felt as if he'd been beat black-and-blue, and wasn't that just the most wonderful way to wake up.

Plus, he had to take a piss.

He would have dragged a hand over his head but he couldn't. There was a light rattle off to his left, and he would have twisted to see what it was, but he couldn't bloody well move.

He opened his mouth and licked his lips, wiggling his tongue a couple of times to loosen off that sock sensation. He had just cleared his throat in preparation to swear profusely at life, the universe and everything, when something small, black and furry landed on his chest.

The kitten sat primly and washed its face.

"Enigma."

The beast didn't move. Didn't twitch.

Chase relaxed and ignored the fuzzy thing. His brain had finally clued in that he had to be in Whitehorse. How had he gotten there?

Hell. The chopper. Shelley was damn tricky.

He cleared his throat. "Hello?"

The word rasped out, and the only attention he got was Enigma coming forward to lick his chin.

Chase sighed. Nice. Pinned in place again by sixteen ounces of black cotton candy.

"Enigma, stop that."

Shelley's quietly spoken words came from Chase's right, and he turned his head as much as he could just in time to see Shelley's face light up.

"Oh God, you're awake." She turned and shouted behind her. "He's awake."

She scooped up the cat, dropped the creature to the floor and leaned over to plant a huge kiss on Chase's lips.

Chase accepted it. Soaked in her flavour. Growled lightly when she pulled away. "You want to unlock me and let us try that again?"

"You need to go slow, dude." Hands worked on unfastening the straps holding him down. Shaun's face angled over him, the wolf's cocky grin upside down.

The expression was more annoying when you saw it from a position of powerlessness.

Chase struggled to get vertical, swinging his legs to let them hang over the edge of the mattress. "You guys run a strict boarding house, tying your guests to the bed."

Concern and worry tightened Shelley's expression. "I know. And we charge extra for it."

Shaun slipped to the side and offered a shoulder. "You've got to be ready to bust a nut. Come on, man, I'll escort you to the little boy's room and you can wring out your kidneys."

"Jeez, Shaun. Just offer to take the man to the bathroom. You don't need to be crude."

"Crude? What'd I say?"

The floor felt uneven underfoot as Chase leaned harder on the other wolf than he'd intended. He ignored the banter trailing after them, concentrating on finding his balance to ensure he could insist on privacy by the time they hit the john.

Shaun paused at the door, peeked a glance behind them. He leaned on the wall as he gestured Chase into the bathroom alone. "It's safe, dude, she's not watching. I'll stand guard from here."

Chase slipped out from the Beta's support. "Are you going to tell me why I feel as if I've been hit by a Mack truck?"

Shaun's laughter carried in from outside the door. "Not my fault. I wasn't the one who dropped you on the tarmac while getting you out of the chopper."

What?

Chase thought as hard as he could, but the memories were foggy. There was the fight, the pain in his body as he lay on the floor in his cabin. The incredible energy it had taken to shift into his wolf and back to human.

Oh, and Shelley smacking his butt with something sharp right before he lost all focus.

There was enough reason to hurt without having been dropped.

"You're being an asshole, aren't you?" he asked Shaun.

Shaun tapped a drum roll on the wall. "That was payback for the little *fucked-up wireless reception* trick you tried to pull on me. Nobody dropped you. You've been flat-out on your ass for a long time, though, so you're bound to feel like crap."

Chase took a moment to use the new toothbrush waiting for him beside the sink. The man in the mirror wasn't pretty but looked a lot better than he expected. There were faint bags under his eyes and fading bruises all over, as if fresh skin covered healing wounds. He twisted to check his shoulder and back, but they were both covered with thick bandages and he didn't want to muck with them right now.

He eyed the shower enclosure. "Do I have time for a quick rinse?"

"You expect me to scrub your backside or something? Dude. You're a grown up. Wash 'em if you want to."

Chase moved cautiously to avoid landing on his ass, but he managed to keep the bandages dry. He dried off, pulled on the pants he found on the counter and stepped out the door to nod at Shaun. "I feel like crap, but walking crap. I'll be fine."

"Hungry?"

The mere thought of food triggered a rumble so loud he swore his internal organs shook.

Shaun gestured to the right. "And that answers that question. Come on. We can grab some burgers."

Food was one motivator, but it was getting to see Shelley that sped his steps.

She turned from where she stood at the front counter of the vet clinic. He glanced over her quickly, making sure she was okay. It was crazy how unsteady his feet felt as she moved forward to give him a hug.

A large furry object stepped between them and blocked his path.

Jones?

The surprise of spotting the wolf was the only thing that kept him from kicking the beast out of the way. "What the hell?"

Shelley sighed. "Look, Jones. I appreciate the gesture and all, but this is Chase. He's not going to hurt me."

Oh God, no. Chase stared at the troublesome shifter in disbelief. "Have you finally flipped your last—?"

"Jones likes watching out for me." Shelley squatted to push the shifter aside. "He's been rather charming, actually. I'm sure you can understand how much I've appreciated having him around."

She glared up at him, and Chase rolled his eyes.

So it was like that, was it? No mentioning to the crazy boy that he was crazy? Tenderhearted females. "Gee, Jones. Thank you for taking care of Shelley while I was unconscious. Now if you don't mind, I'd like to give her a hug. I seem to remember that was on my agenda before someone knocked me out."

Shelley flushed. "You had it coming."

"The hug or the jab in the ass?"

Warm arms slipped around him, and she pressed up close. "Both. You scared me."

"Sorry."

He leaned down to touch their lips together, and that made a lot of the remaining aches and pains ease away. He might not know completely what the heck was going on, but he knew this.

He'd given up during the fight. Planned on lying down and dying when the strange wilderness attack was over because he'd thought she was gone forever.

He no longer had any intention of giving up anything, anytime. While he still had breath, he was going to fight to live. And if there was some way to have Shelley a part of that life he would make it happen.

"Shaun said I've been out of it for a while."

Shelley leaned her forehead on his chest. "Ten days."

"Really? Shit." That would explain a few more things. Like how he'd healed so much from the fight. A flash of worry struck, and he twisted her carefully, tugging at her shirt to try to get at her arm.

"Hey, stop it," Shelley complained, pulling out of reach and adjusting her clothes. "Not now."

Shaun snorted.

Shelley stuck out her tongue at him. "Dirty pervert."

Shaun threw his hands in the air in resignation. "I'm just saying I have no complaints if you want to strip, but if you're going to be long I'll leave you two to it and come back with takeout or something."

Oh *sheesh*. Chase's brain must still be half-asleep. "I'm not trying to get you naked, I want to see your cuts."

She flushed even redder. "Oh."

Shaun snorted again. "Man, Shelley, you're cute. I thought my buddy Tad was the shyest shifter in the country, but you got him beat."

"Do you mind?" Chase glared across the room. He didn't care if Shaun was the local Beta, he wasn't going to let Shelley be teased.

The man sat in a nearby chair and shut up, just grinned as he picked up a magazine and flipped pages. "Pretend I'm not here. I'll take you for grub whenever you say the word."

Shelley had her stethoscope out and tugged him toward the side examining room. "I won't keep us long, but I want to double-check you."

Chase went willingly, but he wasn't the only one going to get examined if he had any say. "Ten days, huh?"

She nodded, pushing him into position and wrapping a blood-pressure cuff around his arm. "You were thrashing around a lot for a while. After you nearly hit the floor, I suggested we strap you down. I hope you don't mind. You didn't seem to mind."

Chase caught her fingers and lifted them to his lips. "You're babbling."

She nodded, stealing her fingers back. "I know."

He let her have a moment's peace. She listened to his chest, took his heart rate. When she peeked under his dressings, he let her without bothering to look himself.

"Now, you." He caught her hand before she could run away.

"I'm fine. Really."

Chase twisted until he had her pinned between his legs and locked in position. He undid her buttons one by one, patting her fingers away when she would have protested. "I want to see."

"Shaun is in the waiting room," she protested.

"Good. He can practice waiting and tell us how much he enjoys it." Chase slipped the material from her shoulder. The pretty blue bra with lacey sheer material that totally let him see her nipples registered—he'd have to be really dead for it not to— but he was more concerned with her arm.

He slipped his fingers up her smooth skin carefully as she willingly turned to show him two faint lines on her skin, the wounds almost completely healed.

"Damn. Did you say I slept for ten days or a month?"

Shelley brushed her cheek against his in a move that totally toppled his defenses. "Your wounds are nearly healed as well. I can leave off the bandages if you'd like."

Chase wiggled his shoulder and back to try to sense any of the pain he'd become so familiar with. Nothing. It felt wonderful. Well, achy and bruised, but not like he was being eaten by fire ants.

"I left the gauze on to protect you while you slept—"

"Healed? How is this possible? You must have found out what was wrong with the shifters."

She grinned at him. "Well, thank you for the vote of confidence. Did I not head north with you to find a cure?"

Chase slipped his hands back around her waist. "I never doubted you. But how?"

She snuggled close. Rested her cheek on his chest, her hands clasped around his back as if she was afraid to let him go. "You were the cure."

"Me?" Chase stroked her hair and let the heat from her body warm him. "More information, please."

"Your wolf. Remember when we first met I threatened to let you sleep for a good long time and let your cat heal itself? It's not common, but it's been a well-accepted last-resort cure over the centuries. Put an animal into a nearly comatose state. The lack of movement gives their body a chance to heal. Your system was fighting to stave off the infection, but with the cougar and the man, your metabolism must have been accelerating the mutations."

He didn't want to admit that most of that had gone way over his head. He held on to her until she moved away and stared up into his face. His confusion must have shown because she smiled and spoke again.

"Let me put it this way. Your cat tried to heal you, then your human. They ended up fighting as to the best way to do that, and if their argument hadn't stopped, your shifter would have basically come undone, not knowing which form to take."

"The miner."

She nodded sadly. "I don't know if the disease started from another wild animal, or was a reaction to something they found in their mine. But while your cat and human fought it out and effectively tried to kill you, your wolf went into hibernation and healed itself. When you shifted, you inoculated yourself."

"And you don't have the germs anymore? You're not infected or contagious?"

She shook her head. "When we got back to Whitehorse, I made contact with my mentor. Between the two of us we came up with the idea of making a serum using your blood as a starting point. It seems to be working—we've passed materials and information along to all the other shifter medical facilities so they're prepared if they see signs of an outbreak. We've been in full production here in Whitehorse with one of the shifter-owned pharmacies to make enough to inoculate basically every shifter we can, including all the outcasts. Shaun knows someone who's adapting a wildlife management pistol so we can dose the reluctant ones from a distance."

Damn. "Everyone I touched during the fight, hell, even Taylor back at Rachel's cabin. He's going to need to be looked after—"

"Already done. Well, Taylor at least." She grinned. "I hear he wasn't too cooperative. The medical team sent from Calgary snuck up on him to get the injection done. Not that I usually approve of underhanded methods, but the disease needs to be checked before it spreads farther."

And he agreed. To a point. "Don't like underhanded methods, huh? What you call stuffing me on the helicopter when I was unconscious?"

She blinked innocently. "Oh, did you have different plans? I was sure you'd told me we would be catching the chopper out."

There was a whole lot more to ask about, like if she knew what had caused the attack in the first place. Like why Jones was wrapping himself around her legs like an overgrown house pet.

Like where did they go from here?

Only when he opened his mouth to begin, the most embarrassing noises gurgled forth, his stomach loudly protesting the lack of food.

She kissed his cheek and wiggled away. "Let's track down some nourishment. I had you on an IV for long enough you've probably forgotten what food tastes like."

"But we will talk as I eat?"

She tossed him a T-shirt from off the counter. "Yes, of course."

"And do we have a chaperone for a reason? I mean other than Jones."

"Shaun?" Shelley shrugged. "There's been someone around from the Takhini pack constantly since we brought you to the clinic. Not sure if it's at Evan's or my sister's insistence. More details than that should probably wait for a full stomach, I think."

He didn't insist. He pulled on his shirt, snagging her wrist before she could run away. "Fine. But before we go? Thank you. For healing me."

Chase kissed her, one hand firm on the nape of her neck in case she decided to run. The willing flutter of her mouth opening to his, the tease of her tongue over his teeth—damn.

It was good to know all the parts of his anatomy still worked.

Food, information. Then privacy. In that order, and as soon as possible.

Chapter Twenty-Two

Shaun pulled up in front of the pack house, and all the horrible memories from the past rushed in to hogtie her. Shelley sat in silence for a moment, not moving, just thinking. After the past couple weeks she would have thought little could make her freeze, but it seemed her bout of bravery had been short-lived.

Jones, who had refused to be left at the vet clinic but also refused to shift and get dressed, nudged his furry wolf head against her arm. They'd crawled into the backseat leaving Chase to sit shotgun.

Chase held her door open, staring down with concern as she hesitated.

Jones nudged her again.

"Yeah, yeah, give me a minute. It's like preparing for a trip to the dentist or something."

Chase squeezed her fingers as he helped her out. "That makes two of us. Pack houses. Hmmm, even the word settles like the sweet sound of nails on a blackboard. Shaun, you sure know how to show your guests a good time."

The Beta grimaced but continued walking, grabbing the front doorknob to let them in. "Not many other choices, dude. Not since we've got the furry beast with us, and there's no fresh food in Shelley's fridge to feed you since she's been basically living at the clinic. This is simpler. Trust me. You'll be fine."

"You'll be better than fine." Caroline stood in their path, arms spread wide.

Shelley accepted her sister's hug eagerly. Chase refused to release her fingers, Jones sat on her feet, and she was completely good with all of it. For a moment she just soaked it in. The love, the caring. Her sister's arms around her, the man she cared deeply about holding her as if he didn't want to let her go.

Maybe this would work out with a happy ending easier than she thought.

Caroline stepped away and looked Chase up and down. "If it isn't the walking dead. Well done, by the way. Sounds as if you personally took out seven bears during the fight. Remind me not to get on your bad side."

Chase nodded, but didn't answer. He was too busy looking around, drawing Shelley close to his side as if ready to protect her.

Someone waved from the corner, and they headed into the wide living space. The pack house was simply furnished, comfy couches and tables grouped in small settings all over the extra-large living room. A spacious kitchen stood on one side with a massive dining room table running along the length of one wall.

Doors led off toward the dorm rooms and downstairs to what had been a game room back when she was young. Ping-Pong, foosball. TV and computer games. She hadn't been in the place for nearly ten years, but it felt far different than it should have.

It felt...warmer. More accepting.

Or maybe that was just her wishful imagination. Being accepted by one group of shifters didn't mean everyone else on the planet who could turn furry was going to instantly be her best buddy.

Either way, she stayed close to Chase and avoided making direct eye contact with any of the pack relaxing in the common areas. They found spaces around the coffee table by the fireplace, massive plates of food arriving as soon as they sat.

Shaun winked as he slipped into a chair next to a pretty black woman. "I called ahead to make sure we wouldn't have to wait."

"He's dealt with shifter appetites before," Evan drawled lazily. "Welcome back to Whitehorse."

"Wasn't how I'd planned on returning, but thanks," Chase responded. "I didn't expect to see you tonight."

Evan shrugged. "My place, you're bound to see me."

Caroline pulled out a chair to Evan's right and scooped nachos onto her plate before staring pointedly at Chase. "Did Shelley say you're ready for normal food?"

Shelley was going to have an attack of the giggles right there and then. She wadded up a napkin and threw it at her sister. "What are you, his personal nurse? Stop being mom."

"What? I'm not allowed to ask a question?"

"Bossy pants."

"Troublemaker."

Bickering with Caroline made her smile. It had been too many days of not knowing if the inoculation was going to work or not. Wondering if Chase would ever wake up again.

He tugged her tighter against his side and filled a plate with one hand. Either he was sticking close for that mutual-protection thing, or he really was claiming a bit of territory.

He settled the plate in front of her. "Eat. You look like you've been sharing my IV."

Great. "Love that you think I'm so attractive," she muttered, sinking a little farther into the couch.

Chase ignored the wolves around them. Ignored that Jones had draped himself over the seat to Shelley's right and had his muzzle resting on her thigh. He cupped her face in his hands and brought them so close together his warm breath fanned past her cheek.

"You are beautiful. Inside and out."

He didn't whisper, which wouldn't have kept his comment private anyway, not with shifter hearing. Everyone in the place still would have heard him. But then he kissed her, drawing her mouth so tenderly against his and giving passionately. Like a blessing and a benediction all at once. She wrapped her arms around his neck and wiggled closer, slipping her tongue along his and breathing in his air. The scent of the wilderness and the taste of freedom—he carried them with him.

The sense of being totally and fully alive welled up until she was ready to burst.

Someone coughed, and she realized where she was. What she was doing. But hell if she was going to stop kissing him a second before she had to.

Chase nipped at her bottom lip right before he tugged her hair gently to draw them apart. He was staring, his bright blue eyes looking straight through her, ignoring everyone else.

His gaze dropped to her lips. "Beautiful."

She blushed again—she felt it in her face. The heat that covered her was so not wolfish, but maybe that was another thing she needed to acknowledge. She was wolf, but not. If she wanted to blush, she was allowed to blush. To feel pleasure in the compliments from a good-looking man who not only lit her senses on fire, but also made her heart come alive.

"Thank you." She touched his cheek briefly before twisting to face the crowd, her chin held high.

Caroline's mouth hung open a little, but her eyes were happy. Evan wore a smirk, plus his *nothing can faze me* expression. Shaun simply ate a chicken wing as the woman beside him turned to speak to Caroline.

Chase linked their fingers together and tugged lightly. "I suppose I should apologize, but I'm not going to."

Evan leaned forward and grabbed a drink from the table. "If you're talking to me, I saw nothing to apologize for."

"I meant Shelley. I should have asked if it was okay to be kissing her in public."

This time it was Shaun's jaw hanging open. "Dude, you cats are weird creatures. Seriously." The woman to his right slapped him on the arm. "Oww, what was that for?"

"For being you." She sat back and crossed her legs. "Ignore them, Shelley. Chase, how are you feeling? I'm Gem, the one responsible for hauling Shaun's butt out of trouble most of the time. He doesn't mean any harm, he's just a puppy sometimes."

"Not housebroken?" Chase drawled.

Evan choked on his drink. When he could speak again, he raised his glass in the air.

"And on that note, welcome to a typical evening at the pack house. Where insults and happy fisticuffs are a common way of saying 'I love you, you fucking asshole'." He glared pointedly at Shaun who flipped him off. Evan laughed. "Yes, I'm talking about you, sweetheart. Hey, Chase, I wanted to mention. You did a good job taking care of the bear issue in your territory with a rather motley crew. Well done."

Chase nodded. "I still need details on what exactly it was that I was doing, other than bleeding."

Shelley laid her hand on his arm. "Remember Frank told you about getting some weird bear call to gather for the jamboree and that he ignored it?"

Chase nodded. "Delton mentioned they'd tried to round up the outcasts before as well. Was that it, the bears?"

"Yes, and no," Evan cut in. "It was bad timing on both sides' part, well, as much as a disease can have timing. The bears left Dawson about when you left the north. They were herding all the loners they could find south to be gathered up and shipped here to Whitehorse for the next set of votes."

"Still say bears are weird, dude. Voting to make decisions?"

"Shut up, Shaun." Evan said it like he'd said it a million times before. "However this disease started, it had already begun to spread through the shifter population of the north, including the bears. Turns out it hits their system differently than the rest of us. Increases their aggression, inhibits the reasoning sections of the brain."

Chase kept eating even as he listened, but now asked Shelley directly. "Did you say that inoculation you made crosses species? Does it work on the bears?"

She nodded. "It's looking positive so far. And the bear council is extremely pleased with you. First, your pack managed to stop a rogue group. Plus, you've probably saved their lives since the infected bears would have rolled right into Whitehorse. They could have started a pandemic amongst the entire bear shifter population with how many clans are arriving in town the next couple weeks."

Chase shook his head. "The north is such a quiet place."

"And for that you should be thankful. They'd only managed to round up a couple dozen captives by the time the posse hit your territory. The men in your pack were more than enough to face them down." Evan rose and reached into his pocket. "That reminds me. This is from the bear head council."

He passed over a cheque, and Shelley leaned against Chase's arm to read it. She'd never seen that many numbers in her life, except on the *Reader's Digest* sweepstakes ads.

"Holy moly. What's that about?"

Chase shook the paper in the air. "Why the hell would they want to give me money?"

Evan leaned back and relaxed, sprawled comfortably. "I'm not going to make any wild assumptions. Assumptions like the bears you caught before they could finish their rampage all turned out to belong to one of the least desirable clans of the entire bear population. Like maybe you having a small part in not allowing said group to get an upper hand in the next stage of votes was appreciated by more than a few people... Or maybe it has something to do with that small detail that you ended up *being* the cure for something that could have wiped out most of the shifter population in the north... But I'd hate to assume."

"I didn't do anything special."

Chase made as if to tear up the cheque. Shelley laid a hand on his to stop him. "Think about it. This isn't for you, it's for the pack."

All eyes turned on her, and Shelley stiffened. Okay, maybe it wasn't her place to say such a thing, but...but...

Chase smiled, a slow melting smile that traveled from the corners of his mouth until she was staring at him, mesmerized. "You're right. You're absolutely right."

He tipped his head toward Evan. "Pass on our thanks."

Shelley finished eating, only partly listening to the continued conversations about politics—wolf and bear. She was far more interested in soaking in the heat from where Chase's body touched hers. Her mind leapt from idea to idea about what should and could come next.

She didn't want him to leave, but she didn't want to force him to stay. Asking him to stop being who he was, stop being there for the men of the north, would be far too selfish of her.

A loud clatter rose from the front door, the wolves who'd answered the door shouting at someone who obviously wanted in.

"What the hell?" Shaun was across the room and dealing with it, but conversations stopped to take in the disturbance.

"I know they're in here."

Frank's deep voice was instantly recognizable, and Shelley shot to her feet. She and Chase headed to the door, Jones dogging her heels.

"Look, go chase your bloody tail. I'm not budging until I see them." The bear shifter was just settling his massive shoulders against the doorframe like an immovable brick wall as they rounded the corner into his view. "Hey, see, there's what I mean. Move it, you mangy mutts."

Oh yes, Frank was so diplomatic.

"Frank? What you doing this far south?" she asked, easing around one of the pack members who'd opened the door. The man sniffed and made a face before turning away.

Frank's huge grin flashed as he held up a set of keys. "Brought your car."

Chase laughed and leaned against Shelley's side. "Told you hiding the keys would come in handy."

Shelley ignored him and stepped forward, squeezing Frank hard for a brief moment. "Thank you so much for doing that."

When she stepped back the big man was blinking hard. "Weren't nothing. Wanted to see what the hell was up with Silver."

Chase nodded briefly. "Still kicking."

"Damn. Means I don't get your cabin."

Shaun gestured into the pack house. "You want to join us? We got food."

Frank sniffed suspiciously before waving a hand. "Ate at the gas station."

Shaun raised a brow. "Really. You want a beer or two instead?"

"Pfft. Beer."

The brief pause was barely noticeable. "Harder drinks? Something to relax you after your long drive?"

Frank straightened off the wall, his grin spreading. "Well, if you insist, I might be able to at that. Stay a while, that is." He eyed the room warily. "Is it safe, Silver?"

Shelley heated with pride that Frank looked for assurance to his Alpha before coming in. She was on the verge of bursting, she was so happy and sad, and didn't know what to think right now.

She tugged on Chase's arm and whispered she was going to the washroom, then slipped away for a moment of alone time.

She'd done what she'd set out to do—she'd discovered a cure for Chase, and in the process found a group of people she truly admired. People who had made their way in the world against all odds and without approval.

And they were doing just fine in the place they'd chosen.

She stared out the window at the bright summer sky and tried to organize all the recent lessons she'd learned. What the things she'd learned about family and friendship and...love...really meant right here, and right now.

Chapter Twenty-Three

Chase remained alert as they headed back to the corner with Frank. Shelley had vanished. He kept an eye on his friend, but whether it was Frank on his best behavior or Shaun on his worst, there wasn't much difference in the language or jokes escaping the two rascals as they sat at the edge of the group and broke open the biggest damn bottle of rum Chase had ever seen.

He wondered if he should warn the wolves about Frank's drinking capabilities, but figured this was one of those things that would work itself out in the end.

The ladies of the group rearranged themselves, letting the guys take over most of the space. Bullshit stories and voices grew louder, and Chase listened in, but kept a lookout for Shelley. She seemed to be taking the longest time.

Something wasn't right.

Didn't feel right.

His body itched, almost as bad as when the bears had approached. The sense of *other* telling him to be careful.

He found himself on his feet and headed back toward the door. Caroline rose to march at his side.

"You took good care of Shelley while you were gone. Thank you."

Chase snorted. "Yeah, such good care she got menaced by a bear, attacked by a puma, stolen by a wolf, and then had to draw me back from being nearly dead with her sheer willpower."

Caroline rocked to a stop. "Really?" She leaned closer. "Really? Dammit, the girl didn't tell me a word of that stuff."

Shit. "Well..."

A loud crash rang out. A picture skittered across the floor followed by a small side table. A decorative vase shattered a second before Shelley landed on the broken pieces.

Chase saw red.

Incredibly, Caroline responded faster than him. She tore forward and in a second had the two shifters who were standing and jeering at Shelley by the necks and slammed face first into the wall. "What the hell do you think you're doing?"

One of the wolves all but squeaked in fear. "She's mutant. Can't you smell it?"

"It's Caroline, you idiot, she can't smell like a wolf," the other moaned.

Caroline smacked their heads together. "Don't need to smell to be able to know you're both assholes. Stand up and shut up."

Chase had Shelley on her feet, the area around them now crowded with bodies.

The two wolves turned their faces from Caroline, fear in their body language. "She doesn't belong."

Caroline stepped forward. "You bet she belongs. My sister can go where she wants to go, you got it?"

"Sister?"

"Shit."

The two backed up, cocky attitudes completely vanished. "No problem. Of *course* your sister is welcome."

The idiots retreated, moving closer to where Chase and Shelley stood, obviously far more afraid of Caroline than they were of anyone else. Chase growled—his anger escaped unintentionally, but damn if he would let that kind of behavior be accepted.

Like hell would Shelley belong just because Caroline said so.

He opened his mouth to suggest they get the fuck out when Shelley pushed herself free and blocked the two chastised wolves' path.

"No. No, you're right. You have every right to question why I'm here."

Caroline sighed. "Honey, don't worry. I've got this under control."

Shelley shook her head. "This isn't about you. This isn't about you being strong enough to make a place in a pack of wolves so that when I show up you can force them to accept me. Because that's not about me. That's you. And damn it, if I've learned one thing these past days, it's that I do not need to be ashamed of who I am. I do not have to strive to be something I'm not because what I am is pretty incredible in my own bloody way."

The circle widened, everyone giving Shelley space as she faced the wolves who'd pushed her around. "You aren't the first to trip me up, but dammit, you're going to be the last. Because you are wrong. I'm not a mutant. I'm not something less than you. I'm something *different*, and that means I've got skills and abilities and experiences that you can't possibly know."

The wolves lowered their chins, unable to look her in the eye.

Shelley nodded, widened her stance and turned to face Caroline. "And you. Lord, Caroline, you are so determined to make me happy, you miss what makes me the happiest—when you just love me. Not when you do things for me, not when you wrangle your way into sleeping with the Alpha to set up a safe haven for me to come home to."

Behind them Evan groaned, but he didn't speak. Caroline's face flushed, but she didn't say a word either.

Shelley twisted again, this time to focus her bright eyes in Chase's direction. He held his breath. It seemed Shelley was on a roll, and it was his turn. What sin had he been guilty of?

Her mouth twitched as she fought a smile. "Even you, although I trust your motivation about the best of the lot, but that he-man Alpha thing? I swear if another one of the Keno shifters refers to me solely as 'the Alpha's woman' or 'Silver's treasure' again, I will start conducting castrations."

All the guys in the room involuntarily squeezed their legs together.

There was a soft cough from the edge of the gathering, and Gem stepped forward. "While I have no idea what a lot of that was about, can I make a suggestion, honey? You've done a fine job of telling them all to go take a hike. But what *do* you want? If you don't want the pack, or your sister, running your life, you're going to have to let us know what you do want." She smiled and held out a hand. "I have no objection to chatting about it for as long as you want. And the rest of them can go sit in the corner because they are rude, nasty beasts."

Shelley laughed. "That was a bit of a production, wasn't it?"

Gem shrugged. "You didn't throw stuff or break out into bad, off-key song. Those are the only two things I vote that should get anyone thrown out of the pack house."

Shelley took a big breath and faced Evan. "You said I was welcome to join the pack. Does that offer still stand?"

Evan nodded, seeming a little distracted.

"I have to think about it more. Is that okay?"

"Take all the time you need." He peered around her to face Caroline. "You were using me? Really?"

Silence hung over the room before Caroline spoke sheepishly. "Well, not *using* using. I told you us being together would make things run smoother around the hotel, and that was true. Things are great, right?"

"Oh, totally. You just failed to mention there were *two* reasons for us to hook up. The hotel, and that in your opinion your sister, who would be returning to the north shortly, would be a lot safer if you were in a position of power. Was that part of your reasoning?"

Caroline sniffed, eying the pack around them warily, but keeping her chin high. "Kind of."

Evan burst out laughing before he zipped across the dividing space to sweep Caroline up and swing her in circles. "Cool."

Chase exchanged confused glances with the rest of them.

Evan put the woman back on her feet and tweaked her nose. "You are so wolf-like it's freaky. Good for you."

"You're not mad?"

Evan considered for a minute then shook his head. "Nope. You didn't really lie. Besides, you're good in the sack—why should I be unhappy? And if I'm not pissed, no one else should be, right?"

He glared around the room, making his point clear. The gathered shifters trickled away until just their core group and the two wolves who started the mess remained.

One of them peeled his gaze off the floor for a fraction of a second. "Shelley? Sorry."

"Yeah," echoed the other. "Sorry."

Shelley stepped forward, close enough she could have taken a slap or socked them in the gut. Or worse things, as Chase noticed her knife handle sticking out from her back pocket.

Hmm, it was never a good idea to piss off a woman with a knife and dissection training.

She jerked her head toward the common area. "Go on, get out of here."

The two scurried away, and a moment's calm settled. Frank squeezed Shelley then willingly toddled back to the table escorted by Shaun and Gem.

Chase waited to see what Shelley wanted to do.

She faced her sister. "I'm sorry for yelling at you in public."

Caroline shrugged. "You didn't say anything that shouldn't have been said a long time ago. And I had told you I was going to stop trying to run your life, remember? Only this thing with Evan I'd already put into motion. It was hard to turn it off."

"Plus, you get a thrill bossing people around, admit it."

"Guilty."

"I can't believe..." Shelley peeked at Evan. "I mean, he's good looking and all, but...really, Caroline? Really?"

A snort escaped Caroline. "Oh, girl, you should see him naked. It's not as if I've been suffering for you."

Evan laughed and grabbed Caroline by the hand. "Come on, troublemaker. Let's go terrorize the rest of the pack. Shelley, you let me know what your decision is whenever you're ready. You're welcome here, and welcome to call me for help without officially joining, okay?"

And then, they were finally alone.

Shelley looked up almost shyly, and Chase hesitated. There were all kinds of ways this could go.

She lifted her keys. "You want to go for a drive?"

He slipped his fingers between hers, and they snuck toward the door only to discover Jones blocking their path, tail thumping the ground like a stick on a snare drum.

Chase groaned in frustration. "You never did explain this bit. Jones? Why don't you shift and stay a while? There's food. And games."

The tail stopped moving. Jones's shoulders drooped, and damn if the boy couldn't pull off puppy-dog eyes. Even Chase who had far more important things on his agenda for the rest of the day than babysitting a feral lupine was ready to crack.

Fortunately, Shelley didn't fall for it. She shook her head. "No, this time you can't come with me. Go stay with Frank."

Jones sniffed sadly then paced away, obviously pissed.

Right now? Chase didn't care. He was going to get time alone with Shelley.

If he could only figure out what he wanted to say.

Chapter Twenty-Four

Shelley took him to her apartment. Maybe it was a bad idea, but this wasn't a conversation she wanted to have in a public place while watching for eavesdroppers.

She wasn't even sure where to start. So she used her usual coping method and got her hands busy. The cupboard opened on a massive supply of cans and she smiled. While she'd been out of town, Caroline had seen fit to stock her kitchen. She grabbed a couple different soups and turned to face Chase.

"Did you get enough to eat? We kind of left before I made sure you were full."

Chase slid onto the high stool on the other side of the breakfast bar. "Soup would be good."

She got everything on the stove before working up the courage to face him.

He wasn't sitting far away anymore. He was standing right behind her so when she turned, she slammed into his body.

The grunt that escaped her lips was oh-so-sexy, she rolled her eyes in despair. Elegant to the very end, that was her.

Chase caught her tight and didn't let her go, and suddenly they were kissing. Her fingers found a way under his shirt so she could dig in and enjoy that chest she was addicted to. He nipped his way down her chin and neckline, sucking on the pulse point in her neck. Her instant response was to shake like a leaf in a strong breeze.

"Chase?"

He straightened, and their lips were together again, his tongue exploring her mouth. The kiss sucked the air from her lungs until she was gasping for oxygen.

"Hungry." The word escaped him with a growl.

She didn't think he was talking about the soup. "I want you too."

Chase stepped back, his eyes wild. "Turn off the stove."

Shelley hurried to obey, slipping the pot to the back burner then spinning around ready to resume the kissing and whatever else it led to.

"*Oh—*" Damn the man. He'd nabbed her before she could move more than a couple feet. "Will you stop picking me up all the time?"

Chase ignored her protests and deposited her on the top of the island. "You might not follow directions, and I have an agenda."

Oh boy.

He batted her legs apart and stepped between them. He settled close against her, lifting her chin until their eyes met. His grin was back, that almost-not-there one that made her legs shake, and suddenly she was very grateful to be sitting down.

"I want to make love to you." He broke eye contact and traced her body with his gaze. "I've been longing for more since we finished the last time, right before we hit the trail. It's like you got into my system, and I'm addicted."

The words slipped over her like a dose of oral foreplay, and a tingle began deep inside. "I want to touch you as well. To be..."

Together. The word wouldn't come.

She couldn't say it because it wasn't fair. Because it was what she thought she wanted, but it was too soon to say. Too much to ask. Other than the physical attraction they felt, how could she want to be together forever after only two weeks, and him unconscious for most of the days?

They were two people who had fallen into each other's paths. The fact they were good in bed didn't mean anything other than they were good in bed.

Chase stroked her cheek. "You're thinking way too much about something."

"I don't want to spoil the mood."

No, wait. She was brave. Determined. Like Gem had told her at the pack house, it was one thing to share what she didn't want, but it was more important to share what she did.

Chase lifted her hand to his lips and nibbled on her fingers. "Hmm. You want to have sex?"

She dragged for courage and nodded.

He drew the tip of her finger into his mouth and sucked lightly before pulling off with a *pop*. "That's not going to spoil the mood. So it's got to be something else. You want to talk first?"

Shelley hesitated, then nodded. "I think we need to."

"Agreed."

He stepped back, and Shelley whimpered her disappointment. She whimpered again when he stripped off his shirt and returned to his close position.

Oh Lordy, that chest needed to be outlawed. "What are you doing?"

He played with her buttons. "Talking. Every five minutes we lose another piece of clothing. I figure we should be done talking about the time we're both naked."

Shelley stared at him. "You're not wearing anything anymore but your jeans and underwear."

"Only jeans."

Shelley nearly swallowed her tongue. "Ahhh..."

"Because I agree, we need to talk, but unless I'm totally wrong, we've got one big thing to talk about. The ton of little stuff can wait until after the sex."

She discovered her fingers rubbing up and down his body without her consciously trying.

"Did you have to say sex?" she complained. "It's hard enough to concentrate."

Chase leaned their heads together. "We talked a lot when we were in the bush. I don't remember it being uncomfortable or awkward. You?"

She shook her head. "You made me feel welcome."

"Ha. I didn't make you feel anything. You were welcome, you fit in. And you made it clear at the pack house you have some ideas about the future."

Oh boy, here it came. "I do."

Chase breathed out slowly. "The only thing I want to know... Does that future you've planned out? Does it include me?"

She wasn't sure how to answer. "It's not that simple, Chase."

His expression was unreadable. "No, it is that simple. I'm not asking you to figure out the details because that's not the first thing. Let me say it this way. I want to have you in my life. When I thought you'd left without even saying goodbye, there was this massive empty spot inside that made me feel truly alone for the first time in my life. I've been lonely, but never enough to want to just give the hell up. I don't want to head into a future without you. How that can happen when I live in the north and you're getting established here in Whitehorse?

That's a down-the-road problem, because the first and most important thing I want to know, no, that I *need* to know—do you want me around?"

It was seriously the longest speech she'd ever heard from him. That alone was enough to floor her.

When he started undoing her buttons she shook her head in happy confusion.

"Chase."

His grin was back. "So what's it going to be? You going to admit that you like this old grump?"

He tugged off her top and discarded it behind him. He stared into her face, waiting patiently.

"You know I like you. I..." All the complications rushed back in, and she growled in frustration. "How could it work? I mean, I don't want just a casual thing, Chase. I really care about you. I think."

He laughed. "You know how to keep a man's ego in check. It's like being the man of the hour for ten seconds at a time."

"We've only known each other a few days."

"And we're shifters."

There was another issue. "And we're not mates. And I can't shift. And you're—"

"Ready to remove another bit of your clothing. Say it, Shelley. Say you like me."

She nodded. "I like you. I admire you. I think...I think I've fallen in love with you."

Sheer relief flashed across his face before delight took its place. "Then we're even. Because I've liked you since I spotted you in the park and you were adamant I leave you alone because we weren't mates. I've admired you since you insisted you were coming north."

Hope quivered inside. "Really?"

He kissed her briefly then spoke against her lips. "And I'm already in love with you. Because when I thought you left, I didn't want to live without you."

She punched him in the gut before she could stop herself.

He gasped and doubled over.

Shit. "Oh Lordy, I'm sorry, but that's for freaking me out and being an idiot. Do you know how horrible it was to have to stand there and watch you act like a berserker? To think you might die and there was nothing I could do? Bastard. That's not how you act when you love someone. You fight to be with them. You *fight* for what you want."

Chase drew an unsteady breath and straightened up, his grin back. "Interesting reaction to hearing a guy say he loves you."

She balled up her fist again and he trapped it in his palm. "No dying on me. No giving up."

"No sneaking out windows with juvenile feral wolves and making me crazy with worry."

"Sorry."

She relaxed into his arms, and they held each other. Just stayed close until their heartbeats synchronized and she was in danger of overheating from how hot he made her.

Mysteriously, her bra hooks loosened, and the fabric was tugged from between their bodies.

She smiled, her cheek resting against his chest. "You managed that very well."

"If you've got to cover them pretty things up, I'm glad you at least use the easy access kind of bra. Like a twist-top beer."

How romantic. "You smooth talker."

He nibbled his way down her neck, over the sensitive curve of her breast and kissed her nipple once as if saying hello. "We okay moving to the next stage of the discussion?"

"To the talking-with-our-hands part? Oh *yes*..." The word trailed off into a hiss of bliss because he'd begun to suckle, and there really wasn't any way to stay quiet as he worked her over.

Talented, determined. Creative. They were both naked, and he had her in the bedroom, and she was ready to tip over the edge, his tongue and teeth and lips never leaving her body. Another brush with his fingers, another stroke twisting deep inside, and she moaned in pleasure as her body obeyed his call.

She was still shaking from her orgasm when he slipped into her.

It was the first time they'd made love face to face. They had romped and played and rioted around the cabin the previous times, but now as he stared down and took her again and again—that expression in his eyes?

If it wasn't love, she wasn't sure what love was.

Happiness and gratitude sprang up. Inside, her wolf was still hiding. It didn't matter right now. Maybe that part of her needed more time, maybe she'd never be able to change, but there was no doubt she was loved in spite of that by the man taking her higher and higher. Tightness grew in her core, shots of desire flashing from everywhere his lips brushed her skin.

"Say it again," Chase whispered. "Say we're a couple."

She could do that. "I'm yours."

"You're mine."

She laughed.

She clung to him as they came together. His eyes closed for a second as he emptied, her body accepting him, her mind choosing him.

Her heart filled with caring for him.

They lay tangled together while their breathing slowed. Shelley stared contentedly at the blue outside the window, her body relaxed and sated, her mind buzzing with possibilities. "We're really going to do this. We're going to work on falling in love."

Chase leaned on an elbow and kissed her cheeks, one at a time, before staring into her eyes. "We're going to work on falling *more* in love."

A shiver of delight raced over her. "For a guy who doesn't talk a lot, you sure do have a pretty way with words, you silver-tongued fellow."

He brushed their lips together, and that was the end of any kind of talking for a good long time.

Chapter Twenty-Five

The cabin came into sight so fast Chase barely had time to think through his to-do list.

"Damn. That's freaky how quick we got here."

Shelley stared at him in confusion before he remembered he had to push the button on the walkie-talkie headset for her to hear him. He'd been pretty quiet the two-hour helicopter trip. All of them had, actually. A nice companionable silence after they managed to make Shaun stop rambling about bears and cancan girls and all kinds of unrelated shit.

At least he hoped it was unrelated. Bears doing the cancan wouldn't be a pretty sight.

He repeated his comment, and she nodded.

"It's incredibly fast and horrifyingly slow. You try it when you've got an unconscious man draped over the seat next to you, and you're hoping he doesn't go into cardiac arrest and need medical attention in the middle of the flight."

Yeah, he could see how that would put a damper on things. He squeezed her fingers. "Thanks for taking care of me."

She nodded then turned to stare out the window as they approached the landing spot to the side of the clearing. There were no signs of the random campers he'd had crashed on his lawn, and the sections where they'd trampled the grass were already slightly overgrown as the land returned to its wild state.

Just like the men, probably. Gone back to *their* wild state.

Shaun broke in over the mic. "Ahh. Hovel, sweet hovel. You guys got everything you need for the next while? Alcohol to dull the senses, paint to watch dry?"

Chase pushed the mic button. He didn't say anything, just let his growl—that low terrifying combination of cougar and wolf mixed with pissed-off human—rumble over the line.

Shaun must have a way to override the system because suddenly his laughter rang like summer bird song, light and refreshing. "Okay, fine. It's a palace. The Taj Mahal of shifters everywhere. Just buzz me when you need a drop. Or a lift. I'll make the time for you."

"Of course you will. Caroline would kick your ass if you didn't," Shelley teased.

Now that all her wild energy wasn't being used to interfere in Shelley's life, Chase could see the humour in how the pack bowed and scraped toward her sister.

He'd seen a lot of things over the past four days while he and Shelley had talked and pondered and planned. Seen how Evan treated his pack with a firm, but rather irreverent hand, never doing exactly what they expected. It kept the group on their toes, and yet they trusted Evan explicitly.

It wasn't a leadership style that would work with the outcasts, Chase mused, but it did affirm one thing. When there was a group that needed a leader, the best leaders adapted.

He jumped out of the chopper and hurried around to help remove the supplies they'd brought. Shaun was back in and lifting off before they'd been on the ground for more than a minute.

Jones sat on Shelley's feet as usual, Enigma perched on her shoulder. Chase rolled his eyes at the pair that insisted on following Shelley wherever she went. They all stared after the helicopter as Shaun banked over the ridge of the hill and headed back to Whitehorse. The rapid pulse of the blades faded to be replaced by far more subtle noises. The rasp of a branch falling from a tree, the scolding of squirrels and the slam of a beaver's tail on the far side of the lake.

Typical ear-filling, body-restoring sounds. Chase took a deep breath of the soft summer air, and smiled.

Warm fingers slipped into his hand as he tugged Shelley to his side and looked around contentedly. "I'm glad you're here with me."

"I'm glad it worked out for me to come as well." She kissed him, then grabbed a box and headed toward the cabin. He watched for a moment, the wiggle in her hips too distracting to turn away from.

She flashed him a smile, and he hurried to catch up, a couple boxes balanced in his own arms. The sooner they were moved in, the sooner they could relax.

The front door opened of its own accord, and Delton's familiar face appeared. He didn't say anything, but the cabin was filled with the most incredible scents. Brownies and stew and fresh baked bread.

Shelley plopped down her box, went straight to the old-timer and hugged him tight. Without a word she disappeared out the door, Jones hard on her heels, Enigma remaining behind to stalk through the living room as if he were casing the place.

The flush on Delton's face could only be caused by Shelley's open display of affection. Chase ignored his friend's discomfort and nodded politely. "Smells good."

Delton cleared his throat. He eyed Chase for a moment then raised a brow. "So. You ain't dead. You want your bed back, don't you?"

Nothing had changed. The pace stayed the same. The acceptance. "If you don't mind."

Delton shrugged. "I'm getting soft. Thought about asking if I could build me a lean-to in the back next to the creek. Like to stay around if you need me."

"Be fine."

Delton opened the box Shelley had dropped and whistled softly. "Fancy grub."

Chase grinned. "She's got a sweet tooth."

The cougar moved to put things away. "You look good, by the way. Not being dead and all."

"It's good to not be dead."

The front door swung open, and Shelley tottered in under a double load, and Chase hurried to help her.

It was hours later they were sitting on the porch, stomachs overly full from Delton's cooking, the sun just starting to pass behind the ridge of the western hills.

Shelley sighed happily, all curled up at his side on the wide couch he'd brought onto the porch.

"You sad you're not getting ready for your grand opening?"

Shelley shook her head. "It makes sense to delay for a bit. Now that I'm going to get a partner so I can split my time in Whitehorse with my time out here, there was no rush to open the clinic." She rested her head on his chest. "Not having to worry about paying the first year's bills also makes it a lot easier. Thanks to you sharing the bear payout cash."

"You did the work. You earned that money more than anyone."

She nuzzled against him. "Did you hear Delton say there are men setting up a camp just around the corner?"

"Yeah." That was a surprise. He'd thought the men coming together had been a one-time-only thing, but they'd decided to make a semi-permanent gathering spot. "Mark's building a hut there. Maybe Frank will when he gets back."

Shelley laughed. "I can't believe Frank wanted to stay in town for the meetings. It didn't seem like him to want to do the civilization thing."

"I can't believe he's staying at the Takhini pack house."

"They won't know what hit them."

Chase lifted her chin and took her lips. The privilege of having her there and willing to put up with an old bastard like him still floored him. The kisses got a little steamier, and she wiggled around and tried to crawl into his lap.

Jones refused to move his head off her knee.

Enough. Chase stared down at the boy. For whatever reasons, the kid had decided he should stay wolf and become Shelley's protector—fine. There was no talking him out of that decision. But it didn't mean Jones could get away with hanging around her like he really was a damn dog. "Go find Delton and sleep with him. If I see you before noon tomorrow, I've got two words for you. Duct tape."

Jones rapidly pranced away.

Shelley finished slinging a limb over him and rested her arms around his neck, their torsos brushing lightly, her butt solid in his lap. "Two months in the bush. In the Yukon agreeing to spend that much time without electricity or running water makes me officially crazy, doesn't it?"

"It makes you officially insane anywhere in the world."

She cupped his face in her hands and leaned her forehead against his. "I love you, Chase Johnson."

The words thrilled him and cracked him up. "Crazy woman admits she loves me. Well, that sounds mighty fine."

She mock glared, moving her grasp to his collar and holding on tight. "Have you been in the bush too long, Chase Johnson? I said I loved you, now you say it back."

"Really?" Chase deadpanned.

A snort escaped her. "Really."

"I guess I need more practice." He kissed her pouting lips until she was completely relaxed and soft in his arms.

Had it really only been a month since he sat on this deck? Alone and wondering what the future would bring? The contented smile on her face as he brushed his fingers over her cheek made his heart pound. Yup, this was most definitely love.

She sighed happily. "I think we can practice all you want."

It was the best invitation he'd heard in a long time.

Somewhere between the *I love you*'s and the other practicing, he was pretty sure they were going to work out just fine. Because they had chosen to fall in love.

His wolf and cat retreated to let the man enjoy his woman.

About the Author

Vivian Arend in one word: *Adventurous*. In a sentence: *Willing to try just about anything once*. That wide-eyed attitude has taken her around North America, through parts of Europe, and into Central and South America, often with no running water.

Her optimistic outlook also meant that when challenged to write a book, she gave it a shot, and discovered creating worlds to play in was nearly as addictive as traveling the real one. Now a *New York Times* and *USA Today* bestselling author of both contemporary and paranormal stories, Vivian continues to explore, write and otherwise keep herself well entertained.

You can learn more about what's coming next and find links to Twitter, Facebook and Vivian's newsletter at her website: www.vivianarend.com.

SAMHAIN PUBLISHING

It's all about the story...

Romance

HORROR

Retro ROMANCE

www.samhainpublishing.com

CPSIA information can be obtained at www.ICGtesting.com
Printed in the USA
LVOW13s1703041013

355483LV00007BA/787/P